World Gone Mad

B. Elizabeth Beck

This is a work of fiction. The events, characters, and institutions portrayed are imaginary. Their resemblance, if any, to real-life counterparts is entirely coincidental.

WORLD GONE MAD

"Prelude" Matthew Zapruder. Used with permission.

All Rights Reserved. No part of this book may be reproduced or transmitted in any form or by any means, electronic or mechanical, including photocopying, recording, or by any information storage and retrieval system, without permission in writing from the author.

Text copyright © 2021 by B. Elizabeth Beck
First published in the United States of America
ISBN: 9798591321154
Imprint: Independently published

Cover Design copyright © by Carter R. Neumann
Caslon CP Font permission obtained from Claude Pelletier

Still madly in love with you, Kevin.

World Gone Mad

1
seasons

Chris stood outside the door and listened for Claire's sobs. There were none. He was relieved. She had been weeping for days. He leaned in closer, ear against the door—not even a whimper. It was safe, so he opened the door and watched Claire struggle to reach her paintbrush to the top of her latest art project. She had been working tirelessly in the studio every day for the past week, barely stopping to sleep and rarely pausing to eat, crying behind the closed door.

    Chris looked down at the box in his hand, hoping her favorite pizza from Mellow Mushroom would entice her to stop for a moment. He opened the lid so the aromas could escape to catch her attention, and it worked. She lifted her head and removed her earbuds before setting her brush down to reach for the box.

World Gone Mad

"You didn't have to do this, you know, but I'm awfully glad you did. I'm starving," she said, kissing her stepbrother on the cheek in gratitude.

Chris said, "This sculpture is one of your best."

"Thanks," Claire said, as she helped herself to a slice of pizza. "Mmmm. You got my favorite. Extra mushroom."

"This is the piece for the marketplace in New York?" Chris asked, walking around to inspect the progress. Chris referred to the marketplace located at Hotel Pennsylvania during the New Year's Eve Phish shows they planned to attend.

"Yes, but it's also my Parsons Challenge piece. I'm in a hurry to add it to my portfolio."

"What's the Parsons Challenge?" Chris asked as he sat next to Claire and grabbed a slice of pizza.

She said, "Parsons requires you to submit one piece of art to explore a theme, including the works connected or leading up or responding to that piece and then, to top it off, write an essay explaining how you developed the idea. My *Charlotte's Web* piece was a comment about the connections people make and the communities built around Phish, right? This piece explains that connection."

Chris looked up to the top of the piece and read, "*Love?*"

"*Love*," Claire repeated.

"It reminds me of Drift," Chris said, referring to a Phish song.

"Exactly. It's self-explanatory for anyone in the know and irrelevant for those who don't. Mounting it at the hotel will provide the context I need. Still, of course, I have to submit the portfolio way before December, so I may ask Karen if I can install it at Calico House and take the photographs there."

"That would be a great background, for sure," Chris agreed. "Have you talked to her since her art show in Chicago?"

"No. I plan to do so tonight at the engagement party. What time do you want to leave?"

"Depends on how long it takes my cheese puffs to rise. Pastry dough is tricky."

"Let me text Taylor to see when she wants to leave," Claire said, reaching for her phone. "I think she said her poetry workshop is over by six, but I can't remember."

"Only Taylor would willingly go to school before we actually go back to school."

"That's because she's ambitious. When we all grow up, she'll publish her collections of poems and win a Pulitzer, and we can say we knew her when."

"Glad you have it all worked out," Chris said, standing. "I'm back in the kitchen. Let me know what she says, and we'll go when you are ready."

"Thanks again for the pizza," Claire said. She picked up her brushes and walked to the sink to rinse them. "I'm heading upstairs to shower. I've done enough for today."

"Today? I think you mean this week. You've been obsessed. It's August. School is going to start, and you've done nothing but work."

World Gone Mad

"Better than lying on my bed, sobbing because I have a broken heart," Claire said. "Is that what you'd rather I'd do?"

"What? No," Chris said. "That's not what I want. I'm just worried about you, is all."

"You have nothing to worry about. I just miss him," Claire lied as she finished cleaning her brushes and placed them into their jars to dry. They walked out of the studio, through the family room, and up the basement stairs into the kitchen, where they caught Claire's dad, George red-handed, stuffing a cheese puff in his mouth.

"Busted," he laughed when he saw them, brushing crumbs from his tie. "But, Son, these are a culinary feat."

"Hi, Daddy," Claire said. He touched a dot of paint on her forehead.

"Still at it?" George said. "How did I get such talented kids anyway?"

"I don't know about Claire," Chris said. "But I was your bonus when you married Mom."

"That's right. Best bonus son I could ever ask for," George said.

Chris beamed as he reached in the cabinet for another baking sheet. "I wouldn't get too excited, though. I mean, I'm just learning how to cook. I'm no chef or anything."

"Not yet," George said. "What I know is that when I was your age, I wasn't doing any of this cool stuff you kids do. I didn't tour with Phish or learn to cook or make art projects. I was boring."

"No," Chris said. "You were just doing this weird thing called studying to become a surgeon. No big deal."

"It wasn't a big deal," George said. "Obsessively studying is not creative or adventurous. I guess I wish I had taken some risks at your age because once you grow up, responsibilities weigh you down, and you'll look back and be glad you had the experiences you had now. Or if you're lucky like me, you'll have kids to live vicariously through. Of course, I was raised by a father who claimed there were only three fool-proof careers in the world. Plumber, doctor, or funeral director. My choices were limited, kids."

Chris furrowed his brow and said, "Because people always shit, get sick, and die? That's a twisted way of thinking, for sure. Better include chef into that list, though. People always have to eat, too."

Claire watched her dad loosen his tie. He looked tired, so she reached over and hugged him.

He asked, "Are you heading out tonight? I have to go up and change. Boots and I are expected for yet another fundraiser, I'm afraid."

"Yes, we're going to Calico House for an engagement party," Claire said.

"Karen got engaged?" Dad asked.

"She did," Claire said. "Luke proposed when they were in Chicago for her art show. It was very romantic, and tonight we get to celebrate them."

"Sounds like fun. I read about her success in *The Tribune*. Well-deserved. She sold out the entire show?" George said.

"She did," Claire said. "Goals."

World Gone Mad

"Have a good night," George said as he walked out of the kitchen. He paused in the doorway and said, "Home by midnight, okay? And no—"

"Drinking and driving," Claire and Chris finished the sentence in unison.

Claire watched her dad with affection as he retreated from the kitchen. He worked around the clock ever since being appointed Chief of Surgery at Maywood Hospital, and Claire noticed how thin his hair was on top these days. Meanwhile, Chris's mother, who had been Claire's stepmother for the past ten years, a towering redheaded woman named Beatrice Cutler, known as Boots, reigned queen of the country club and acted on several charity committees.

Most embarrassing was that Boots considered herself a micro-influencer, running a blog on Gracious Living (capital letters intended) and posting endless pictures for her Instagram followers. Claire and Chris endured cotillions when they were in middle school, but Claire drew the line at the coming-out party Boots dreamed of. Claire had absolutely no interest in being a debutant. She refused to wear a white dress and elbow-length gloves, abhorring the idea of a ceremony to be officially presented to society, whatever the hell that meant. It was enough that she and Boots participated in the annual mother-daughter Junior League fashion show. Luckily, her dad stepped in, and the matter was settled, even though Boots never missed a chance to express her resentment by raining shit on Claire's head at every turn. It was exhausting. Only one more year to endure, and Claire would escape to college in New York. Reunited with Sam.

Claire turned to Chris and said, "I'm going to wash this paint off. I should be ready in an hour or so, okay?"

"Sounds good," Chris said, waving her away and setting the timer on the last batch of puffs in the oven.

In her bedroom, Claire stripped off her paint-splattered clothes. She stepped into the shower of the adjoining bathroom she shared with Chris, tilting her head up to the blast of water. She closed her eyes and let tears escape down her cheeks. Missing Sam was like a throbbing bruise she fought to paint through. Their summer romance evolved into more serious of an affair than Claire anticipated when she first approached Sam two months ago at the co-op community art show. Only two months? How could that be? It felt like a lifetime, not just a season.

The moment she saw him, she fell instantly in love. Karen told Claire and Chris to look out for her nephew, Sam, who would be staying at Calico House for the summer, so Claire anticipated befriending him. She just didn't count on falling for him. She never expected Sam to join them in Chris's RV, affectionately named *Suby Greenberg*, and travel with them to see a dozen Phish shows. It was the best experience of her life. Sam fit right into their phamily as if he had always been here with them. Now he was back in New York with his father before he moved back into the dorms at St. Philips, the boarding school he attended, and Claire was stuck alone in Maywood, Ohio, dreading senior year, feeling lonely and forlorn.

Claire allowed herself a few minutes to cry before turning off the faucet and wrapping herself in a towel. She gave herself over to the process of drying her hair. Since it was so long, her arms ached from brushing it all out with the hairdryer. A quick application of the mascara wand and a dab of lip gloss, and she was ready. After she had pulled on her favorite pair of jeans and a loosely woven white cotton tunic, she stacked several bangles on one wrist and tied a beaded flower bracelet on the other. She stepped into sandals, grabbed her patchwork bag, and walked downstairs to meet Chris, who was storing the last of the puffs to take to the party.

Taylor knocked twice before opening the kitchen door. Unlike many petite women, Taylor wasn't afraid of the maxi dress. Hers was a flowing multi-colored halter style that revealed her collar bones and long neck.

"You look so elegant," Claire said as a greeting.

Taylor said, "Thank you. Your hair looks cute."

Chris looked over and said, "The opposite sisters."

It was what Claire and Taylor always called themselves. Claire was tall, had pale skin, and had always worn her thick, curly, blonde hair long. In contrast, Taylor was several inches shorter than her friend; charming freckles scattered her light-brown complexion, and she wore her hair in a natural tight afro once she had abandoned her braids in elementary school. They had always been best friends even when in high school, Claire joined the art club and helped build set designs for the school plays while Taylor joined the literary club and wrote for the school paper. Otherwise, they were inseparable.

"Before we leave, can I take a peek?" Taylor asked Claire, heading down the stairs to Claire's basement studio before she could say yes. The girls tromped past the family room furnished with sectional sofas arranged around a large fireplace, a bar, and a pool table, to the studio.

Since it was a walk-out basement, two glass doors lined the back wall, allowing natural light. Claire's dad had the carpet removed and tiles installed, which were more practical. One wall was devoted to cabinets, below which stood a large sink and counter. A closet served as storage, and in the rest of the area, Claire's paintings hung from the walls, and the large objects Claire used in the mixed media conceptual phase of her artist's life leaned against the walls.

For her homage to E.B. White's *Charlotte's Web,* Claire had converted hula-hoops into spider webs that were held upright by a peg she hammered into the wall. She installed that piece in the lot at SPAC in July. Their friend and fifth companion on the ride that was Phish tour, a beautiful soul named Alex, had taken hundreds of pictures of that installation while Claire greeted the phans and encouraged them to participate by writing their childhood best friend's name on a paper tag. Once the webs were full, the tags appeared like dewdrops at the end of the afternoon. Of course, the perfect July skies enhanced everything that day, one of the best days of Claire's life. The piece she was currently constructing, the work she called *Love,* took center stage. It would be the reflection piece to the *Charlotte's Web* piece included in the portfolio.

As Taylor walked around the four panels, she asked, "How did you choose the colors?"

Claire said, "I knew I wanted the three primary colors, but then of the three secondary colors, green just made the most sense to me over purple and orange. I am questioning myself, though. Maybe I should have chosen purple."

"No," Taylor said. "I like the green. It works."

A tall pole anchored the piece on a round stand in the center. Suspended from the poles were four large triangular arched panels descending to the ground like a giant umbrella. Large weights staked down each arch, which was tall enough for a person to walk under.

"I haven't begun adhering the objects yet," Claire said, sweeping her arm to the table. There, she had collected Matchbox cars, Army figures, plastic dolls, trucks, jacks, marbles, woodblocks, LEGOs, Slinkys, pick-up sticks, skeleton keys, dozens of multi-colored pinwheels, two Jack-in-the-boxes, and a Raggedy Ann doll.

"It's taken all of my energies to work the panels into the plastic tubes, so they arch. Plus, I need to make sure it's sturdy yet movable since we're lugging it to New York and around the city to get it installed," she said. "It can't be too heavy nor too cumbersome."

Taylor beamed at her friend. "It's going to be amazing when it's all done. Completely different from the webs that were ethereal and white and floaty. This is dense and colorful."

"That's the whole point. Each panel represents each musician, see? Trey is green. Fishman is red, of course. I think Mike should be yellow, and Page is blue, but I'm not sure yet, and I don't know if it even matters. I'm not printing their names on the panel. I just like to know for myself as I start adding the objects."

"Exactly how are we going to transport them, though?" Taylor asked, furrowing her brow.

Claire lifted a sizeable black fabric drawstring bag. "These, see? I have four of them. Each panel fits in each one of these bags. The tubing pulls out of the hems I sewed."

"More sewing?" Taylor interrupted. "I thought after the webs you'd never sew again."

"I know, but I can't seem to get away from it, can I? Thank God for seventh grade home ec class," she said. "Anyway, the poles will be labeled and stacked together. I'll tie them together with these Velcro bands so we can carry them as a bundle. Other than that, we just have to carry the center stand and the four weights, and we'll be good to assemble."

"You can count on me," Taylor said, putting her arm around her friend.

2
only rule

Calico House looked inviting, its windows lit, and glowing lanterns suspended from the eaves of the porch when they drove up. As soon as Claire opened the car door, she could hear the Grateful Dead playing from the outdoor speakers. She noticed the bonfire was stacked, ready for later in the evening when the drummers began their rhythms and the dancers responded with hula hoops and by lighting poi. Chris carried the food he prepared to the tables on the lawn in front of the patio facing the sacred elm tree. He added his cheese puffs to the food on the table, including plates of vegetables, a bowl of hummus, two full charcuterie boards, a carved roasted chicken, a bowl of pasta salad, another of fruit, and a platter of brownies.

"Enough to feed an army," Alex remarked as he sidled up to Chris.

"Hey, man," Chris said, turning to hug his friend. "What did you bring? Don't tell me these are your mother's tamales."

"No such luck this time," Alex said. "Fresh salsa made with tomatoes and cilantro from my mother's garden and guacamole from the restaurant."

"Sounds divine," Claire said as she kissed Alex hello. "Want to go down to the elm tree to smoke this?" She held up a joint.

"Lead the way, lady," Alex said.

He, Claire, Chris, and Taylor walked the few feet down to the elm tree. Under its comforting branches, Chris held a lighter for Claire, who dragged before she passed the joint to Taylor.

"Just in time for sunset," Claire sighed, looking over the pond where pink streaks painted the sky as the sun dipped over the green hills. "One of my favorite places in the world."

"Have you spoken with Sam?" Alex asked.

"Of course," Claire said. "Every day. It's hard, though. But it's only for a year. I mean, what's a year, anyway? And besides, we'll see each other before then, too. Like at New Year's Eve when we go to New York for the show."

"I think you're being very mature about it," Taylor said after she hit the joint. "Some people would be a wreck, but you just keep doing your work, and that is what matters. Work."

"What's a year?" Alex said. "I mean, what happens in a year?"

World Gone Mad

"We will be reunited in college," Claire said. "If all goes as planned, that is."

"Let's go up and say hello," Chris suggested before Claire got too emotional. This tree was her and Sam's sacred space all summer, so smoking a joint here was fine, but they needed to move on before Claire could dwell. The four met Karen on the patio.

"Congratulations," Claire said, hugging Karen and then asking to see her ring. She and Taylor squealed appropriately and began asking questions about the wedding. Chris leaned over to kiss her cheek, and Alex hugged and congratulated her, too. Chris wandered into the living room where guests were already gathered, drinking and talking and smoking, while Alex stopped to greet friends in the kitchen.

Chris did a double-take when he thought he spied Grant Fields sitting at the end of the sofa. He had never seen Grant outside school and certainly did not expect to see the football player at Karen's house. The only reason Chris even knew who Grant was, apart from the rest of the team, was his status as *the* openly gay player. Everyone at school knew Grant.

"Hey, man," Grant said. "It's Chris, right?"

"Yes," Chris said, reaching to shake Grant's hand. "What are you doing here? I mean—"

Grant laughed. "No, it's alright. Luke invited me. I've been working part-time for him this summer, so he included me, but I don't know anyone here. Like, are all these people from Maywood? How come I've never seen any of these people before?"

Chris said, "You have. It's just different when the hippies all gather together versus just seeing us individually in town, right?"

"You may be right. It's not my typical scene, but everyone seems nice."

"Have you eaten yet?" Chris said. "I made cheese puffs you've got to taste."

Grant stood and said, "I could eat." He followed Chris back outside, where they loaded up their plates with food. They took their dishes to the picnic table on the lawn to eat.

"These are good," Grant said, tasting the puffs. "When did you learn to cook?"

"Just now," Chris said. "I decided to learn a few things after we went on tour to see Phish this summer and almost starved to death because nobody actually cooked, you know what I mean? We reheated and microwaved, but you miss real food after a few weeks on the road."

"You went on tour with Phish?" Grant said.

"Yes," Chris said. "Have you heard of them?"

"I listen to them. Matt and Joe turned me on to them this summer at football camp. Do you know them?" Grant said, referring to two guys on the team.

"I know of them," Chris said. Their graduating class was only a hundred and fifty students, most of whom had gone to school together since kindergarten. Almost everyone knew everyone else. Chris had known Grant since sixth-grade gym class, a memory too embarrassing to mention. Middle school was not kind to Chris, who was not athletic by nature and, therefore, an easy target for bullying. Not wanting to rehash those days, Chris steered the conversation by asking Grant about the upcoming football season, which worked as Grant was eager to discuss the team. When they had finished eating, Chris offered his dab cart to Grant, who accepted it.

"I didn't know you liked to get high," Chris said.

"Usually, I'm pretty good when I'm in season, but tonight I'll make an exception," Grant said as he hit the cart.

"When in Rome," Chris said, laughing.

Grant looked confused. "Rome?" he asked.

"That old expression," Chris said. "When in Rome, do as the Romans? You've never heard of it?"

"Who said that?" Grant asked.

"You know what?" Chris said. "I haven't the slightest clue, now that I think about it." He and Grant looked at each other and cracked up just as Taylor approached them.

"What's so funny?" she asked.

"Nothing," Chris said. "Taylor, do you know Grant? Grant, this is Taylor."

"Yes," Taylor said, sitting next to Chris on the picnic table bench. "We had Chemistry with Penrose together last year."

"Penrose is the best teacher in the school," Grant said. "I hated Science until I had his class. That dude is hilarious."

"And smart," Taylor agreed. "I'm taking Physics with him this year. I hope it will help my writing. One of the guys in my writing workshop is a retired Physics professor, and he is our in-house expert on all things dealing with science in our poems."

"You just want to be like Tracy K. Smith," Chris said.

"Why not? She's my hero," Taylor said, arching her neck. "I wouldn't mind winning the Pulitzer."

"Where's Claire?" Chris asked.

"She's up there, talking with John Lackey and his wife," Taylor said, indicating to the front porch where Claire was sitting across from the artist and his wife, talking animatedly with her hands like she does when she gets excited talking about art.

"I think I'll join them. I just wanted to see where you were," Taylor said, leaning over to kiss Chris, who ducked.

"Are you okay?" she asked.

"Of course," Chris said, pulling Taylor down so he could kiss her cheek. "I don't know why I did that. Sorry, babe."

"Babe? Okay, bruh," Taylor said, raising an eyebrow before walking away.

"So that's your girlfriend?" Grant asked.

"Not really," Chris said. "I don't know. It's complicated."

"What isn't?" Grant said, standing. "I'm taking off. See you later, man."

"Yeah, see you," Chris mumbled, looking down and not meeting Grant's eyes.

Grant hesitated a moment and then walked away. Chris remained at the table alone, watching the party spill out from the house onto the porch. A few people wandered their way to the bonfire that Luke was lighting, and Chris could hear the first beats of the drums, so he followed them. When he approached the circle,

World Gone Mad

Alex signaled for him, and he gratefully took a seat next to his friend and accepted the djembe drum Alex offered. Chris focused on the rhythms emerging and let his body relax, distracting his thoughts of Grant and how inexplicably happy Chris was to have talked with him until only the patterns of the drum existed.

3
signs

Although the walk to Taylor's house was only two houses away, Claire was sweating in the heat of the August afternoon by the time she rang the doorbell. She gazed at Mrs. Thompson's flower gardens that seemed to shimmer in the sunshine. Claire knew the inground sprinkler system Mrs. Thompson insisted on having installed kept their gardens and lawn from turning brown and withering like most other yards in the neighborhood. Her hand itched to sketch the blooms on thick paper before smearing translucent watercolor to achieve the liquid light. She could sit on their front porch and let the hours slip by as she concentrated on reflection and shadow, but there was no time. She and Taylor only had twenty minutes to drive across town for their appointment.

World Gone Mad

Claire made a note of this urge, as it had been too long since she had simply painted. The desire to strip down to the basic elements of drawing was potent. She would unearth her watercolors and locate a pad of paper when she returned home, even though she was still immersed in adhering the found objects on the panels of the *Love* sculpture. Perhaps she could carve a few hours each afternoon or even in the mornings while she drank coffee and wasted time on social media. Only these last weeks before the first day of school, which was further complicated this year with the common application, the essay, and FAFSA. Not to mention a full load of classes. It was enough to make Claire's head spin, and the only way she knew to find clarity was through drawing.

Taylor opened the door, and their Goldendoodle, Woodstock, barreled her way past Taylor to greet Claire with slobbery kisses. Claire bent down to pet her in response. The dog was like a giant stuffed animal, her fur so curly and soft. She was the friendliest dog in the world.

"Woodstock! You bad dog! Get back into the house," Taylor said, shooing her pet inside before closing the front door.

"You ready?" Claire asked as they walked down to her house to retrieve her car.

"As ready as I'm going to be," Taylor said. "I don't know about this, Claire."

"What's to know?" Claire said as she pulled the car out of the driveway. "It's a reading. It's going to be fun and maybe even a little bit true."

"But you don't completely buy into this, do you?" Taylor asked.

"I do, and I don't. What I mean is that I believe that some people are more intuitive than others and can read more about their auras. I mean, come on. We've watched enough shows about psychics to know that some of it is real and some of it is gleaned from the other person's responses, so our best bet is to play poker-faced and try not to feed her too much from our expressions and responses and see what she has to say."

Claire drove past the shopping plaza where the co-op art gallery was on the outskirts of town. She parked on a side street in front of a small white bungalow nearly obscured by two giant weeping cherry trees.

"How do you know this is it?" Taylor said nervously.

"Her address is printed on the mailbox. See?" Claire said as she turned off the ignition and dropped the keys into her bag. "Come on, silly. Karen wouldn't send us anywhere that wasn't safe."

They climbed the rickety stairs to the front door and rang the bell. The door swung open almost immediately, revealing a large woman wearing a caftan and several layers of beads around her neck. Her gray hair was loose and wavy, and her eyes a sparkling blue that crinkled in the corners when she smiled her greeting at the girls.

"Welcome," she said. "Claire and Taylor, right? I'm Theresa. Come in. Come in."

They followed Theresa into the front room, including a large round wood table and two chairs. The room's only other furniture was a faded maroon velvet settee sofa placed under the bay window that faced the street. Panels of crocheted lace curtains covered the windows, allowing sunlight to penetrate while providing privacy. What was most interesting about the room were the plants that dominated every inch of space. There were towering palms, bamboo, and schefflera lining every wall. Varieties of ivy, ferns, and cascading philodendron draped from macrame hangers in front of every window and the corners. Across the mantle of the fireplace stood a collection of violets in various states of bloom. Between each plant on the mantle and scattered across the windowsill were different crystals and stones. A beaded curtain separated the room from whatever was in the back of the house. The effect was like a Victorian-style jungle of sorts, Claire thought as she looked down to see a large tabby cat wind its way around her ankles.

Theresa sat at the head of the table, her back to the mantle, and gestured for one of the girls to sit across from her. "Who's first?" she asked.

"Me," Claire said, pulling out the chair while Taylor settled on the sofa.

Theresa struck a match, lit a large white pillar candle, extinguished the match with a wave of her hand, and placed it on the corner of a china platter, which held four white crystals, a small bowl of what looked like salt, a blue glass jar, an amethyst crystal wand, and a charred bundle of sage. Claire breathed in deeply, recognizing the scent of a recently smudged room.

Theresa smiled to see Claire breathe and asked, "My dear, is there anything in particular you want to ask, or are you here for a general reading?"

"General reading, I suppose," Claire said. "Are you going to read my cards or my palm or?"

"Would you like me to?" Theresa asked.

"I don't know," Claire said. "I've never done this before."

"Why don't we start with the crystals and the flame first and see where it goes," Theresa said.

She picked up the four crystals and placed them in a line between her and Claire. "Please place your palms on each crystal, but don't pick them up. Just cup your hand around each to allow them to feel your vibrations."

Claire did as she was told, placing her palms on the crystals to feel their edges and planes. They felt cold. After she had touched each one, she rested her hands on her lap and waited. Theresa closed her eyes and seemed to be concentrating. Claire watched as the flame of the candle expanded and contracted and wavered. She thought she saw the fern fronds dance from her peripheral vision. Theresa opened her eyes. She reached for the first crystal in the row and pushed it toward Claire.

"Let me begin by welcoming the presence who would like to greet you," Theresa began. "She's entering from your maternal side, but I can't quite make out what she's saying because I think she may be speaking in French or Portuguese, maybe? No, it's French."

Claire concentrated on keeping her face placid, but her heart skipped a beat. Her mother was French, but she was alive as far as Claire knew.

"I think it may be your grandmother," Theresa said as if Claire had spoken. "She seems familiar. She watches over you, and I sense a deep love and pride for you. Does this make sense?"

Claire said, "My mother is French. I didn't know her mother, though."

"Let's move on. I see that you are suffering heartbreak. Wait, not so much your own as your beloved's. Perhaps you broke up with him? He misses you very much," Theresa said. "There is longing in both your hearts, but I also see another presence. Someone from your past, perhaps? He holds a brush of sorts in his hand. He is a bright star but not to be trusted. I see he does not have your best intentions at heart."

Claire shook her head but knew who Theresa was referring to. Her ex-boyfriend, Michael Preston, someone she absolutely did not want to discuss.

"Is he the reason for your breakup?" Theresa asked.

"What breakup?" Claire said. "Sam and I may be separated right now, but we are very much together."

"Let's move on," Theresa said. She returned the first crystal, pushed the second in line toward Claire, and closed her eyes. After a few seconds, she opened them and said, "This is your last year at home. You are leaving Maywood for a city. Chicago? No. Oh, New York, of course. I wouldn't mistake that smell anywhere. You're going to New York."

Claire said, "That's the plan anyway. I'm applying to schools in New York."

"You'll be accepted," Theresa said. "Love will carry you through. Does that make sense? I don't know how else to say what I'm hearing. Love. Love. It's bright like a rainbow."

Claire sat perfectly still. It was one thing to guess she had a grandmother spirit, a heartbreak, and would be leaving for college next year. Theresa could have said that to any teenager in this chair, but to describe Claire's art Theresa couldn't know anything about was another. She waited for Theresa to continue, refusing to make eye contact with Taylor, who she could feel was zapping laser beams to her from her perch on the sofa. They were such best friends that one slight look was enough for Claire to understand that Taylor was freaking out a bit. So was Claire.

Theresa positioned the second crystal back in line, pushed the third toward Claire, and closed her eyes again. When she opened them, she was frowning. "I'm having trouble reading this third crystal because your grandmother's voice is so urgent. I'm struggling to understand her message. It sounds like *letra ta mare*. I'm sorry. I don't speak French. Let me try again," she closed her eyes again. "*Letra ta mare.* Mare like in horse only I don't see a horse; I only see white. A white horse, perhaps?"

Claire sought her friend's eyes. Taylor smiled reassuringly. Theresa shook her head and began again. "The third crystal indicates a change to come."

"Like graduating high school and attending college in New York as I plan?" Claire said archly. She was starting to find this whole reading amusing. Perhaps she had even talked about her plans at the Red Tent circle at Karen's house. There had to be a logical explanation for all of this. Not that Claire didn't believe in energy, but she was starting to doubt these crystals. Maybe she should have insisted Theresa use Tarot cards or read her palm instead.

"Yes, of course," Theresa said. "But I'm reading a change not so much to you, but your twin. You have a twin?"

"No," Claire said. "I do not have a twin."

"Your brother. He's your age, no?" When Claire didn't speak, she continued. "I assumed he was your twin, but I see he is your spiritual twin, not your biological twin, but you are the same age. He is emerging. Discarding. Almost like a snake sheds its skin, and you must be there for him. He needs your guidance and assurance during this vulnerable transition."

"Transition?" Claire interrupted. "Like death?"

"No, not like death. Not at all. More like a shifting or, like I said, a shedding of one identity to another. In fact, he has a strong life light. You don't need to worry about that." Theresa returned the third crystal and pushed the final toward Claire. "This crystal is open to opportunity. You may ask a question now if you like."

Claire thought for a moment but couldn't come up with a single question she wanted to ask. She was still processing the jumble of information about Chris, trying to make sense of it in the scheme of real life. Perhaps Chris was entering into his life as a chef? Who knows? There were multiple ways to interpret this reading. Claire felt frustrated. "Should I ask if I'm ever going to get married and have kids?"

"No, because that's not what you really want to ask," Theresa said. "You want to ask if your work will ever get recognized. You want to know if the art you make matters. If going away to study painting and pursuing your dreams in New York is the path for you. That's what you care about now. Those are the questions that keep you awake at night."

She was right, of course. Claire could do nothing but nod in agreement.

"Well, the answers are clear. You know your path, and you must follow it," Theresa said, moving the last crystal back into line.

"Now, I'd like to take a break to change the energy before I start with your friend. Would you two care for a glass of iced tea or water?"

Both girls asked for iced tea, and Theresa indicated that they stay behind while she walked through the beaded curtain to the back of the house, where presumably, the kitchen was located.

"Strange, right?" Taylor whispered. "I'm checking my phone now. She was not talking about a horse; I'll bet. What was the phrase again? It's going to be hard to find it phonetically, but we can try, right?"

"*Mare* means mother," Claire said. "I understood that much. Not *mare* as in horse, but *mare* as in mother. So, look up what *letra* means. Oh, forget it. It means letter. The phrase is, write to your mother."

Taylor dropped her phone back into her bag and looked at her friend, who seemed a bit pale. "Are you okay, Claire?"

Claire sat next to Taylor on the sofa, patting her knee. "Your turn."

As Taylor positioned herself in the chair at the table, Theresa returned with two glasses of iced tea the girls gratefully accepted. It was sweet with lemon.

Theresa settled across from Taylor and waved her hands around the flame to pull its energy toward her. She gathered the four crystals in her two hands and placed them again in a line, asking Taylor to palm each crystal, like she had Claire do. When she closed her eyes, Taylor caught Claire's gaze, and they lifted their eyebrows simultaneously.

"The presence I feel comes from your paternal side, but the energy is maternal," Theresa began. "It's a young spirit, though. Before you were born, taken too soon in life, but she says she loves you and has always danced next to you. Does that make sense?"

"Yes," Taylor said. When she failed to elaborate, Theresa continued. "The first crystal indicates the love that you haven't experienced yet. What you've felt has not been entirely real. Perhaps a crush? Someone at a distance? Whatever it is, it's not real. Your real love is yet to come."

"Chris will be sad to hear that," Taylor joked to Claire. "Are you going to tell him he's not real, or should I?"

"I see," Theresa said. "You are involved with her twin. Now it makes sense. I don't usually break a reading to give advice, but my dear, he is not your true love. Don't worry. It's still out there."

"I'm not worried," Taylor insisted. "And I never thought that Chris was my one true love either, but he is my boyfriend."

"Things are not always what they seem," Theresa said. She moved the first crystal back into place and pushed forward the second.

"This takes no effort; the energy is so strong—your words. You have been gifted with language, I see. There are a host of elders hovering over your shoulder. All you must do is listen. They are poised to channel their stories. How wonderful." Theresa beamed at Taylor. "I've worked with a lot of writers, my dear. None of them have the ancestors like you. It is a gift to be treasured. You have many words to write."

"The third crystal reveals family. You come from a strong family and are destined to have a family of your own. There are pets. Dogs, not cats. Gardens and laughter and puzzles, like those million-piece table puzzles and books. Shelves and shelves of books."

"Hopefully, some of those books will be my own," Taylor joked.

Theresa looked serious and said, "I have no doubt. Would you like to ask a question of the fourth crystal?"

"May I ask it silently?" Taylor said.

"Of course," Theresa looked a bit smug, but amused, not irritated like Claire, who was avidly watching the reading from the sofa, was afraid she'd be.

World Gone Mad

Theresa said, "The answer is yes. Quickly. Meaning, whatever answer you seek will come in response quickly. You will not have to wait. I hear the word, *early*?"

Taylor sat quietly with her head bowed. Theresa waited a minute and then said, "I hope you girls are satisfied with the readings."

Claire rose from the sofa and reached into her bag for her wallet to pay Theresa's fees. Taylor remained silent as Claire thanked Theresa as they walked through the front door into the late afternoon heat. Once they had settled into Claire's car, blasting the air conditioning and cueing up Billie Eilish, the girls' recent musical obsession, Claire asked Taylor if she was okay since she hadn't yet said a word.

"I'm trying to convince myself Theresa memorized the word *early* to read for any high school senior. I mean, we all want early acceptance. That's a no-brainer," Taylor said.

"But is that the question you asked silently? For early acceptance?"

"Of course, that's what I asked," Taylor said. "I only care about Kenyon, and if I get early acceptance, I won't have to argue with my parents about their never-ending argument for me to attend Spelman, Howard, or even Wilberforce."

"Are you sure you don't want to go to a historically black college? Aren't you curious?" Claire kept her eyes on the road as she drove as an excuse not to directly look at her friend.

"Look. If Kenyon happened to be a black school, it would be so much easier. But I didn't choose Kenyon for any other reason than it's where I've always wanted to go and because it has the best writing program for what I want to do. I mean, *The Kenyon Review*? Come on. It's only one of the most reputable literary journals in the country. My parents are just going to have to accept that. They have those two they can push into their dreams," Taylor said, indicating to TJ, which was short for Anthony, Junior, and Tristan, her little brothers who were running through the front yard to their bikes on the driveway as Claire pulled up and parked the car.

When the girls walked into the house, Mrs. Thompson greeted them hurriedly, her high heels clicking against the hardwood floors. "Girls, just in time. I've got a showing in fifteen minutes. The boys have eaten lunch and are waiting for you so they can swim. I'll be home before dinner. If you could take the chicken breasts from the freezer to defrost, I would appreciate it. Daddy and I have chamber practice after dinner tonight. Will you be home?"

Taylor said, "Sure, Mom. I've got it."

Claire followed Taylor into the kitchen so she could unearth the chicken from the freezer. Ivy Thompson was one of the busiest realtors in Maywood and one of the chicest women Claire had ever met, as far as she was concerned. Mrs. Thompson wore her hair in a chignon most days, dressed in severely tailored suits with a simple strand of pearls, and carried designer handbags as she drove clients around in her Mercedes from house to house. She and Dr. Thompson had been married forever. Everyone called him Dr. Tony except Taylor, who rolled her eyes. Although he was a dentist and Mrs. Thompson worked in real estate, what bonded them together was their music. She played cello, and he played violin for a small chamber music group with other local musicians. Sometimes they had salons on Sunday afternoons where the Steinway in the living room came to life, accompanied by the strings. Claire loved to listen to the music and the conversations the musicians had after the performances.

TJ and Tristan burst into the kitchen, demanding to be allowed to use the pool. "Mom promised," TJ whined.

"Just give me one moment," Taylor said. "We want to change into our suits, too. Go play Minecraft for a few minutes until we come back down, and don't even think about going outside until then, okay?"

As Claire followed Taylor through the dining room, she noticed the jigsaw puzzle in progress on the large table. Theresa was right about her reading of Taylor's family. Taylor stopped midway up the hall staircase to point out a picture on the family gallery wall.

"That's my aunt Tyfini. She was my father's little sister. A stray bullet killed her. She was caught in cross-fire while dancing in her own front yard," Taylor said. "I couldn't respond to Theresa when she talked about Tyfini. It was spooky. I didn't even know who she was talking about first. I never met Tyfini, of course. She died when she and my dad were just kids, but he talks about her sometimes, and I know that experience seriously motivated Dad to work hard to become a dentist and raise his own family outside of the 'hood' where he grew up in Dayton."

"There is little risk of stray bullets in Maywood, that's for sure," Claire agreed.

The girls walked the next flight of stairs to Taylor's attic room. It was one of Claire's favorite rooms in the world; its ceiling eaves slanted, punctuated by multiple dormer windows. Braided area rugs covered the hardwood floors, and one wall was lined entirely with bookshelves that were bursting with books stacked seemingly haphazardly, but Claire knew Taylor could locate any book in minutes if she needed. Taylor's bed was an old-fashioned brass bed covered with a patchwork quilt and multiple pillows. Under the bed was a trundle, which pulled out whenever Claire spent the night. Lines of poems Taylor admired, written in ink on various pieces of paper, and slid between the mirror and the frame hung over her dresser. Over the years, scraps were removed and replaced with whatever new poem Taylor adored.

After the girls had changed and released the boys from video games, they settled into their chaise lounges next to the pool to continue their conversation with large tumblers of ice water and a bag of grapes while making sure the boys stayed afloat. Not that they needed to worry, both boys and Taylor had been swimming since birth. Literally. Mrs. Thompson loved to tell stories of her home births in tubs of water if you were unfortunate to be around when she felt nostalgic. Because she was a champion swimmer in high school and college, swimming was such an important part of their family life.

"I'm not quite sure what she was talking about regarding Chris," Taylor said. "But there is something I need to talk to you about. Keep it in the vault, yes?"

World Gone Mad

"Yes," Claire said. Anything that was stated *in the vault* was promised to be kept secret by the other. It was a pact they made in elementary school that both girls honored for each other.

"You know Chris and I haven't been doing that great. I mean, going on tour together was kind of like a test of sorts for me. I wanted to see if maybe we would connect the way I hoped we could."

"But you couldn't," Claire said.

"Right," Taylor said. "I don't know if we ever truly had a connection. I mean, I am deeply affectionate of Chris, and I did find him attractive, but—"

"I get it," Claire said. "He kind of went off the rails with his drinking."

"It's not even that. It's that he never connected with me. It was like he was playing a role or something, but it wasn't real. I could sense the distance, even as we were doing it. Eyes closed. Disconnected. Not to mention, we have absolutely nothing in common other than Phish. I don't know if that's enough. Am I making any sense?"

"Of course. Sounds awful."

"Here's the thing," Taylor said, sitting up to take a breath. "I've met someone else."

Claire sat up, too. "You did? Where? Who? Tell."

"His name is Josh. Joshua Gentry, and he's from Lima," Taylor said, referring to a neighboring town. "And he's black. He was the only other person my age in our writing workshop, so it was natural for us to start talking. He's a poet, but also a tennis player."

"Tennis player? The only black tennis player I know—"

"Arthur Ashe," Taylor said.

"Nope," Claire said. "I was thinking of Venus and Serena Williams."

"Good point. Josh is working on a persona collection from the voice of Muhammad Ali. He also does found poems from Ali's poems. It's brilliant."

"And cute?"

"Doesn't begin to describe him. I was surprised to see him in workshop when we first met. I mean, he's so athletic; he has muscles. Didn't seem like a poet to me. But he is! He's smart and plans to study English. Creative writing like me. His first choice is Wilberforce."

"Sounds like your parents are going to adore him. He sounds perfect," Claire said. She turned her attention to the boys in the pool. "Hey, guys! Don't hit each other so hard. Stop."

"I know," Taylor sighed. "He's never even heard of Phish, but who cares?"

"He can always learn about Phish," Claire said. "He sounds nice. I'm happy for you. When are you going to tell Chris?"

"I planned to talk to him at the engagement party, but he was busy talking with Grant Fields all night, which was odd, but whatever."

"You know, now that you mention it, Grant has been hanging around lately," Claire said.

"Are you considering writing your mother a letter?" Taylor asked.

"Wasn't that bizarre?" Claire said. "I mean, how would she know my mother was French? It seemed obvious Theresa didn't speak the language, so I have to admit that freaked me out a bit."

"Maybe," Taylor murmured. "Have you talked with Sam lately?"

"Just this morning. We video call every day and text non-stop. We are fine," Claire said. "Tell me more about Josh. I want to hear every detail of how you two met. Start at the beginning."

The sun warmed Claire's body as Taylor lit up to relive every detail of her new romance. The boys abandoned horseplay to challenge each other to swim contests across the pool. The afternoon at the pool was exactly the break Claire needed from the studio, and she appreciated these last few hours of summer in her friend's backyard.

4
eyes open

Claire emerged from her studio exhausted from the solid three hours she worked. Her arms ached from holding objects in place while the adhesives she applied dried to secure everything to the panels. In the kitchen, she found the ever-present Grant sitting at the island watching Chris at work. The stove was covered in pots simmering, and scattered across the counter surface were various bowls, whisks, a carton of eggs, a block of butter, and chopped herbs on cutting boards. At the doorway, she hesitated in the shadow to listen.

"I'll never perfect these five stupid sauces," Chris whined, holding up a wooden spoon. "Béchamel, Velouté, Espagnole, Hollandaise, and Tomato. The five Mother sauces of French cuisine can kiss my ass."

"Don't give up," Grant said as he accepted the spoon Chris proffered, tasting the sauce.

"My Tomato is perfect, but my Hollandaise keeps breaking," Chris said, frowning over the pot.

"Water," Grant read, peering over a digital tablet. "It says here to whisk in water when your sauce breaks."

"Doesn't make sense, but I'll try. I don't know why that would work. The sauce doesn't even have any water in it, to begin with," Chris said, pouring water and whisking vigorously. "It worked. Look, my sauce coats the spoon. You are a genius."

Grant beamed in return. Claire looked back and forth at them suspiciously. Were they flirting? Chris leaned over the counter and swiped his towel across Grant's cheek, where a sauce had smeared. Just as it looked like they were going to kiss, Grant spotted Claire.

"Hey, guys. What's up?" Claire breezed in as if she had not just been busted eavesdropping. "What are you cooking tonight, Captain?"

"I'm working on the five French sauces," Chris said.

Grant jumped up. "I've got to run. I'll catch you later."

Chris looked downcast but said, "Bet," before returning to stirring his sauces. He arranged his face and switched gears. "So, how was your fortune reading today?"

"Good," Claire said, rummaging in the refrigerator. "Some of it was obvious, of course. But some of it was a bit eerie. She referenced Love and rainbows when she 'saw' my art. She said I needed to write a letter to my mom, but she misunderstood and thought Sam and I had broken up, which couldn't be further from the truth. I don't know."

"She said you needed to write a letter to your mom?" Chris repeated.

"In French, no less. And she didn't even speak French, so she thought it was about a white horse. Mare. Mother. Strange."

"Are you going to do it?"

"What? No," Claire said, lifting the lid from a container of yogurt and digging in with a spoon. "Between finishing this project, uploading the pictures for my portfolio, and writing the essays, I have enough on my mind to add a distraction like that. Too complicated. No time."

"I hear you," Chris said.

"And what's with these sauces anyway? You can't even make a burger or meatloaf or even roast a chicken, Christopher. Why don't you start with something people can actually eat?"

"You're in a mood," Chris said. "What's with you?"

"Did I just see you almost kissing Grant?"

"What? No," Chris said, flustered. He knocked over a pan, and sauce splattered all over the cabinets and floor. "Look what you made me do."

"I didn't make you do anything," Claire said as she turned on her heels and left Chris to clean up his mess. The entire kitchen looked like a disaster area, and she didn't want to be anywhere near when Boots came home and saw it.

World Gone Mad

Back in her room, she tried to video call Sam, but he wasn't answering. She wondered how long this would last until the frustration that they couldn't be together and uncertainty of the future would settle in, and either she or Sam or both decided to call it quits. Recognizing her foul mood, she decided that only a scalding hot bath would help. She liked to do that sometimes. Fill the tub to the top with as hot water as she could stand, pour in lavender-infused Epsom salts, and float until her body succumbed to sleep. It was the best meditation she could think to do in her current mood. Problems cluttered her brain: the eerie reading with Theresa, Taylor's news of her new love, and wondering what was going on with Chris.

While she soaked, her mind finally calmed enough that she could fall to sleep, so she dried off, pulled Sam's CBGB t-shirt over her head, and settled under the sheets. She slept until four a.m. when she abruptly woke. She tossed and turned in bed for twenty minutes before giving up hope of falling back to sleep. She got out of bed, pulled on a pair of yoga pants from the floor, and quietly crept downstairs, stopping in the kitchen for a glass of water before she planned to trudge to her studio to see if she could squeeze out a few hours of work. Instead, her father interrupted her plans. He was sitting in the dark at the kitchen table, a glass of bourbon at his elbow.

"What are you doing, Daddy? Can't sleep?" Claire asked, settling in a chair at the table with him.

"Sweetie. What are you doing up?"

"Same as you, I suppose. Too much on my mind," Claire said.

"Care to share?" her dad asked.

"Just the regular stuff. College applications, and FAFSA, and this new piece I'm finishing for my portfolio," Claire said.

"I'll help you with the FAFSA, of course. You, Chris, and I need to schedule a time where we can all sit together and crank it out. So, let that be off your mind, at least. As for your art, I don't think you have anything to worry about. Have you uploaded all the pictures yet?"

"All but this last piece."

Her dad rose. "Let me see."

"Now?" Claire asked.

"Why not? Will you show me?" He offered his hand, and she took it and led him to her studio and flipped on the light.

The piece was so colorful, it almost glowed. Her dad chuckled when he started walking under the panels, examining the objects Claire had painstakingly adhered. He turned to her and asked, "You plan to install this in New York? How?"

She gestured, "It collapses. See? Each one of these panels can fit into these drawstring bags so we can carry them in. It will be hard work, but I hope we can pull it off."

He said, "It's incredible, honey. I'm always amazed by your work, but this is stunning."

"Thanks, Daddy."

When he retreated upstairs, instead of grabbing her tube of glue, she reached for a sketchbook and packet of pencils, indulging her desire to draw until the sun began to rise on the day, and the sounds of the house awakening intruded her studio. It was seven, and

World Gone Mad

she was exhausted. Good thing it was still summer break, she thought as she bypassed the kitchen, returned to her bed, and finally fell asleep.

5
breathe

The evening of Holler, the poetry series Taylor attended each month, Claire stopped her work in the studio early to take her time getting ready. Not that it was any special event, but more because she was willing to try anything to lift her spirits. What started as missing Sam had progressed into more of a depression than Claire liked to admit. She knew it was stupid to be forlorn, but she couldn't help the way she felt. Hopefully, when school started next week, she'd be too busy to be so sad. Spending endless hours alone in the studio probably was not helping her feelings, which is why she was anxious to agree to attend Holler with Taylor. Plus, she wanted to finally meet Josh, Taylor's new love interest, even though Chris was still out of the loop.

World Gone Mad

While Claire set her hair in beach waves, she thought about reading a poem of her own tonight at the open mic. She had never read one of her poems in public, though. She had never even read any of her poems to Taylor, so she wasn't sure just signing up for open mic was a good idea. Best to stick with what she was good at, making art, which was public enough.

Feeling sad and heartsick, Claire turned up the stereo to let Billie Eilish console her. She loved everything about Billie, from her atmospheric music to her profound lyrics, to her baggy clothes and dyed hair. Maybe she'd dye her hair pink or blue to cheer herself up. That would be something to do before school started Monday. She wanted to avoid sinking so far into depression that she landed back into the hospital as she did two years ago. That was an experience Claire never wanted to suffer again.

The term "hospital" was a joke. It was more like a prison than anything else. They locked her up. The food was so terrible; she could only nibble on Saltine crackers and sip Sprite by the end of her stay, causing her to lose weight her frame could not afford to spare. Strenuous dieting was part of her depression, to begin with. The other patients were so horrifyingly violent; she was terrified the entire stay. The nurses were mean, and the doctors never spent anything longer than ten minutes a day with their patients. The facility itself was so filthy; Claire yearned for a scalding shower as soon as she returned home to her private bathroom. Therefore, she needed to do whatever she needed to do to not succumb to despair so far that her father would be forced to send her back there. She would rather die first. No, not die. She knew better now.

Although she felt heartbroken from Sam leaving, she did not feel suicidal. After learning that Sam's mother took her life, Claire had a different attitude to what used to be her "last solution." It was not the final solution, and it took too much of a toll on her loved ones to ever contemplate that idea again. Sam was still heartbroken, even after three years of grieving the loss of his mom. There was a difference between thinking and feeling, though. Knowing that didn't make the depression lift. The gray cloud still hovered around her head, even after the hot shower she hoped would wash it away. She knew not to feel depressed, but she couldn't convince herself not to if that made any sense. Surely life would not be as bleak as it seems now. She didn't tell Sam about her hospitalization and was grateful Chris kept his mouth shut for once. Sam didn't need to know how Claire struggled, and besides, being with Sam was the best medicine she ever had. Not once during the summer with him did she feel depressed. Not until he left, that is.

She took a deep breath and reminded herself that college and life after Maywood would be better. It was a matter of getting through this phase of missing Sam and pushing through senior year. She just wanted this cloud of depression to lift. She picked up a picture of her and Sam in a sunflower field and kissed it, remembering their kisses and assuring herself that she and Sam would be together in New York for New Year's Eve. These weren't forever, her feelings of despair. It was a journey she needed to travel, is all.

Feeling bolstered, Claire hurried downstairs to find Chris before she drove to Mellow Mushroom, the local pizzeria that hosted

Holler every month. She found him, Grant, and Drake in the garage where *Suby Greenberg* was parked, listening to music, and passing around the cart, getting high. She accepted the dab cart and took a long drag. Getting mildly buzzed before hearing poetry was almost a rule as far as she was concerned.

"Have you guys been hanging out all day?" Claire asked Chris.

"Yeah, man," Chris said. "And did Taylor tell you? We broke up."

"You did? When?" Claire said, pretending this was new information.

"Earlier today. She came by to return a box of my things and to tell me we were done. Whatever. I was going to break up with her before we started back to school anyway."

Claire knew he was fronting, but she didn't say anything. Chris didn't seem too broken up by it, though. He seemed content with his friends. She was sure she'd hear more about it all later, but it was time to get going if she wanted to be on time for Holler, so she bid the guys farewell. After ducking into the house for her handbag and phone, she used an app to request a ride to Mellow Mushroom.

She found Taylor sitting at a booth with her customary two glasses of water. She slid into the booth and asked, "Is he here yet?" as she looked around the restaurant. Nobody looked to fit the description Taylor had given her the other day at the pool.

"Not yet," Taylor said, consulting her phone. "He just texted he would be late and asked me to sign him up for the open mic, so I did. He'll read after me if Eric follows the order. Sometimes he mixes us up, though."

"Who is the featured poet tonight?" Claire asked. "Anyone I've heard of?"

"I'm not sure. I mean, I know the feature. It's Jay McCoy. I'm not sure if you've ever heard of him. He was one of the teachers at my writing workshop, so some of us are here tonight to read for him on the open mic and then hear him read from his new book. It should be good. He's wicked smart."

Before they could continue the conversation, Eric Sutherland, the host of Holler, took the mic and launched the show with a poem of his own about the devastation of Australia's fires before he called the first reader to the mic. Claire ordered a soda and pretzel bites from the server with a million piercings who worked at the restaurant for as long as Claire could remember.

As soon as Josh walked through the door, Taylor lit up and raised her hand to wave him over. He slipped into the booth next to Taylor and kissed her on the cheek. Once the poet ended, Taylor introduced Josh to Claire.

"Nice to meet you," he said, shaking her hand.

"I'm excited to hear you read," Claire said, but that was all they could say before the next poet was called to the mic. Eric kept a brisk pace, which was a good thing, especially nights when the list seemed longer than what two hours could afford, and who could listen to more than two hours of poetry at a clip? Taylor, maybe, Claire thought. Maybe this Josh dude, too.

What Claire liked most about Holler was the audience. Unlike other poetry readings where everyone was silent and didn't even clap after someone read, the Holler audience cheered, and clapped, and were as rambunctious as they pleased, like a poetry slam. Only there was no judging at Holler. It was more like a poetry reunion, mainly because the poets knew each other after reading and writing at workshops together for years.

Josh beamed when Eric called Taylor to the mic. She looked so elegant in her purple top and white shorts, gold chandelier earrings in each ear. She was chic, like her mama.

Taylor took a deep breath, looked directly at Josh, and launched. "This poem is called *Evidence*." She paused and then read her poem, all the while keeping her gaze steady on Josh.

> If you want to get with me,
> write a poem that kisses
> me so deeply, I lose my mind.
> Compose while you drift to sleep.
> Sculpt me with your breath.
> In fact, start at the back
> of my neck. Let your idea
> of me distract your thoughts
> and interrupt your writing until
> you can only scribble my name
> over and over and over.
> Paint me as your muse. Make
> love an act of choreography.
> Direct the tempo. Sing down
> my spine and remind me why
> lovers write in verse.

Claire stole a look at Josh while Taylor was reading. He was concentrated on each word, a private smile firmly in place. The room erupted into raucous applause when Taylor had finished reading, which made her smile shyly as she made her way through the crowd back to their booth. Before she could take her seat, Eric called Josh's name to the mic. Claire was disappointed. He read a poem from the voice of Muhammad Ali's boxing glove. It was odd, yet good, but Claire wished he had responded to Taylor with a love poem of his own. Taylor didn't seem fazed in the least, though. She beamed while he read and clapped loudly at the end.

Before Eric introduced the featured reader, he called a brief intermission, so Claire turned her attention to Josh. Not only was he as good-looking as Taylor had described, but he was also charming and funny, too. Claire was happy her friend had found such a great guy, so she was utterly unprepared for the wave of sorrow she felt overcome her senses. She excused herself, paid her tab, and waited for a ride she requested from the app. on her phone, feeling regret for missing the featured reader but knowing if she didn't leave, she would burst into tears.

It was awful to feel disconnected from everyone, isolated in her grief. Here she was, sitting with people who were happy to see each other, and share their poems, and applaud each other with exuberance when all she wanted to do was curl up in a ball on her bed and sob. She didn't even bother to wipe away the tears streaming down her face. Who cared if her mascara ran anyway? She didn't want to see anybody and didn't care what she looked like, so once the driver pulled in the driveway, she walked past the garage where she was sure Chris and his friends still were and entered through the kitchen, intending to make a beeline to her bedroom. What she didn't count on was having to deal with Boots, who Claire studiously avoided as much as possible.

"Claire. Come here," Boots said, not turning away from her laptop. "Right now."

"Can it wait, Boots? I'm exhausted," Claire said, turning to the stairway.

"No, it cannot wait, young lady," Boots began, but stopped short when she saw Claire's face. "What happened to you?"

"Nothing," Claire said. "Can I go now, please?"

"I suppose so," Boots sighed. "It's always something with you, I swear. I have never met a more dramatic—"

But Claire had already turned the corner and was walking up the stairs, so she didn't hear the rest of the boring tirade Boots repeated any chance she had to berate Claire. Not one time in the years she and Dad had been married had Boots had anything nice to say to Claire. Instead, Boots seemed to take perverse pleasure in torturing her stepdaughter. Claire was lazy. Her art created too big a mess in her house. She wasn't responsible. She was selfish and spoiled. The list went on and on, and Claire didn't need to hear what current misdeed she had inadvertently committed. She already felt like a failure. She didn't need Boots to detail her flaws right now. She just wanted to sleep.

She didn't even have the energy to slam her bedroom door shut. Instead, she quietly closed and locked the door and flopped face-down on her bed, but after a moment, she realized she needed to use the bathroom, so Claire rose and walked to the one she and Chris shared between their rooms only to find a half-naked Grant standing in front of the toilet.

"Oh! Excuse me," Claire said as she quickly exited the bathroom, closing the door firmly behind her. What was that? It wasn't unusual for Chris to have his friends spend the night, but they usually camped out in the basement family room, and she had never stumbled upon naked boys in her bathroom. She crept into the hallway to use the hall bathroom before returning to her room, where she cued up "Horizon" by Pigeons Playing Ping Pong. Claire firmly placed in her earbuds and turned up the volume as high as it would go, hearing be damned. She could worry about going deaf another day.

6
trust

"Claire just saw me," Grant said as he returned to Chris's bedroom. "She walked in as I was taking a piss."

"What did she say?" Chris asked.

"Just 'Excuse me,' and then she walked right back out. I didn't say anything," Grant said, climbing under the sheet to reach to console Chris, who sat up and swung his legs over the corner of the bed. With his head in his hands, shoulders slumped, he groaned, "Not good. I've meant to talk to her, but there's been so much going on."

Grant touched Chris's back. "What are you going to tell her?"

"Don't pressure me," Chris said, standing to break contact. "I've told you, I'm not ready to commit. Taylor just broke up with me. I'm not sure I'm ready for anything serious."

Grant got out of bed and pulled his jeans on before shrugging into his t-shirt. "Then I don't know what I'm even doing here. This isn't for me. I've already done the whole coming-out exploration bit. You do what you need, and then come find me."

"Grant," Chris began as Grant opened the bedroom door and hesitated, but he stopped. There wasn't anything else to say. He wasn't ready to commit to Grant. He wasn't even sure what the hell he was doing, so he let Grant close the door behind him. Chris stood still as he heard Grant's steps descend the stairs and close the front door behind him before he flopped back down on the bed.

It wasn't that he wanted to experiment as Grant assumed. It was worse. How could Chris explain that Grant was not someone he wanted to get serious with, although he was attracted to him. Chris was ashamed of the fact that Grant was not someone he wanted to date openly. He was handsome, no doubt about that, and very charming when he chose, but the fact of the matter was, he and Chris had very little in common. Grant could care less about academics other than getting the minimum GPA for eligibility to play. He admitted to never reading any books assigned to him at school and has no interest in music, art, poetry, anything that wasn't about football, carbs, weight-lifting, and reliving games.

Chris cringed when Grant used words like *irregardless*. Once, Grant said, *exemplarary*. Chris wanted to scream, "It's exemplary. Exemplary." Grant didn't take any AP classes and would barely graduate with the minimum requirements, and it showed. He couldn't keep up with the steady banter Chris was used to with Claire and Taylor.

But it was wrong to sleep with someone you didn't want to date publicly. Chris knew this from the Medieval Courtly Rules of Love he studied in tenth grade Western Civ class, which he and Claire liked to mock. Still, when you reread them and applied them to your relationship in real life, they're surprisingly accurate. Chris wasn't ready to introduce Grant as his boyfriend. He wasn't prepared to come out as gay. Chris knew it was time to break it off with Grant, but he gave in to desire at every turn. Those muscles. What was wrong with him to want a guy who made him cringe?

Grant wasn't the first boy Chris was attracted to, but he was the first boy he had ever slept with. Before, attractions ended with stolen kisses. Once he mutually masturbated with a boy at summer camp, that boy avoided him the last few days before their parents all retrieved them, and Chris never saw him again. Then Chris fell in love with Taylor and spent the previous year involved exclusively with her. He never even thought about boys except in the most private space in his mind until he saw Grant at Calico House, and something sparked between the two that intensified until it evolved into something Chris wasn't sure he could handle.

He dreaded the conversation with Claire he knew was inevitable. She would want to overanalyze every detail, and Chris didn't have the heart to do that right now. It was terrible, but Chris didn't want to start school with everyone knowing he was *the* openly gay football player's latest boyfriend. Grant may be out, but Chris wasn't even sure what he was and loathed the idea of trying on labels or identities like outfits to be worn once and discarded. Better to break it off with Grant now and keep his sex life as private as possible. He wasn't even sure he wanted a sex life. It was complicated with Taylor, and now it has been complicated with Grant for entirely different reasons.

Overwhelmed by the drama of it all, Chris flipped his laptop open and immersed himself in studying Gordon Ramsey's video of how to cook the perfect filet mignon. Chris had spent so much time perfecting his bearnaise sauce; it was time to learn to prepare the perfect steaks. Someone in the house would eat it.

7
a way

The morning Claire loaded her installment into her car and drove it to Calico House to photograph for her Parsons portfolio was bright and clear. The sun proved its power well before noon, and the humidity so intense, it felt like swimming through the air, as it does in Ohio in late summer.

Although Claire could have easily photographed the piece at her own home, she wanted to test the pieces' movability in their bags before lugging them up to New York. She also wanted to set the work in two radically different settings: the pastoral beauty of Calico House against the austerity of a conference room at Hotel Pennsylvania. Rural versus urban. Taylor offered to help, but Claire declined. She wanted to be alone in the process. She felt confident in her photography skills, slinging the same Nikon around her neck her father bought her years ago when she first started cataloging her work.

It was quiet when Claire parked in the driveway and began unloading and assembling the installment on the lawn near the elm tree facing the pond. Other than a few chickens who wandered over to greet her, Claire was alone. Karen was working in her studio or away from Calico House for the moment, but she replied to Claire's texts last night confirming permission. Claire pulled her hair into a bun on the top of her head, yet she was soaking wet with sweat and frustration by the time she finished. The sculpture assembled without a hitch, but the pictures weren't working, meaning no matter what angle Claire chose, she wasn't pleased with the results.

In harsh daylight, the piece lost its magic, for lack of a better term. The painted toys looked garish and cheap. The glitter reflected poorly, and she needed a ladder or something to take pictures from above. Claire glanced up at the elm tree. She had climbed it before and wondered if climbing it now would achieve an angle that would photograph correctly, but she was a little afraid of heights. She felt almost nauseous from the heat of the day and the disappointment that this critical piece had failed. It didn't make sense. Nearly the exact opposite effect from her *Charlotte's Web* piece that burst into life the moment the sun reflected on it in the lot at the SPAC show. What was the difference? Where was the problem, and what would she do if this didn't work for her portfolio?

Feeling demoralized, she carefully placed her camera against the elm tree, stripped down to her bra and underwear, and walked to the edge of the pond. The water wasn't cool this time of the late summer season, but it was refreshing to submerge her body, so she slowly swam to the center and floated with her face lifted to the sun. The tree frogs croaked their deep songs, and dragonflies flitted on the surface of the pond, while Claire studied the clouds in the sky.

Claire heard Karen call her name and turned to see her waving at Claire from the shore. She took her time swimming back while Karen walked around the piece, inspecting it. It was the first time Karen had seen the sculpture, and Claire was anxious to hear what her mentor had to say.

"I brought you a kimono, honey," Karen said, indicating to the silk robe laying at the base of the elm.

"Thanks, Karen," Claire said as she tied the robe closed around her waist. "It's not working."

"It just ties," Karen said, still studying the piece as she walked around each panel and under it.

"Not the kimono. The piece," Claire said, smiling a little for the first time all day.

Karen looked up abruptly and said, "What's wrong with it? I think it's lovely." She walked to the elm tree base and sat next to Claire, who picked up her camera to show her the failed shots. Karen didn't speak until Claire had scrolled through all the photos.

"I see. What prompted you to want to photograph this installment here?" Karen asked. "Is it because of the tree?"

"Yes, in part," Claire said. "Sam and I spent a lot of time under this tree. I miss him."

"I know. This tree has become sacred in many different ways over the years, I suppose. It's our very own Tree of Life, so to speak. When we moved to Maywood, our father hung a swing from a branch of this tree, which broke off in an ice storm years and years ago. Maggie was so distraught when that happened. Dad never hung another swing, though. Then, I scattered Maggie's ashes around the base of the tree, and although Sam didn't know that was where he could find his mother's spirit, he was drawn to this tree all summer. Finally, you and Sam fell in love under this tree. There's history here."

"Also, because my *Charlotte's Web* piece looked amazing when we installed it outside. I thought, I mean, I hoped this sculpture would gain life like that when I brought it here."

"I understand," Karen said. "I remember the pictures, and they were beautiful. But let me ask, other than photographing this piece for your portfolio, where did you tell me you planned to install it for the public?"

"Hotel Pennsylvania in New York," Claire said.

"So, it's an interior piece," Karen said.

"I guess I never thought of it that way, but that makes perfect sense. I mean, I've never analyzed it that way, but yes. When I made *Charlotte's Web*, I had a picture in my mind of what it would look like outside against the green of nature, how the sunlight would reflect off the strands of the web, and how people would walk around it, hanging their friendship tags that looked like dewdrops when it was all done. I guess I didn't realize the entire time I was making this *Love* piece that I pictured it in the hotel. I only chose to bring it here to photograph because my portfolio needs to be submitted now. I can't wait until New Year's Eve."

"And because you were missing Sam, you thought to bring it here," Karen finished. "You could have set this up in your backyard for the same effect."

"And failed," Claire said.

"Not failed. Learned. Come on, Claire. You know this by now. Making art is a series of problems and solutions. Each stroke of the paintbrush provides a new problem you need to solve as you create. You brought it here. Photographed it. Learned in the process that an outdoor setting doesn't work, which reinforces your understanding of the place of the piece. Now you have to solve this problem."

"What's the solution?" Claire asked.

Karen laughed, brushed the dust from the back of her jeans, and handed Claire her clothes. "No way, kid. You're not getting off that easy. But I will help you tear this down and load it into your car."

Claire dressed and showed Karen how to fold the panels and slide them into their pockets while Claire carted each of the five bases and the center pole to her car.

Just before she got behind the wheel to drive home, she said, "I think I've got it. The solution that is."

Karen leaned in and hugged Claire. "I knew you would."

Claire drove home slowly, almost in contrast to the rush she felt to unload the pieces and reassemble them the way she now knew it had to be photographed. She felt a surge of joy like she always did whenever inspiration hit her, so she cued up "Blaze On" by Phish, pulled her Baba Cool shades on her face, and sang along at the top of her lungs. Her hair blew around in the wind from the open car seat, and dusk settled on yet another Ohio summer day.

She was so exhilarated, she would have begun reassembling if she weren't so physically exhausted and hungry, but she was. The bags felt heavier in the four trips it took to haul them from her car into the basement studio. She trudged her way upstairs to the kitchen to rummage something from the refrigerator only to be surprised by Chris, poised over a cast-iron skillet at the stove.

"You're home," Chris said as Claire peered over to see what he was making. "I've been waiting for you to cook these steaks. Have a seat. Everything else is ready. Are you hungry?"

"Famished," Claire said as she opened the fridge and retrieved a bottle of water. "You're making steaks?"

"The Gordon Ramsey method," Chris said. "Now that I've perfected my béarnaise sauce, I thought it was time to learn to cook something people could actually eat."

Claire looked at Chris, but he didn't seem angry. He concentrated on heating the oil to the right temperature before he dropped the steaks into the skillet. Claire watched him add a dollop of butter to the pan, and then a clove of garlic, and what looked to be a leaf that Claire assumed was an herb of sorts. In a double boiler on the stove was what appeared to be his sauce. The timer chirped, and without missing a beat, Chris grabbed two potholders and opened the oven to retrieve a steaming pan.

"Potato casserole," he announced.

"Christopher, this is a feast," Claire said as they sat at the table with their plates. Chris had even prepared a green salad with mustard vinaigrette. "Thank you. I needed to eat. I don't know the last time I've sat down to a complete meal and not just grabbed something on the go. This is delicious."

"Thank you," Chris said. "But I think I need to work more on my technique with these steaks. It's a process."

"Where's Grant?" Claire said as casually as possible, not looking up to meet Chris's eyes.

"I don't know," Chris said. He retrieved his phone from the kitchen counter. "But we've got more important topics to discuss."

"So, it's like that, huh?" Claire said.

"The first is Trey Band in Kentucky in September, and the second is Trey acoustic in Dayton in October," Chris continued as if Claire hadn't spoken. "I think we should plan to take *Suby* for the weekend in Kentucky. Make it a little road trip of sorts. You know, break up the monotony of school until New Year's by planning these two shows to get through the Fall. I mean, if we have to miss Dick's, at least we'll have these two shows on the horizon. What do you think?"

"I think that sounds great," Claire said. She knew Chris wouldn't talk until he wanted to talk. She also knew planning shows was what he did, especially when he tried to avoid whatever topic was at hand, so there was no need to force it out of him. She would have to be patient and wait for him to come to her. He had been her stepbrother for ten years. They were best friends and partners in their family dynamic, which often felt like Dad and Boots in one bubble and Claire and Chris in the other.

Even though they had paired off this past year, Chris with Taylor and Claire with Sam, she knew she could rely on her brother. She also knew something was off with Grant, who had practically been living here for the past month, and now was persona non grata, so as Claire cleared the table and started washing the dishes, she pushed one last time. "Who all is going?"

"The usual, I suppose. Me, you, Taylor, if she wants to, Alex, Drake," Chris said.

"Grant?" Claire couldn't help but push.

"It's during football season," Chris said as he walked out of the kitchen. "So, no."

Claire returned to her studio, wasting no time unearthing the black fabric rolls she needed to create a box of sorts. Instead of photographing the piece in natural light, she would do the opposite. Create a black box devoid of natural light, and it worked.

She began with a panel of the black fabric on the floor, then ran clothesline to make a square before pinning each of the four panels. She finished by draping one panel over the top before finally reconstructing the installment. Contained within the black box, the objects in the piece suddenly sprang to life, and their magic sparkled again. The colors of the work photographed in rich hues and the lines were clearly defined. The effect was satisfying, and within hours, Claire finally had the pictures she needed for her portfolio. As she exited the studio, she resolved to abandon large installment pieces and return to drawing and painting for the fall season. She would especially avoid any projects that had to do with fabrics and sewing; exchange her glue gun, needle, and thread for a simple pencil and a paintbrush, thank you very much.

8
dawn

The first days of school were always grueling, but this year it was particularly difficult to wake when Claire's alarm rang at six forty-five each morning, but she dared not miss a beat. AP History and AP English were her first two classes every day. Her art studio classes were scheduled in the afternoons. Claire appreciated the schedule. Focusing on her two academic courses in the mornings before relaxing in the art studio at school in the afternoons suited her rhythm, she told Taylor at lunch in the cafeteria.

"My days are not as peaceful, that's for sure," Taylor said before she bit into her apple. "I don't know what I was thinking, taking Physics. It's the first week, and the math is already killing me. I know everyone says after the first few weeks of grinding math, it gets fun. We get to do experiments and whatever, but until then, I just don't know."

"Have you thought about the shows?" Claire asked, changing the conversation. "The plan is to stream Dick's this weekend and then take off for Kentucky, which is only three weeks from now."

"Yes, I've decided not to go with you to Kentucky," Taylor said. "I know I'm disappointing you, but I'm just not ready to spend an entire weekend with Chris in an RV. I'm just not. I will, however, promise to go to Dayton with you in October. And I will come by this weekend for the streams. You're doing it in the backyard, I assume?"

"Unless it's raining. Then we'll just hang in the garage," Claire threw the remainder of her lunch in the can. The bell was going to ring. "It's okay. I understand. See you after school to ride home?"

"No," Taylor said, following Claire out of the cafeteria. "I have my meeting for literary club today. We have to choose our editorial staff for the journal for the year."

"See you later, editor-in-chief," Claire bid her friend farewell as she tucked into the art studios for the remainder of the day. She was grateful for the sanctuary and for the consistency her art world provided her. Mr. Shohayda had been her art teacher in middle school, yet when Claire arrived in high school, he had applied for the high school position and moved with her, not because of her but coincidentally, which suited Claire just fine. She had only had two art teachers in her life, him and Karen, who she used to take lessons from while in elementary school. Of course, Mr. Shohayda and Karen knew each other; Maywood was so small. It made her happy to know these were two people she could count on as Taylor drifted away in her literary world and her romance with Josh.

Meanwhile, Chris decided he had to ride his bicycle to and from school every day because his culinary adventures were making him fat. He hated all forms of exercise except bicycling, which left Claire alone in the car at the end of the day, unlike last year when she toted Chris, Taylor, and sometimes Drake, too. Was this senior year? The beginning of the inevitable drifting apart? Claire didn't anticipate having to miss her friends while she was missing Sam.

Fortunately, the last three hours of the day in the studio flew by as Claire drew a still life Mr. Shohayda had set up for his freshman art classes. She was content focusing on her fundamentals, concentrating on negative space and line, and shading with a simple pencil on paper. Her sketches were satisfying in their simplicity, and Claire was pleased with the composition. She thought about how fortunate she was to be an artist because she felt a sense of accomplishment as she lay down on her bed for a nap after school.

What was supposed to be only an hour's rest became three hours. Claire was startled to see it was already seven o'clock in the evening when she opened her eyes. She was surprised Boots hadn't bothered to interrupt her nap and wondered where Chris was, too, so she splashed water on her face and wandered downstairs to see where everybody was. The kitchen was empty, and before she could explore any further, Sam video called her.

"Hey there," Sam said, standing in front of his building. "Are you ready for our walk date?"

"I completely forgot," Claire confessed. "I fell asleep after school and just woke up. I'm not even sure where everybody is."

"Okay," Sam said. "Do you want to reschedule?"

"No," Claire said. "I want to walk with you, but is it okay if you walk and I rest? I feel guilty. I had planned to walk around Mayfield, starting at the library or Dairy Queen. I can't believe I forgot."

Sam said, "Stop worrying so much. Okay, so here is my building," he said as he panned the screen so Claire could see. There were so many people on the sidewalk. Crowds walked briskly past each other, some with earbuds in place, others with cellphones to their ears, and everyone in a hurry.

"Okay, let's start this way toward my favorite bodega, and I can even show you the deli that serves the world's greatest heart attack sandwich, a New York specialty you must try when you come here for New Year's."

"Heart attack sandwich?" Claire repeated. "I'm not sure about that, but okay." She reached for a bag of blue tortilla chips, a jar of salsa, two mandarin oranges, and a Sprite and walked to her room, where she settled back on her bed. All the while, Sam continued walking, the streets of New York loud and crowded, which made her heart soar with anticipation. In one year, she would be ensconced in art school in New York, holding Sam's hand while walking those streets. She couldn't wait.

"Here it is," Sam said. "Rico's Pizzeria. The best slice in town. Pepperoni or plain cheese?"

"Plain cheese for me. Pepperoni for you," Claire said, laughing. "This bag of chips with salsa is nothing compared to New York pizza. I'm jealous."

Sam opened the door and got in line. When he got to the front, he said, "Hey, Rico. Say hello to my girlfriend."

An older gentleman, sporting a handlebar mustache waved and said, "Hello, girlfriend. Whattya have today?"

"Pepperoni," Sam said. "She'll have to live vicariously through me."

"And where is girlfriend now?" Rico asked as he used a sizeable wood-handled shovel to retrieve a steaming slice of pizza from the oven.

"Ohio," Sam said, handing him the money and accepting his slice.

"Ohio," Rico said. "You got yourself a country girl, Sam?"

"You'll meet her in person when she comes here for New Year's Eve. See you later, Rico," Sam called as he exited the shop and returned to the street, phone in one hand and his slice in the other. He folded the pizza lengthwise and took a huge bite.

"Heaven," he said, with his mouth full.

"Where are you taking me now?" Claire asked.

"To the park," Sam said. "Would you like to see inside Gramercy Park?"

"You know I would," Claire said. Only residents who lived on Gramercy Park had a key to the private garden. Sam grew up there, and Claire was desperate to see. She relished the idea that the same park enchanted both her and Sam's mom. Even though it was dusk, Claire could see the park clearly as Sam navigated his way through, pointing out details he promised to show her in December. After they ended the call, Claire clutched her phone to her chest, which felt dramatic but fitting for the longing she felt in her heart.

Meeting Sam was a defining moment of her life. Of course, everyone was excited when Karen told them her nephew was visiting for the summer. Maywood was so small, anyone new was exotic, but knowing Sam was from New York held an extra appeal. What Claire did not anticipate was falling in love so quickly and so profoundly. Michael Preston was the only other adult romance of her life, and what she felt then paled in comparison to what she felt for Sam. Since Michael was also an artist, there was always an element of competition between them until Michael won the game by applying and being accepted to the Savannah School of Design, leaving Claire behind to finish two high school years. Her depression spiraled out of the grief of Michael leaving, and a week in the hospital was enough to catapult Claire into climbing out of her depression through making art. Work would be her salvation, and it proved successful as Claire felt stronger.

Last year, Claire devoted herself to exploring installation art, and the gray cloud of depression lifted the further she progressed in her work. Then, when she was not expecting romance, she met Sam. The summer was incredible. They practically lived at Calico House when they weren't on tour with Phish. Inseparable, their romance gained momentum, and Claire prayed it would hold firm until they could be reunited next year when Claire moved to New York for college. That was the plan, anyway. Claire looked at her calendar and counted the weeks until New Year's Eve when she could finally kiss Sam again until she got discouraged. Seventeen weeks seemed eternally far away.

9
play on

"It's crooked, Claire," Chris said, exasperated. "Hurry up. The show is going to start any minute."

"Relax," Claire said. "It's Colorado time. You keep forgetting. We still have another hour."

She pulled on the screen they had hung in the backyard while Chris double-checked his laptop connection to the projector. Claire had strung battery-operated, tiny fairy lights around the bushes and in the bottom branches of the ornamental trees. She lit citronella torches strategically placed around the stone patio. She and Chris rearranged the patio furniture to create a dance area. Alex, Taylor, and Drake had already arrived, bringing snacks and coolers they deposited at the table Claire had covered with a red and white checked tablecloth.

Streaming the three consecutive Dick's shows from Colorado was an epic event. They were the last shows of the summer, closing the tour, and nobody wanted to miss a moment. The weather held steady in its oppressive late summer humidity, but Claire was just grateful for no rain. Taylor would not have felt comfortable cooped up inside the garage to stream the shows with Chris, and Claire wanted her girlfriend there to dance with.

"Josh didn't want to come?" Claire asked Taylor.

"It's not really his scene, and I don't feel like having to navigate an evening with Josh and Chris quite yet," Taylor said. "It's another reason why it's good Josh lives in Lima and doesn't go to school with us. There's a clear distance between my relationship with him and my friendships here."

"I guess that is good," Claire said. "I just wish there wasn't so much distance between Sam and me. I don't know how I will make it through four months before I can hug him again. I know we're supposed to be mature about it all, but it's hard. Sometimes video calling with him is almost worse than not seeing him at all. It's like I want to reach through the screen and magically transport myself into his arms."

Before Taylor could respond, Chris yelled, "It's starting!"

They turned their attention to the screen as the members of the band entered the stage. That familiar feeling of delicious anticipation tingled through Claire's fingertips, momentarily piercing through her lovesickness. She turned to Taylor and said, "You wore silver."

World Gone Mad

"Of course! I had to celebrate the silver anniversary of Dick's," Taylor said. She wore a sparkly silver top with black shorts. Claire had wrapped a silver scarf shot with metallic strands around her neck and wore a white t-shirt, a silk patchwork skirt, and silver earrings.

"But your hair!" Claire said. "It's gorgeous. When did you get it done?"

"Mom and I went together," Taylor said. Her hair was braided into six rows of solid plats. Interspersed down the braids were little gold hoops that sparkled. "I haven't worn braids since elementary school."

"I love them," Claire said before Chris interrupted when Phish launched into the second song.

"Did you hear that? He said, *flea*, not Free, *flea*. Hilarious."

Alex raised his beer bottle to toast Chris and said, "Hilarious, yes." After he took a chug, he continued, "But it's no joke, man. This could have been another Curve Ball disaster. Seriously, this virus is real."

"Real to prairie dogs, maybe," Chris said. "But I don't think humans can catch this plague."

"Plague," Claire repeated. "How bizarre. Makes me think of Shakespeare or the Bible or whatever. I mean, what plagues do you actually hear about in real life?"

"They restricted overnight camping, but at least they went on with the shows," Alex said.

"And no vending either," Chris said. "Seriously, though? No plague could ever stop Phish."

"I'm going to video call Sam so we can all say hello," Claire said, reaching for her phone. She knew he was streaming the shows on his laptop at home in New York. Even though school started in Maywood, Sam's boarding school in New Hampshire didn't begin until after Labor Day weekend. His dad planned to drive him up Tuesday. He answered the call right away. She wanted to kiss the screen when she saw his trusty red hunting hat firmly placed on his head, his favorite show apparel. Instead, she passed the phone to Chris, who greeted Sam, handed it to Alex, and then to Taylor before returning to Claire. She settled into a chair on the patio to watch the end of first set with Sam. Almost as good as being at the show together. Almost.

At set break, Claire and Sam hung up, promising to call back for second set. Claire wanted to use the bathroom alone, and when she returned, she was grateful to see Alex and Chris setting out the snacks because she was hungry. Alex brought tacos from his family's restaurant, which was called "Miss Elva's Cocina." His mother, Miss Elva, was a comforting presence, busy in the kitchen and supervising her staff, including Alex, his two sisters, two brothers, and Luis, padre of the family. Luis was charming and gracious, so he handled the front of the house while Miss Elva held court in front of her stove, monitoring tortillas baking in a stone oven. Claire's dad made fast friends with the Dominguez's when they first moved to Maywood. Good thing or they would have starved. Unlike Chris, Dad wasn't much of a cook. Chris had prepared guacamole, bean dip, a nacho platter, and three different salsas the night before. Taylor tore open the bag of tortilla chips and dumped them into a basket on the table.

"So, nobody is going to Kentucky with us? It's only a three-hour drive, and I even made a reservation at an RV park nearby," Chris said.

"I thought I told you. I can go," Alex said. "Especially since it's just overnight. I can work Friday, take Saturday off and not have to report back until Sunday. It's in two weeks, right?"

"Three," Chris said. "Saturday, September twenty-first."

Taylor remained conspicuously silent, focusing on searching through the cooler for a drink. "Are there any Sprites left?" she asked.

Chris plunged his hand into the cooler and unearthed one. "They're at the bottom," he said as he handed her a dripping can.

"Thanks," she said, not meeting his eye.

"I guess this means you're not coming with us to Kentucky?" Chris persisted.

"Leave her alone," Claire scolded. "She's got other plans."

"I'm not bothering her. I just want to know who is going and who is not so that I can make plans," Chris said, attempting to look innocent.

Claire stared him down as Taylor excused herself to use the bathroom, probably just to get away from the situation. Claire didn't blame her one bit. She reprimanded Chris when Taylor went inside.

"Leave her be, Chris. What does it matter to you, anyway? I thought you were seeing—"

"They're back," Chris said, pointing to the screen where the band was returning to launch second set. Claire sighed, but she took her plate and returned to her chair to redial Sam to watch the second set together. Taylor smiled at Claire when she returned outside and sat in the chair next to her.

They sailed through "Everything's Right" and danced together virtually to "Sand." Claire cried a little when the band launched "What's the Use" because the song's melancholy tones always pierce through her soul. By the time they were singing to "Say It To Me S.A.N.T.O.S.," Claire was grateful she and her friends were able to dance together, streaming the show in the backyard, Sam on video; all seemed right in the world for the moment.

The next night Alex had to work, but Taylor returned. "I can only hang out again tonight. Not tomorrow," Taylor said, as she handed Claire a platter of hummus and vegetables. "My mom made this for us. She says hello."

"Are you seeing Josh tomorrow?" Claire asked.

"I'm going to his family barbeque," Taylor said. "I'm so nervous, though. It will be his whole family, cousins, aunts, uncles. I don't know."

"It will be great," Claire said to reassure her friend. "Just be yourself. They're going to love you."

"Are you going to call Sam?" Taylor said as they took their seats from yesterday to launch the show. Chris and Drake emerged from the garage where they were hitting the cart, getting high. Unlike last night, Boots and Dad were home, so they had to be more subtle with the weed.

"No," Claire said. "He is visiting his grandparents with his dad tonight. If they get back early enough to stream second set, he will call."

Drake approached them and asked, "Do you want a drink or anything?"

"No, but thank you, Drake," Claire said. "How are you?"

"Fine," he said. "Glad to be here tonight to blow off a little steam. I don't know about you, but senior year is already kicking my ass, and it's barely even started."

"I know, right?" Taylor agreed. "I'm just glad you're in Physics with me. The math alone is killing me."

"I'd be happy to help. Just call me," Drake said just as Chris began shushing them that the show was going to start. Claire was glad Taylor had asked Drake for help. Drake may seem like a stoner idiot, but he was truly a math genius of sorts. Claire guessed he was probably going to study engineering in college. As she watched her friends dance, she thought about their history. Claire and Drake were dates for prom last spring to double with Taylor and Chris, but then Taylor snuck off and kissed Drake, which caused a huge drama. Not for Claire. She didn't care about Drake romantically, but Chris was furious. He eventually forgave Taylor, and they stayed together until just a few weeks ago when Taylor met Josh, and Chris started hanging out with Grant. Typical small-town chaos.

Because there were so few kids at school who liked Phish, they would come together for shows and even find a way to be civil to each other regardless of their history. Taylor laughed at something Chris said, pushing his shoulder. Claire rose and joined her friends dancing. No time to ponder life when Phish was insisting all their attention from a stage in Colorado all the way to their small town of Maywood. She was completely content until the last song of the set. "Drift While You're Sleeping" was Sam's favorite song, and she felt lonely without him.

Claire's dad emerged at set break. "Hey kids," George said, dipping a carrot into the hummus. "How's the show?"

"Not as good as last night," Chris said.

"Are you kidding me?" Claire disagreed. "That Drift was amazing."

"Yeah, you're right. The Drift was good," Chris conceded.

George turned to Drake and asked, "How are you these days, Drake?"

"I'm fine, Dr. Cutler," Drake said. "It's nice to see you again, sir."

"Got a full load this semester?" George asked.

"Yes, sir. Physics, Calc, Trig, Anatomy, and English," Drake said. "And History. American Government."

"Sounds rough," George said. "But it's good to double-down senior year before college. Do you know where you are applying?"

"Daddy, come on," Claire interrupted. "It's a show. We don't want to be bogged down with college stuff right now."

George laughed. "Okay, I hear you. Alright, you kids enjoy yourself. Chris, don't forget to bring the projector to the house tonight. It might rain. And don't forget your laptop, too."

World Gone Mad

"I won't," Chris promised, but Claire knew she would have to remind him like she did last night. Alex was working, and she knew she couldn't count on Drake to help lug the stuff back inside. Per usual, by the end of the show, he would be too wasted or passed out on the basement sofa to be of any help.

Second set proved to be as consuming as Claire hoped. Even though they were only streaming the shows, there was something powerful about seeing how many thousands of other people were streaming to their ends of the world, all at the same time, connected to the twenty-five thousand people in the stadium. All for Phish.

After seeing a dozen shows this summer, Claire was confident this music would be the soundtrack for her life. She would always listen to new music, like her obsession with **Billie Eilish**, but her heart would remain true for Phish, especially when she needed solace or inspiration. Not to mention, it is the only music complicated enough to contain all her mental attention. Life could be so chaotic; only a Phish show could completely distract Claire, for which she was grateful. No space for worrying about college, FAFSA, and the common app. No room to think about the next art project. But nothing could erase her intense longing for Sam, so she was delighted when he called just as Phish launched into "The Wedge," which segued into "Slave to the Traffic Light." Of course, it was nothing like actually being together at a show, but it was the best they had for now. Just seeing his face, the cowlick that pushed his hair from his forehead that was so darling to her, she spent hours tracing in her mind, was soothing.

He stayed on the call with her until the end of the show, during the task of lugging the equipment and empty food trays back into the house, so they could fall asleep together, each of them clutching their phones under the tent of the blankets they created in their respective beds. "Sweet dreams, my love," were the last words Sam spoke to lull Claire to sleep. Once her breathing steadied, he quietly disconnected, rolled over, and chased the images of her into his dreams.

10
with me

Taylor fought the urge to bite her nails on the drive to the pavilion in the public park, where Josh's family hosted their annual summer reunion.

"We have to meet here," Josh explained in the car, on the drive over. "Our family is too big for our backyard, so this park works perfectly. Mom can't ever say no. She invites everyone every year. You could be a distant third cousin twice removed and still be considered family if Mom has ever even so much as hugged you."

"That's sweet," Taylor said. "What does she do for a living?"

"She runs Sunshine House, the homeless shelter in Lima," Josh said. He signaled the right blinker. Taylor could see the park as they made the turn.

"And your dad?" Taylor asked.

"Judge is a lawyer," Josh said. When Taylor looked confused, he continued. "That's his first name. Well, nickname. He's not a judge. Just a regular lawyer, but somehow, he got the nickname in law school, and it stuck. Everyone knows him as Judge Gentry. And when I say everyone, I mean it. Lima is a small town. Everyone knows everybody else and is in everybody's business."

"I get it," Taylor said. "Maywood is the same way. I can't wait to leave for college."

"You and me both," Josh said as he parked the car in the lot. "Ready?"

Taylor mumbled under her breath, "in omnia paratus," the phrase she and Claire adopted to get them through tough situations. The Latin phrase was inscribed in marble over the Maywood Library entrance where Taylor and Claire used to go for story hour as children. Then, they heard the phrase used in their favorite television show, *Gilmore Girls*. The phrase meant, ready for all things, which Taylor was decidedly not, but she pulled the visor down, applied a bit more lip gloss, and opened the door. Josh held her hand as they walked toward the pavilion.

Mrs. Gentry greeted them with a smile, revealing charming dimples indenting both cheeks. She was a lovely woman with a smooth complexion and light brown hair. She reached up to hug her son and turned to Taylor with an outstretched hand. "So nice to finally meet you, Taylor," she said.

"It's nice to meet you, too," Taylor said. "Thank you for inviting me."

"Of course," Mrs. Gentry said. "Judge, come over and say hello to your son. He's brought a friend for us to meet."

Judge Gentry wore a crisp white shirt, suspenders, and a bow tie. He lumbered over from a game of cornhole to say hello, his large hand engulfing Taylor's and his eyes peering from behind glasses to inspect her. "How do you do, young lady?"

"I'm well, sir," Taylor said.

She recognized the resemblance of Josh to his father. Before she could say anything further, Judge pulled Josh away while Mrs. Gentry said, "Taylor, honey, now you come over and tell us a little bit about yourself."

"Mama," Josh cried over his shoulder. "We can't stay long. Remember? I told you we were just stopping by to say hello."

"And that's all I'm asking your friend to do. Go on, now," Mrs. Gentry waved her son away and patted next to her on the picnic table bench. "Josh says you're from Maywood?"

"Yes, ma'am," Taylor said, sitting. "Josh and I met on campus in our writing workshop."

"What do you write, honey?" Mrs. Gentry asked.

"I write poetry," Taylor said.

"Like Maya Angelou, huh?" Mrs. Gentry smiled at her knowingly.

"I wish," Taylor said. She looked at the other women busy chatting with each other as they organized the platters of potato salad, macaroni and cheese, green beans, baked beans, cornbread, deviled eggs, and collard greens. Scattered down the center of the gingham checked tablecloths were centerpieces of red and white gerbera daisies in galvanized steel planters. Several men were operating the grills while groups of younger people played corn hole. Children ran around with squirt guns, occasionally screaming until one of the women would yell to pipe it down. R&B streamed from the portable speakers, a soothing background surrounding the scene. Taylor hummed along to the familiar refrain of "End of the Road" by Boyz II Men. It was summer. It was hot. It was a traditional family barbeque, much like the reunions Taylor attended with her extended family in Dayton. She felt comfortable listening to the women's banter while chatting with Josh's mom.

"We've got to go, Mama," Josh said, pulling Taylor's hand.

"You just got here," Mrs. Gentry protested. "You haven't even gotten a plate yet. You've gotta eat before you go."

Josh looked at Taylor. Before he could speak, she interrupted. "That would be lovely, Mrs. Gentry. What can I do to help?"

"Honey, I think we've got everything ready. You're our guest. Go get yourself something to eat, and then you two can take off for your next stop," Mrs. Gentry said.

After Taylor and Josh had loaded their plates, they sat at a picnic table to eat. A young man plopped down across from them and said, "You aren't even gonna introduce me, brother?"

Josh laughed. "Yes. Taylor, this is my little brother, Jason."

"Little is a relative term," Jason joked, pulling his shoulders back. "I think I may even have shot up a couple of inches since you weren't looking, man."

"You can be as tall as you want. You'll still always be my little brother," Josh said. "What was your handicap today?"

"Don't even ask," Jason grumbled. "I'm gonna make myself a plate. Taylor, it was nice to meet you."

"Nice to meet you, too," Taylor said.

Josh answered her unasked question. "Jason plays competitive golf. He just made the varsity team, and he's only a freshman."

"Tennis and golf?" Taylor asked.

"Yes," Josh said. "I'm not kidding when I say our bedroom was wallpapered with posters of Arthur Ashe and Tiger Woods. It's Judge's rule. Either golf or tennis. I chose tennis. Jason chose golf."

"Not football or basketball?" Taylor teased.

"Especially not football or basketball," Josh said. He wasn't laughing. "No stereotypical sports for the young black men in the Gentry family. No siree. Gentry men learn to play white men sports for the purpose of business and because you can play tennis and golf your entire life."

"What does your father play?" Taylor asked.

"There's the irony of life," Josh said as he lifted their empty plates to deposit into the trash. "He doesn't play shit."

Taylor trailed after Josh to say good-bye to his mother. She thanked her profusely for the food and said she hoped to see her again soon. Judge was nowhere to be found, so she quietly followed Josh back to the car.

After he started the ignition, he turned to her. "So, that's my family."

"That's your family," she repeated. "I like your mom very much."

"She's good. She works hard and takes care of everyone," Josh said as he pulled the car in reverse to exit the parking lot. "I'm grateful she supports my writing."

"Where are we going now?" Taylor asked.

"We've been invited to a party at a lake house," Josh said. "Have you ever been to Grand Lake?"

"In Celina?" Taylor asked, referring to the town further west of Lima.

"That's the one," Josh said. "It's hosted by this woman I met on campus. Petra Kirk. Have you ever heard of her? She's married to Damian Kirk, the software genius. They claim to be philanthropists and patrons of the arts. Word is if they like you, they will underwrite whatever project you pitch to them."

"What are you trying to pitch exactly?" Taylor asked.

Josh grinned. "Nothing at the moment, but these connections can't hurt, right? Plus, it's so hot, I thought it might be nice to be on the lake."

It was a lovely idea to be on a lake this hot afternoon, and Taylor admired the mansion that emerged as they pulled up to the semi-circle driveway in front. She could see the lake shimmering behind the house. A large green lawn sloped down to the edge of the water.

World Gone Mad

As she and Josh entered the front door, she silently thanked herself for wearing a sundress. Worried it was too dressy for a family reunion, she was now grateful as they entered the party full of well-dressed, older white people. Josh wore a seersucker button-down shirt tucked into khaki shorts and a needlepoint belt detailed with tennis racquets. She glanced down at his shoes, driving moccasins; no socks, much like many of the other men at the party. Josh paused a waiter, who was circulating with a silver tray of champagne flutes. He handed her a glass and clinked just as a large black woman with an oversized afro wearing a flowing Kente cloth caftan exclaimed, "Joshie! You came!" She air-kissed him on both cheeks before turning to Taylor. "And who is this delicious creature, pray tell?"

Before Josh could introduce them, the woman was interrupted by a nervous young man who whispered in her ear. "Sorry, darlings," the woman said as she followed the young man into the crowd.

"That was Petra Kirk," Josh said.

Taylor raised an eyebrow in response. She took a sip of champagne and asked, "Joshie?"

"Let's make our way to the patio and see the lake, shall we?" Josh said.

"We shall," Taylor teased, following him closely through the throngs of guests and was grateful for the lake breeze when they finally made it to the patio. Taylor was used to being one of the only black women in groups after growing up in Maywood. Still, these white people were different from the hippies who gathered at Karen's Calico House, and not at all like the country club set Boots and Dr. Cutler socialized with either. Determining their age to be in their thirties, they were flamboyantly dressed. Many women wore large hats one would expect to see at a horse track. Most men wore bowties, crisp dress shirts rolled up to their elbows, and shorts, an unusual combination of business and casual. A few women wore flowing gowns, and Taylor thought she spotted one woman wearing a tiara. Another cluster of women sported neon-colored dyed hair and sparkly cocktail dresses usually worn at nightclubs. Feather boas, leopard print, zebra stripes, stiletto heels, and sequins seemed to be the rule. Taylor unconsciously reached to finger one of the gold rings in her braids, grateful for their adornment in this glittery crowd.

"You look beautiful today," Josh said. "I meant to tell you that earlier, but you look pretty in that dress."

Taylor smiled at Josh. "Thank you. This is—" She didn't know what to say, lacking the words to describe the lively crowd, shouting to be heard over loud disco music from the massive speakers. Servers dressed in all-black circulated with trays of hor d'oeuvres consisting of little sandwiches topped with caviar, sashimi, and sushi rolls. Josh gestured to a server holding a tray of champagne flutes, replacing their empty glasses with crisp, new bubbly.

"Would you like to walk down to the water?" Josh asked.

Taylor gratefully accepted, and they made their way through the crowd without spilling too much champagne in the process. Once they had walked almost to the shore, the sound receded, and Taylor took a deep breath. The water was glorious, the sun glinting off the small waves sparkling like diamonds. There were almost no clouds in the sky, and the humidity of the day diminished as the breeze from the lake cooled them down. Taylor studied the sailboats in the distance.

She asked Josh, "Are these your friends?"

"No," Josh said. "I've never met any of those people before. As I said, I met Petra on campus at the gallery opening for the artist, Kiptoo Taurus. Do you know him? He's from Nairobi but lives and works in Kentucky. You just have to see his art. Phenomenal. Anyway, after we met, I'd run into Petra on campus from time to time. She asked me last week, and I thought it might be nice to spend some time on the lake. I don't know."

"It is," Taylor said. "The lake is beautiful, but I think I was more interested in spending time getting to know your family more than talking with these people. I mean, I wouldn't even know where to start."

"Why don't we use this opportunity to talk to each other and not worry ourselves with anyone else," Josh said, pulling Taylor to sit next to him on the lawn. "We have everything we need right here, and I can't think of a more perfect place I'd rather be right now. Could you?"

Taylor was so unaccustomed to his steady gaze; she didn't answer right away. Instead, she felt a warm glow begin to radiate her entire being. Josh frowned and began to stand. He said, "Or we could go back."

Taylor tugged his hand. "Of course not. Come here."

He took that as an invitation not just to sit but to kiss her. She felt the world melt away as he held her head with both hands, almost cradling her. It was such a tender gesture, Taylor wished the kiss would last forever. She also liked how casually the kiss ended with Josh gazing at her, leaning back on his elbows to recline on the lawn and watch the lake, like kissing was an ordinary act they did all the time. She felt herself relax for the first time all day.

He asked, "I feel like I know you so well through your writing, but I also feel like I don't know you at all yet. Tell me about you. Where are you applying for school?"

"Kenyon," Taylor said. "I'm applying for early decision; I want it so bad. What about you?"

"Wilberforce, for sure," Josh said. "My dad graduated from Central State and then did law school at the University of Cincinnati for their human rights program. He has definite plans for me."

"Will you play tennis for Wilberforce?" Taylor asked.

Josh said, "Can I confess? I'm not very good. So no. I don't even know if Wilberforce has a tennis team, and I don't plan to play in college anyway."

When Taylor looked confused, he continued. "My parents require us to play a sport only to become a 'well-rounded individual.' They don't mandate it's a life goal or dream of us playing professionally. In fact, just the opposite. Too many young black boys think their only ticket to success is through sports. Academics and only academics are the focus in our house. Play a sport, join clubs at school, volunteer in the community, and get straight A's. It's that easy."

When Taylor asked, "Is it?" he smiled as she hoped.

"What in life is?" Josh said. "Easy, I mean."

World Gone Mad

"You are my parent's perfect dream," Taylor said. "They would die for me to want to go to Wilberforce. That or Spelman, or Howard. I am required to apply to those schools, too."

"Don't you want to go to an HBCU? I do. Aren't you tired of being the only black person wherever you go? At least my family is not the only black family in Lima."

"It does bother me, but I've lived in Maywood my entire life. I won't say I'm used to it, and I don't plan to go back home after college either. It's just that Kenyon has been my dream school since I first knew I wanted to be a writer. I can't picture anything but that."

"Lemme give you another vision to consider, please?" Josh paused when he saw the look on Taylor's face.

She said, "Mm-mm. Go ahead. I'm listening."

"What if you went to Wilberforce, Spelman, or Howard for undergrad and then went to Iowa for your MFA? I mean, there can't be anything more white or more prestigious for writing than Iowa, right?"

Taylor laughed. "You have a point. Is that what you plan to do? Apply for an MFA?"

"No," Josh said. "I'm going to study philosophy, not writing. I'm an existentialist. I'll use my writing skills for publishing papers, of course. But my goal is to go all the way for my Ph.D. but in philosophy. I want to teach. It's all I've ever wanted to do, be a professor. However, I couch it to my parents by explaining that I'm studying philosophy to prepare for law school. They don't have to know everything all at once. I'll let it unfold and take it as it comes if that makes any sense."

"It makes complete sense, and you may even change your mind once you get into college," Taylor said and then asked, "What's an existentialist?"

"In the most boiled down sense, it means to believe in existence before essence. Meaning, every single person is their own self. Individuals can make their own decision, act independently, and even be responsible for those actions regardless of their essence. The essence is the labels and roles used to contain and label people. I mean, it gets a lot more complicated than that, but that's the general idea. I contemplate the concept of existence. I read and study Sartre, Kierkegaard, and Nietzsche. Have you ever seen the movie *I Heart Huckabees?*"

"I don't think so," Taylor said.

"It's a great movie to learn about existentialism, and it's funny as hell. I'll have to show it to you sometime. I like the analogy that the universe is a blanket, and everything is part of that blanket. Everything in the universe is a strand woven into the fabric of one blanket. Like, everything is connected to everything else, and everything is everything. I'm not explaining it right. You'll have to see it. It's about a guy who has an existential crisis, so he hires Dustin Hoffman and Lily Tomlin, who play existential detectives. Have you heard about dismantling reality?"

Before Taylor could reply, they heard Josh's name called from the patio of the house. Well, not Josh, but that obnoxious, "Josh-ie, Josh-ie." It just bugged Taylor.

World Gone Mad

Josh saw her expression and said, "Let's leave, okay? I barely know that woman. You don't mind, do you? Let's just say our goodbyes and get out of here."

"Please," Taylor said, taking his hand to stand. They retrieved their empty champagne flutes and slowly walked back to the house. Petra Kirk was waving at them from the balcony like she was waving down a bus or even an airplane; her gestures were dramatic.

"Joshie, dahling," Petra said. "Come here, my pet. There are people you absolutely have to meet."

"I'm sorry, Petra, but we have to leave," Josh said. "I appreciate the invitation. It's been great."

"The lake is just beautiful," Taylor said, but Petra barely glanced in her direction.

"You just got here," Petra continued, but Josh grabbed Taylor's hand firmly and began retreating down the patio stairs outside, not back through the house, much to Taylor's relief.

"Next time. Thanks again, Petra," Josh said, not stopping his tracks. When they made it to his parked car, got in, and turned up the air conditioning immediately, they looked at each other and burst out laughing.

"That was just weird," Taylor said.

"Really weird," Josh agreed. "Let's get you home, okay? What would you like to listen to?"

Taylor looked at him, thought about what he said about dismantling reality, and asked, "Have you ever heard of the band, Phish?"

11
take notice

Sam arrived at the restaurant in Chinatown earlier than he anticipated, so he walked around Little Italy to kill time. He was in no hurry this last week in New York before returning to school. He wanted to immerse himself in the city as much as possible, so he stopped to examine books an August West-looking dude had spread out on a tarp on the sidewalk when he spotted a copy of *The Road* by Cormac McCarthy.

"Five dollars," the man said.

Sam reached into his jeans pocket and pulled out three crumpled dollar bills, "I'll give you three."

The man grunted but grabbed the money, so Sam tucked the book under his arm and walked away. He paused at a rack outside a boutique, fingering the delicate lace scarves in an array of color, inadvertently pulling one loose.

"That's seven dollars," a woman barked. "You pay me now."

"I was just looking," Sam protested.

"You not looking. You touching. You buy," she insisted.

Instead of arguing, Sam handed her a ten-dollar bill, and she quickly returned three. It seemed funny and odd that these three bills appeared to replace the three dollars Sam had just paid for the book. Money changed hands over and over, and there was no telling whether one bill was a bill that you had previously spent or had never seen before. Sam wondered if it was possible never to receive the actual bills one spent in a lifetime, or if every bill was always new. What if he marked one hundred one-dollar bills with some symbol and then circulated those bills just in New York City. Would any of those bills ever return to him?

"Sam, great to see you, man," Haynes said. He and Sam exchanged a handshake, half-hugging before they entered the restaurant. "Have you ever been here before? Best dim sum in the city."

Haynes Topper and Sam attended St. Philips together. Although they were both from Manhattan, they had never seen each other outside of school. Haynes had texted Sam earlier in the week to meet tonight for dinner, and Sam agreed, more so out of curiosity than anything else. Not that Haynes wasn't a nice guy, it's just that he typically hung out with his own friends at school and had never done anything more than nod at Sam in the hallways.

"Ready for school?" Haynes said after they had placed their order. "I can't believe we go back already. Of course, spending the summer in Europe makes the time fly by even more. What did you do?"

"I went on tour with Phish," Sam said.

"Phish," Haynes said. "How was it? I saw Dead and Company last summer at Citi Field. It was wild. I mean, I'd been there for Mets games before, but this was something else."

"I get it," Sam said as he used his chopsticks to skewer a dumpling and dip it into soy sauce. "We saw Phish at Fenway Park. I've never seen the Dead. How was the show?"

They talked about music, and then Haynes cracked Sam up with stories of his misadventures on trains he traveled around Europe, struggling to speak French and Italian.

"And I only took Spanish after our required year of Latin," Haynes joked. "I'm glad we did it, though. Life-changing experience."

"Who's we?" Sam asked.

"Max Donegan, Reid Yates, Tate Hughes, and me," Haynes said.

"Archer Bates didn't go with you?" Sam asked.

Haynes frowned as he unwrapped his fortune cookie. "No. Archer summers with his family on Nantucket." He pointed at his fortune and read, "You are better than your biggest dreams. What does yours say?"

"Watch for clouds in your sunny sky," Sam read. "Gloomy fucking fortune if you ask me."

World Gone Mad

Haynes laughed as the boys split the bill and then walked down the sidewalk to the subway. A few days later, as Sam unpacked his clothes in the dorm room at school, Haynes knocked on the open door.

"Hey, bruh. We're back," Haynes said. "Heard you got my pal, Winston, as a roommate this year."

"I can't even tell you how happy that makes me," Sam said. "I don't know if Chip is your friend, but he was a horrible roommate."

Haynes said, "He's a jackal and definitely not my friend, but Winston is. Do you know him? I told him we hung out in the city last week and that you were cool."

"Thanks," Sam said. "I know who he is, of course. I look forward to getting to know him this year. Especially if he's your friend."

"Bet," Haynes said. He picked up a double-framed picture from Sam's desk and asked, "Who's this? Your girlfriend?"

Sam said, "Yes. That's Claire, and that's my mom at a Dead show years ago."

"Your mom at a Dead show? Seriously? And your girlfriend is hot. Where does she go to school?"

"Thanks," Sam said. "In Ohio. She's back in Maywood, but we'll see each other in New York for New Year's Eve."

"That's a long time from now. So what are you into? Want to come with? We're going to get pizza. Are you hungry?"

"Sure," Sam said, dropping his socks into the top drawer. "Let's go."

He followed Haynes down the hallway to Max and Reid's room, where he knocked on their door. The boys acted like Sam had been hanging out with them all the time. After Winston moved in, Sam was swept into the group of friends. During the first weeks of school, whenever they walked to the dining hall, threw a frisbee before dinner, or popped popcorn after returning from the library in the evenings, Sam was included in everything.

Not only that, but Sam was engrossed in his classes this semester and busy searching for the crescent moon symbols he saw all over campus. Scratched into the wood of a bench, inked with Sharpie inside a toilet stall, penciled on a desk in a classroom, Sam kept finding the image. He asked Haynes about it over lunch one afternoon, but Haynes frowned in confusion and said, "What symbols?"

"A crescent moon," Sam said.

"Waxing or waning?" Haynes asked.

"I don't know," Sam said. "What's the difference?"

"If it's waxing, the points face left. If waning, they point right."

"I guess I'll have to pay better attention," Sam said.

Haynes picked up his empty tray and said, "You do that, man. See you later."

Sam returned to the places where he had seen the symbols, but they were no longer there. Erased or painted over or something. Even the crescent scratched into a classroom desk had disappeared. It was confusing. Sam spent the week searching to no avail. After

World Gone Mad

breakfast on Saturday, he returned to the dorm room to find Winston rummaging in the closet.

"Have you seen my goggles?" Winston asked, not stopping his search to look at Sam.

"I can't say that I have," Sam said. "Why do you need them?"

"We're all going to Lake Winnipesaukee so we can meet some Brewster Academy girls. Want to come?"

Although September twenty-first was officially the start of autumn, the day was unseasonably hot, so Sam quickly accepted Winston's invitation. He didn't have any interest in meeting girls. He just wanted to escape the heat, and the idea of a cool lake sounded enticing. Haynes drove, and Sam piled into the car with Winston, Max, Reid, and Archer. They stopped at a local sandwich shop and loaded up with chips, sub sandwiches, and sodas to bring to the lake, where they spread out quilts Haynes had in the trunk. They passed the afternoon snacking, swimming, and chatting with the Brewster girls, who were friendly but sporty, athletic types who were more interested in challenging the boys to swim contests than in flirting and kissing, which suited Sam just fine.

Amid horseplay, Archer pants-ed Winston, who was standing at the edge of the water. He taunted, "Look at wittle Wee-Wee. Wee-Wee's wittle wee-wee."

Of course, everyone broke out laughing at poor Winston, stripped bare-assed, his white legs like sticks holding up his concave chest and shriveled dick. Sam didn't laugh. Archer was a bully, and Winston was his roommate. As he strode from the lake to get to Winston, he purposefully brushed against Archer.

"You're a fucking douche," Sam said, loud enough for everyone to hear.

"What's your problem, asshole?" Archer snarled.

"You," Sam said. "You're my problem."

"Alright, alright," Haynes interfered. "Time to go, guys. Let's gather up and get out of here. It was just a harmless prank. No foul."

Sam disagreed, but he kept his mouth shut and kept walking to get to his roommate. Winston had pulled on a sweatshirt, his face hidden inside the hoodie, and was leaning against the car. He didn't say a word the entire drive home, even when Archer offered a limp apology. "We cool, bruh? It was just a joke."

Winston didn't look up to meet his eye and only half-nodded as he hurried out of the car and hustled back to the dorms. Sam let him go and didn't prod him to speak the rest of the evening. But he heard his roommate crying quietly into his pillow that night. Sam vowed to get that douchebag, Archer, back. His steely resolve was the only thing that kept Sam from embarrassing Winston even further by letting him know he could hear him crying.

12
fool

"Well, we're definitely not at a Phish show," Chris said, as he, Claire, and Alex walked around the Bourbon and Beyond Festival in the hot September afternoon. Trey Anastasio Band wasn't slated to play until seven that evening, so they had time to wander around the fairgrounds that were converted into a music venue for the event. There were two main stages next to each other, and the musicians would rotate, so the audience didn't miss a beat. They were trying to figure out which stage TAB would perform to find a place near the front for that set.

"Definitely stage right," Alex said, looking up from his phone. "Alison Krauss is slated. She's sung for Phish before. Wonder if she will sit in with Trey."

"She also sang with Robert Plant," Chris added. "Maybe we'll hear her sing all three sets."

"That would be cool," Claire agreed. "Let's get some waters first and find our way down."

They stood in line for waters, and because the smell of barbeque was so enticing, they chose to order food as well. They were able to cluster around a bourbon barrel that stood upright as a table to eat, looking around at the older rockers wearing Led Zeppelin t-shirts, men in cowboy hats and bandanas, and women in sundresses and cowboy boots. Not a hippie in the crowd. No tie-dyes, no patchwork, no red sequins to be found. Many people were sitting in folding chairs, even back where you couldn't see the stage if you were sitting, and nobody was dancing.

"This is strange," Claire murmured as they wound their way down closer to the stage. Alison Krauss walked out in an ethereal outfit and took the mic. Alex led them as far as they could go before hitting a barrier reserved for VIP tickets.

"What?" Chris demanded. "You can't even ride the rail here? What the hell is this?"

Alex patted his back. "Relax, man. We'll be alright. This is good. We are here to see Trey, remember?"

A heavily tattooed skinny dude with short black dreadlocks leaned over to Chris and said, "It's typical, man. Kentucky. The haves and have-nots, you know what I mean?"

World Gone Mad

"I just didn't know you had to upgrade your ticket to get up to the stage," Chris whined. "But I don't know if that would have mattered. We only came to see Trey. I could care less about the rest."

"You don't dig Led Zeppelin?" a woman with the dude said. She was as skinny as he. "I'm Twizzler. This is Bones."

Claire, Chris, and Alex introduced themselves as Trey, and the band walked on to the stage while Alison sang her last song. Trey was beaming his customary grin, and Claire felt herself relax. It was going to be like sinking into bliss for the next hour, and she counted on following that familiar feeling as the crowd applauded Alison as she took her bows, and Trey launched into "Set Your Soul Free." Indeed. "Mozambique" was a huge crowd-pleaser. She overheard Bones yell to Twizzler, "The horn section is blazing." Almost like an omen, the band launched right into "Blaze On." Claire just smiled to herself. She was long used to the alchemy that was Phish.

By the time the last note of "Sand" resounded in her soul, Claire was grateful they had come to Kentucky. It was a different scene from a Phish show, but she looked around at the faces. Some people were dancing, and everyone was at least nodding along.

Incredible how quickly an hour zoomed by, and before she was ready, Trey was taking his bows. Claire felt a wave of sadness, a let down the set had ended so quickly as she stood with Chris and Alex, who were talking with Bones and Twizzler. They decided to move out of the standing pack of people and find a space to sit. Once they were situated, Chris and Alex left to replenish their waters and to use the restroom. Claire sat with Twizzler and Bones and talked about music. They were locals who had scored free tickets for the festival from their landlord or boss or someone. Claire wasn't sure because it was hard to make out their words. Twizzler spoke in an almost whisper, and Bones tended to mumble. Both had thick Kentucky accents.

"Have you ever heard of these guys?" Claire asked, referring to Hall and Oates, the band on stage.

"They're on the radio sometimes. *Mumble mumble.* Heard it in the holla. At Pappy's *mumble.*" Claire heard Bones reply.

Twizzler looked down at her lap and stayed silent. She answered questions but never asked anything or volunteered anything to the stilted conversation Claire had given up on, pretending to be interested in the band. She was relieved when Chris and Alex returned with bottles of water. Twizzler suddenly stood, leaned toward Claire, and whispered, "Do you want to go to the restroom?"

"Sure," Claire said, following Twizzler to the line of port-a-lets. When it was Claire's turn, Twizzler said, "Let me hold your bag for you so you can use both hands in there."

"Thanks, Twizzler," Claire said. She hurried to pee, yet Twizzler wasn't standing there like Claire expected when she opened the port-a-let. Figuring she probably got a chance at another available stall, Claire walked away from the stench but stayed close, watching the doors for Twizzler to emerge. It would have been nice if Claire could have held Twizzler's bag for her turn.

The crowd roared as Robert Plant took the stage as headliner of the evening. Claire sang along as he launched, "What Is and What Should Never Be." Memories of middle school flooded her being. She and Taylor would lose entire afternoons, lying under the

World Gone Mad

Thompson's dining room table, listening to whole albums, Led Zeppelin, the Beatles, Joni Mitchell, Carole King, the Kinks, and The Rolling Stones, until they had memorized and infused their souls with music. They learned that albums were created like books, including a beginning, a middle, and an end, and were devout in their pursuit to concentrate on each song in deliberate order. She made a mental note to steal Taylor for a nostalgic Sunday afternoon under the Thompson's dining room table again before the school year ended, and they'd be separated at different schools, in different cities for the first time since they'd met.

As soon as Robert Plant cried about a mama and the way she grooves, Claire was frustrated. Figuring she must have missed Twizzler coming out of the port-a-lets, she made her way back to Alex and Chris, who were singing their hearts out.

"Where's Twizzler?" Claire yelled to be heard.

"I thought she went with you," Chris said.

"She did, but I lost her," Claire said. She looked past Alex and asked, "Where is Bones?"

"I don't know. He took off a while ago, I think. Here, do you want some water?" Alex said, handing Claire his bottle. After she had taken a swig, she pulled Chris's sleeve.

"I think Twizzler took off with my bag," Claire said. "She offered to hold it for me while I used the toilet, but when I came out, she was gone. She's gone. Bones is gone. This is bad, Chris."

"Was your phone in there?" Chris asked. People started shushing them, so he pulled Claire and Alex back to the vending areas across from the port-a-lets.

"No," Claire said. "I have it in my back pocket, but my wallet was in the bag. Driver's license, ATM card, library card, and about fifty bucks in cash."

"Let's walk around and look for them," Alex suggested. "Maybe they just went to get something to eat or are hanging out in the back or something."

"Or maybe I've been robbed blind," Claire snarked. "I'm so stupid. It's not like she's a Phish Chick or anything. What was I thinking anyway?"

Missing the entire Robert Plant set, they walked around the fairgrounds' perimeter, scanning the lines for concessions, and circling back to the entrance with no success. Disheartened, Claire felt foolish and disappointed in herself. She had known that Twizzler chick for exactly two minutes and willingly gave her all her stuff? Why would she be so naïve? Alex led them back to the stage area behind the port-a-lets. Suddenly, he stopped and pointed. Slumped like a rag doll against the chain-link fence was Twizzler. As they approached her, Claire scanned for Bones. He was nowhere to be found. Claire screamed and pointed to her bag, lying next to the girl who looked to be dead. Alex quickly walked over, picked up the bag, and slung it over his shoulder, pushing Claire and Chris to turn around.

"Follow me," Alex ordered. Claire was too stunned to reply. She looked back at Twizzler's face that appeared almost gray and waxy. Her eyes were closed, and her mouth was slightly agape.

Alex pushed Claire and Chris back to where the bourbon barrel tables were and demanded, "Check your bag. Is your wallet in there? Your id?"

Claire's hands were shaking, but she did what she was told. Everything seemed to be intact except for the cash. It was missing, but her driver's license, ATM card, and even her library card were still tucked into their little slots inside her wallet.

"Let's go," Alex said, still taking command.

"What the hell, Alex?" Chris said, finally coming out of his shock.

"Trust me," Alex said. Claire and Chris followed him as he made a beeline to where three police officers clustered, watching the crowd.

"There's a chick passed out by the port-a-lets. She looks bad, so we're coming to you to help. I think she may have overdosed or something."

Two of the officers started walking immediately in the direction of the port-a-lets. A third officer grabbed his radio and requested the EMT's. Alex took advantage of their quick response to hold Claire by the hand and slowly edge them back into the crowd watching the show.

"Quiet. Move slowly. Act casual until we disappear," Alex whispered into her ear. Claire kept her head down and followed. Chris weaved away from them for a moment, then made his way back as they stopped in the middle of the crowd, who was delirious, singing along to "Ramble On."

"This has got to be the encore, so we need to make our way out of the venue now. Slowly. Casually," Alex directed. Claire and Chris followed. Once they had made it back to *Suby Greenberg*, Claire locked the door behind them as they slumped inside with relief.

"That was crazy," Chris said in a shaky voice. "Do you think she is dead? Like, dead, dead?"

Claire burst into tears.

"I don't know," Alex said. "It's okay, Claire. We got her help. She may be okay."

"How'd you know what to do?" Chris asked. "I mean, to keep us out of it?"

"I didn't," Alex confessed. "I just acted on instinct. It's not our fault we met some junkies who robbed Claire. Why should we have been involved if we didn't need to be? I saw the bag and grabbed it without thinking. Once we determined nothing but cash was missing, my instincts to flee just kicked in, man."

"Well, I'm glad they did and that you got us out of there," Chris said. "I just want to get the fuck home, though. Do you guys mind? I don't want to stay the night in Kentucky. Let's go."

Claire looked up through her tears and said, "I agree. Let's go home, please."

Because it was only three hours from Louisville to Maywood, it was an easy drive. Chris cued up "Ghosts of the Forest" as Alex took the wheel. Claire reclined on the sofa and tried to let the music wash the image of Twizzler's dead face from her memory. She was afraid it would take more than an amazing album to do that, though.

It was well after two o'clock in the morning when they finally rolled into Maywood, so Alex decided to crash at Chris and Claire's house. "No need to wake my parents this late," Alex said. "They think we're still in Kentucky anyway, and my mother is such a light sleeper. I don't want to wake her."

"Of course, dude," Chris said as they tiptoed into the house. Claire pulled out a sheet and an extra pillow from the linen closet and brought it downstairs to the basement family room sofa where Alex could crash.

"Thank you for everything, Alex," Claire said. "I don't know what we would have done without you."

"I'm glad you'll never have to find out." He reached over to kiss Claire on the cheek in a brotherly gesture. She patted his arm before trudging back to her bedroom to collapse. Only then did she allow the tears to stream. She knew she wouldn't be able to fall asleep, so she just lay quietly in her bed until the pink streaks of morning dark emerged.

13
regrets

Career Day at Maywood High School was a joke to the seniors. It was too late for most of them, who had submitted their common applications the week before, but for whatever reason, the day always landed in the second week of October. Claire always assumed the seniors skipped school entirely on Career Day, but now she realized that seniors were still head-down in classes because this was the last semester that "counted" for college. At least, that was what Claire did all morning. She attended her classes before stopping in the cafeteria. She devoted her afternoons to the studio, and she needed to eat something since she didn't have time for breakfast before school. Instead of just grabbing an apple, string cheese, or a yogurt, Claire decided to go through the actual cafeteria line for once, searching for anything that looked appetizing.

"Hi, Claire, honey," Mrs. Whitaker, Drake's mom, said. "Would you like some meatloaf?"

"No, thank you. May I have the rice, though?" Claire said while also reaching for a prepackaged salad. No elaborate salad bar at Maywood High.

"Of course," Mrs. Whitaker said, piling rice onto the plastic tray and handing it to Claire. "Have a good day, dear."

"You, too, Mrs. Whitaker. See you later," Claire said as she moved to the end to swipe her student id to charge the lunch to her student account. She stopped for a spork and napkin, then carried her tray through the cafeteria to the outside courtyard, where she chose a spot on a bench. It was a warm and sunny day. The first time Claire had been outside since her commute to school in the morning. Grateful to be breathing fresh air, she lifted the lid of the salad and speared lettuce on her spork. Before it made it to her mouth, Drake approached.

"May I sit with you?" he said, holding his lunch tray.

Claire scooted over and said, "Please. I just saw your mom. When did she start working in the cafeteria?"

"Just this year," Drake said. "She lost her job when Dr. Farbman retired last spring. It's not so cool for your mom to be a cafeteria lady, but I'm glad she has a job."

"There's nothing un-cool about being a cafeteria lady," Claire said. "It's good work."

Drake tilted his head and said, "If you say so. It's different. She started working for Dr. Farbman before I was even born. I practically grew up running in and out of his office, you know? He's almost like family; we know him so well. We kids called him by his first name, Dr. Howard, like everyone calls your dad, Dr. Tony. Stand-up guys, for sure. But she doesn't get paid to teach Sunday school, so landing this gig has been good."

"Do you remember the time when your mom had us make cotton ball lambs at Easter, and Chris ate so much paste, he looked like he was foaming at the mouth? Your mom thought he was having a seizure."

Drake chuckled. "Yes. Those were good days when you guys used to come to church. I wish you'd come back."

"We do," Claire said. "We're there every Christmas and Easter like the good Episcopalians we are."

"Ah, yes. C and E Christians," Drake teased. "Mom has plenty to say about that, but she's always had a soft spot for you."

"All the moms love me. I'm the poster child for motherless children," Claire said.

Drake laughed and then changed the subject, "Chris said some shit went down in Kentucky at the show."

"Yes," Claire said. "It was bad. We met these people who turned out to be shady as fuck. Did he tell you the girl stole my bag and then overdosed or something?"

"Yes. He said it was gruesome, but that Alex got you guys out of the situation safely."

"Thankfully, yes. I don't know what we'd do without his quick instincts. It was horrible, though. We didn't even spend the night in the RV park. We came right home; the whole thing wigged us out. I don't even know if that girl is dead or alive."

"It's not your fault, though," Drake said to reassure Claire.

"It's not, but I still feel bad. I scan the news, but nothing was reported about anyone dying at the festival, so maybe she's okay."

"I'm sure she is," Drake said. "I'm just glad you're okay."

Claire paused for a moment. Then she stood with her tray and said, "And with that, I'm out of here. Got too much to do in the studio this afternoon. Thanks for hanging out with me. We don't see each other enough in school. Let's do this again, okay?"

Drake grinned. "It's a date. I mean, yes. Cool."

Every time he talked with Claire alone, which wasn't often, he was always tongue-tied. He'd had a crush on her since back in the days of Sunday school, not that he'd ever admitted that to anyone. She had a boyfriend. What would be the point in declaring his unrequited love now? He had the chance when they went to prom together last year. Even though it was just as friends, it could have developed into something more if he hadn't lost his head and made out with Taylor. He didn't plan that at all, especially since she was Chris's girlfriend and date for the evening, but she kissed him. Of course, he kissed her back. Not many girls had ever thrown themselves at him. To be honest, no one had ever kissed him like that. He was only human.

What did anyone expect him to do in response? Luckily, he and Chris made amends last summer before they left for the Phish shows. Drake stayed behind, just like he had to stay back for the Louisville show. His parents disapproved of Phish, and there was no way they'd ever let him take off with his friends for weeks at a time to follow a band. That would have to wait for college, and Drake couldn't wait to escape his strict Christian parents and finally be on his own, making his own decisions. He pledged to see as many live concerts as possible. But first, he had to pass Calculus, so he carried his empty tray back into the cafeteria and walked to class.

Claire pulled the tray of leaves she had collected down from the shelf marked for her supplies in the studio. Throughout the month, she had pocketed different leaves she brought to the studio and pressed them between wax paper in an old Jansen art history book that was huge enough to press hundreds of leaves.

Each day, Claire chose a leaf to study. She sketched and painted over some of the drawings with watercolors. Others she chose to shade with colored pencils. She was inspired by Georgia O'Keefe, who blew up small flowers to a large scale to stop the viewer and force him or her to notice what people typically pass by without a second glance. She often leafed through a copy of Walt Whitman's *Leaves of Grass* she kept in her home studio to remind herself the truth of the universe is found in a single leaf of grass. She contemplated incorporating lines from "Song of Myself" because they floated like songs in her mind.

Most of Claire's sketches retained the integrity of the leaves, and others appeared as abstracts. She wasn't sure which way the project would evolve. She just knew that returning to drawing and contemplating objects of nature soothed her, now that she had photographed her installment pieces and she had submitted her portfolios. It was a relief to make art for herself again, not just to create for her college portfolios. The pressure of completing the three major sculptures drained the joy from the process she was reclaiming in her series of nature drawings, which she loved.

"Well, imagine running into you here," Michael said, standing over Claire at her worktable.

At the sound of his voice, Claire's hand froze over the paper before she lifted her eyes to see him. She should have known he'd be at school today. College Day was an opportunity for the recent graduates to return to high school as a sort of a visiting celebrity. They got to greet their teachers, talk with the students about their own experiences in college, and walk the halls knowing they had already succeeded in escaping and moving on in life. And Michael Preston liked nothing more than being in the spotlight.

He looked good. He always did, though. Michael was the kind of guy who took the time to not only think about wearing a scarf but coordinated it to his clothes that looked artistic and not fussy. Today, he wore a frayed-edged corduroy blazer over a black V-neck shirt, jeans, and Gucci loafers, without socks, of course. Claire looked down at her off-the-shoulder beige sweater and jeans, pleased she had chosen to wear that today. She had pulled her hair into a messy bun and had taken time to put on a bit of make-up. Not because of Michael necessarily, but because she knew many graduates would be returning today, and she wanted to look good.

Silently chiding herself for even caring what Michael thought, Claire pulled her shoulders back and sat up a little taller.

"Michael Preston, how are you?" she said, instantly regretting not calling him Mike, a name he hated, just to get a perverse pleasure in seeing him grimace. Why is it she could never think of quick retorts until after important situations like this?

"Good. You're looking good these days," Michael said. When she didn't respond, he continued. "What are you working on? A new series?"

"Something like that. I'm not sure yet, though. I'm letting it evolve," Claire said.

Michael sneered. "Enjoy that. Once you get into college, they don't let you wander around art, letting things evolve. It's all deadlines and due dates. Formal critiques suck because your classmates will do anything to tear your art to shreds. Seriously brutal."

"That sounds horrible," Claire said.

"It's almost like they want to squeeze all the creativity out of you so they can remold you the way they want you to be as an artist. It's exhausting," Michael said. When Claire remained silent, he continued. "I mean, it's not that bad. I don't mean to make it all doom and gloom. I've learned a lot, that's for sure."

"What are you doing here today?" Claire asked.

"I was asked to speak to Mr. Shohayda's classes, and I also talked with Mr. Penrose's students, too," Michael said. "But I'm done for the day, so I thought I'd come to find you."

"Well, you did," Claire said. "Here I am."

"Here you are," Michael said, pulling the stool across from her and picking up a leaf. "Do you mind?"

Claire handed him a sheet of paper. "Be my guest."

They worked silently for the following hour, much like they did two years ago when Claire was a sophomore and Michael was a senior, and they were a couple. Claire had forgotten that she liked to draw with Michael in companionable silence. Art was a mostly solitary endeavor unless you were working next to another artist. When the bell rang, signaling the school day's end, Claire looked at Michael's sketches. They were masterful, of course. It was what attracted her to Michael in the beginning, her awe of his natural talent. College did not vacuum Michael's creativity if these drawings were any indication. He had an instinct for line she always envied. As she gathered her materials to store for the day, he asked her if he could give her a ride home.

"I usually drive to school," Claire said. "But this morning, I rode with Taylor, so okay."

He had driven his dad's convertible since the weather was still mild in early October. When he cued up his music, Claire frowned. Now she remembered one big disconnect between them. Michael had horrible taste in music and refused to listen to anything she liked. Claire sighed and figured she would endure it until they reached her house, but he turned the opposite way.

"Where are you going?" she asked.

"Thought we'd stop at the trestle," Michael said. "Just for a minute, maybe? For old time's sake?"

Although she knew better, Claire just said, "Fine," and followed him after he parked the car.

They walked past the picnic tables and grills to the actual trestle. Claire thought about Sam. This was where they took him his first night in Maywood. Claire looked down at the water below and remembered his shocked expression when they both jumped in, fully dressed. She had yelled, "in omnia paratus." She had also kissed him full on the mouth in her excitement of leading him to jump with her, so she wasn't prepared when Michael leaned over and kissed her. She fell into the kiss for a moment before she smelled his breath and her brain kicked back in. Claire pulled away and said, "What are you doing?"

"Missing you," Michael said, pulling out the charm. "You're still so damn pretty. I just love your hair," he said, reaching to touch the curls that had escaped from her bun. "I missed your geranium perfume so much. Don't you miss me?"

"Not exactly. Not anymore," Claire said.

Claire turned abruptly and stormed back to the car. She felt stupid. She should have known better than to agree to come here. The park was deserted, of course. Kids only came to the trestle at night to party. She didn't know if anyone else even came here any other time. She leaned against his car, waiting. She would insist he take her back to her house right now.

"Come on, Claire," Michael said. He stood in front of her, put his hands on her jeans' waistband, and pulled her against him. When he kissed her neck, she put both her hands on his chest and pushed.

World Gone Mad

"Take me home, please," Claire said, reaching to open the car door. "This was a mistake."

Michael stood there for a moment, frowning, and then sighed. He walked to the driver's side as she sat in the passenger seat, waiting. He didn't talk as he started the ignition and backed out of the parking lot.

"The only reason I even agreed to do this stupid College Day was to see you," Michael said.

"Then you wasted your time. There's nothing to see here." Claire stared straight ahead, refusing to face him.

"Is it true?"

"Is what true?"

"That you cracked up when I left for school?" Michael said. "They said you had to go to the hospital; you were so upset."

"Not that you cared. If you knew, why didn't you reach out?"

"Because I was already at school. I figured it would be better for you if I stayed out of the picture," Michael said.

"Then you needed to stay out." Claire kept her gaze focused on the windshield. She was frozen with shame that he even knew she was in the hospital. They remained silent until he pulled into her driveway. Claire didn't speak as she retrieved her backpack and got out of the car.

"Wait, Claire," Michael called from behind the wheel. Claire didn't turn back. She raised her middle finger at him as she walked to the front door and slammed it behind her. Then she retreated to her bedroom and locked the door.

What the hell was she thinking? She should have played sick and stayed home today. That's what she had done last year, so she didn't even know if Michael had returned and didn't ask. Why she thought she could deal with him now was beyond her. She felt stupid and ashamed of how proud she was when Michael complimented her looks and her art. His opinion shouldn't matter to her, but it did, and that pissed her off. It was bad enough that she was fighting depression. Did she need to be a masochist and revisit old wounds? She glanced at her phone that read several unopened texts from Sam, which made her feel guilty. Not that she had done anything wrong, per se. But Sam was so good, and she was a bad person for wanting Michael's attention.

She would never confess this afternoon to Sam. Nothing good would come out of it. She would swallow her guilt and forget Michael had ever come back. It was too late anyway. Her heart belonged to Sam. To be brutally honest, she only wanted to know if Michael was still attracted to her. What was wrong with her, anyway? He was a pretentious ass. It's unnerving to see someone you once thought you loved. Maybe they could look as good as they once did when you first met them, but in this case, they could also repel you by bringing out the worst version of yourself you wished you could forget and move beyond. It was uncomfortable seeing him now when she had been working so hard to fight the flashbacks from the hospital

Remembering her resolve, Claire pledged to work the tools she knew worked to fight this depression. She would forgive herself for one stupid kiss with Michael. If anything, it reinforced what she knew to be true. That she loved Sam and nobody else. She would focus on her art, concentrating all of her energies into drawing to sharpen her skills, especially if it was as vicious in college as Michael warned. And she would focus her time and energy on her friends this last year together in high school. It was the end of the world she'd always known. It was time to dig deep and find the joy that she felt all summer. If only she could convince herself.

14
listen

It made no sense to Sam when he began to see those crescent moon symbols around campus again. He saw them in the first weeks of school, and then they disappeared. Suddenly, this first week of October, they seemed to be everywhere again, even scribbled on a scrap of notebook paper tucked into his copy of *The Dakota Winters*. Sam asked Winston about the symbols, but he was no help. He just shrugged and asked, "What symbols?"

"The crescent moon symbols I see in graffiti around campus," Sam said.

When Sam encountered a crescent moon drawn on the cafeteria tray under his plate, he took note. The points faced left. He spotted Jayden, his roommate freshman and sophomore years, and took the seat next to him. It was the first time this school year Sam had a chance to spend a moment with Jayden, and he was glad to see him.

Jayden looked up from his bowl of tomato soup, pointed to the symbol, and said, "All points left, huh?"

Sam turned to him and asked, "What does it mean, though?"

Jayden craned his neck to look around like a spy before he shares top secret information. Sam smiled at his seriousness until he noticed Jayden wasn't smiling back, so he leaned in to hear what his friend had to say.

"Quill and Toth, man. Or QT is how they refer to themselves," Jayden began.

"They, who?" Sam asked.

"The QTs. It's a secret society. Top secret. I mean, I've only ever heard about it. I don't even know if they exist."

"How come we've never heard of them? I mean, we've been here four years, and this is the first I've ever seen a moon or heard anything about a secret society or whatever."

"You must know more about the QTs than anyone else."

"What do you mean? I don't know anything. That's why I'm asking you," Sam said.

"Bruh, you know we don't roll like that. Until this year, I didn't know you even knew Haynes Topper, and now you're like with their crew all the time."

Sam stopped eating his turkey sandwich and looked at his friend. Jayden was right. Until this year, the two of them had been, if not friends, then at least friendly. Sam never questioned it until now and felt terrible. He offered, "Whatever. Do you want to hang out after dinner tonight or something?"

"You might be too busy chasing moons," Jayden said, laughing.

Sam relaxed and asked, "So what else do you know about this?"

"The myth is when you see a crescent moon pointing left; it means you're about to get tapped."

"What's tapped?" Sam asked, biting into his sandwich, studying the symbol on the tray.

"Initiated into the society," Jayden said. "Only a select few ever get initiated, and they aren't allowed to tell anybody until their funerals."

"Funerals?" Sam asked to clarify.

"Yes, it's that secret. They can't admit to anyone because secret societies aren't allowed but exist in schools. So, at the funeral, the QTs send a flag to reveal they've been in the secret society all along," Jayden said.

"Well, their families know, right?"

"Not until their funerals," Jayden said. "All of the Ivies have these societies, too. It doesn't end in high school. The hell will continue for another four years of college until you can finally escape it all."

"Still not a fan of school, huh?" Sam said as Jayden gathered the remains of his lunch on his tray.

World Gone Mad

"Not a fan of elitist bullshit is all," Jayden said. "I like the classes. I hate the rest. See you, man."

Jayden was from a Long Island suburb; Sam forgot which one. They had never socialized outside of school. As one of the few scholarship kids at St. Philips, Jayden wore a proverbial chip on his shoulder. He was a prodigy in sciences, most likely headed to MIT or Harvard to become one of the geniuses in a governmental think tank or build rocket ships for NASA or something. He and Sam were roommates for the first two years until Sam got unlucky enough to wind up with that douche, Chip, last year. He was grateful Winston was his roommate this year but felt a little sentimental about Jayden now that he saw him again at lunch. He would have to make a point to hang out with the dude since this was senior year, their last chance before they scattered all over the country for college.

Sam considered secrecy as he left the cafeteria and walked to his afternoon classes, spotting two more crescent moon symbols on his way. He'd have to look up Toth. He didn't even know what it meant. If he was going to be tapped, as Jayden claimed, he needed to learn more.

15
caution

"Are you absolutely sure you want us to use the tickets?" Taylor asked. It was Sunday afternoon, and she and Claire were perched on the stools in the kitchen while Chris cooked. Since they had submitted their college applications the week before, they all felt relaxed. No more pressure to get everything done and the anxiety of waiting had yet to kick in. That wouldn't happen for a few weeks for Taylor's early decision for Kenyon, not for a few months for Claire's applications to Parsons and NYU. It was the first afternoon of freedom since senior year had launched, and it felt wonderful. Boots was at her Junior League meeting, and Dad was at the hospital this weekend, so they took the opportunity to smoke a joint in the backyard. Claire studied the colors of the trees that had flourished into autumnal majesty, as they do in mid-October in Ohio before they followed Chris into the kitchen so he could cook. He was teaching himself to make homemade marinara, which filled the air with garlic, basil, and oregano. Claire's stomach rumbled.

"How much longer, Christopher?" Claire whined. In response, Chris pushed a plate of herbs in her direction, lifted an olive oil bottle, poured it on top, and then handed her a loaf of bread.

"Here. Snack on this. My sauce won't be ready for a while, and I still need to boil the pasta," Chris said. Then he turned to Taylor. "It would be great if you and Josh could use the tickets. Really. I can't miss this seminar." He referred to a cooking class he had signed up for that conflicted with Trey Anastasio's solo show in Dayton, Ohio, on Wednesday.

"Claire?" Taylor asked.

"I think it's the perfect show to introduce someone to Phish," Claire said. "The Victoria Theatre is a small venue, and it should be a chill scene. You and Josh make a date out of it. Get into town early. Grab a bite. Take him to see Trey. It's perfect. And you can teach Josh the love of a miracle."

"That would be fun," Taylor said. "I've never miracled anyone."

With four tickets in her hand, when Josh picked her up after school Wednesday to make the drive to Dayton, she felt a familiar tingle of excitement. The tradition of asking for a free ticket stemmed from the Grateful Dead, whose song "I Need a Miracle" was kind of an anthem. People flooded Grateful Dead and Phish shows without a ticket to walk the lot before the show with one finger raised as a request and hoped for the miracle of a free ticket. Taylor couldn't wait to experience the joy that would come from bestowing a miracle, and Josh would better understand her obsession with Phish.

"Well, it's not Phish exactly," Taylor explained to Josh as he merged onto I-75 South. "It's going to be wonderful. Just Trey, stripped down with only his guitar, but he's a storyteller. We're in for some good stuff, and he'll play Phish tunes, of course."

"Whatever you like," Josh said. "But read me another poem, please."

Taylor had brought two books with her for the drive; the first was Ross Gay's book, *The Book of Delights*. She and Josh loved Ross, mostly since he was from Ohio, too. Taylor had never been to Youngstown, but it was Ohio, and that was inspiring. The second book was Matthew Zapruder's *Come On All You Ghosts*, which included poems so funny, the first time she ever read them, she literally laughed out loud, which is a rarity in the poetry world for sure.

"Let me read you, 'The Prelude,'" Taylor said. "It's my favorite." She launched, 'Oh this Diet Coke is really good.' Let me stop there for a minute. Isn't that brilliant? What poem starts with Diet Coke?"

Josh smiled. "I don't know. I'm not sure why it's funny, though."

Taylor said, "Let me start again, and I'll read it all the way through, okay?" She used what she called her "reading voice," started again.

World Gone Mad

Oh this Diet Coke is really good,
though come to think of it it tastes
like nothing plus the idea of chocolate,
or an acquaintance of chocolate
speaking fondly of certain times
it and chocolate had spoken of nothing,
or nothing remembering a field
in which it once ate the most wondrous
sandwich of ham and rustic chambered cheese
yet still wished for a piece of chocolate
before the lone walk back through
the corn then the darkening forest
to the disappointing village and its super
creepy bed and breakfast. With secret despair
I returned to the city. Something
seemed to be waiting for me.
Maybe the "chosen guide" Wordsworth
wrote he would even were it "nothing
better than a wandering cloud"
have followed which of course to me
and everyone sounds amazing.
All I follow is my own desire,
sometimes to feel, sometimes to be
at least a little more than intermittently
at ease with being loved. I am never
at ease. Not with hours I can read or walk
and look at the brightly colored
houses filled with lives, not with night
when I lie on my back and listen,
not with the hallway, definitely
not with baseball, definitely
not with time. Poor Coleridge, son
of a Vicar and a lake, he could not feel
the energy. No present joy, no cheerful
confidence, just love of friends and the wind
taking his arrow away. Come to the edge
the edge beckoned softly. Take
this cup full of darkness and stay as long
as you want and maybe a little longer.

When she finished, she held the book to her chest. Zapruder's poems opened a whole world to her. Learning John Ashbery inspired him led her down research wormholes for days, something she loved to do. Ashbery had won every major award for poetry, and Taylor dreamed of winning even one of the accolades he achieved. Her new poems included pop culture references, just like Zapruder's Diet Coke. Before she could explain more, Josh had entered downtown Dayton, and they busied themselves looking for a place to park.

He said, "Okay, Uno's Pizza or this other place called Flying Pizza. What do you think?"

"Flying Pizza, please," Taylor said. "How can we resist that name?"

"I know. I already see a poem forming in your mind," Josh said, as they held hands and walked to the restaurant, which was so close to the theater, they could take their time to eat before the show.

After they had placed their order, they talked about Zapruder's poem, Josh's new poems about Muhammad Ali, and Taylor's obsession with Button Poetry, a YouTube channel devoted to the latest voices in the spoken word scene. Although Taylor didn't write slam poems, she loved to watch them. She had only been to a slam once, years ago, at the Kentucky Women Writer's Conference in Lexington, Kentucky, when her freshman English teacher had taken a group of honors English students on a field trip to see their first slam. It was inspiring. Of course, until that, the only slam poetry she knew was from Saul Williams, her secret poetry fangirl crush she didn't admit to Josh. She wished she could have seen him, but she was only eleven years old when he performed in Lexington, and Taylor didn't even know who Saul Williams was when she was in sixth grade.

"How do you reconcile being the only black person at these shows?" Josh asked as they stood on the sidewalk in front of the theater. He pointed to a white dude whose blonde dreads fell to the middle of his back and whispered to Taylor. "I mean, really?"

Taylor giggled and said, "Wait until I tell you about this chick named Willow Alex picked up on summer tour. You won't believe. But first, look around. Do you see anyone holding up a finger like this?" She demonstrated.

"Come on, let's walk around a bit. Here," Taylor said, handing him two tickets. "I want you to give the tickets away. Giving a miracle is the best feeling. Trust me."

Unlike a Phish show, the crowd for this solo concert was mostly older people, and the scene was very relaxed. There was no vending. No lot. Just a bunch of older white people chatting with each other, smoking their last cigarettes or nicotine vapes. The smell of pot smoke was conspicuously absent. Taylor and Josh walked around a little bit. There was still fifteen minutes until showtime, a fact she reminded Josh when he complained. Suddenly, as if appearing from nowhere, two girls about their age approached them, each holding up a finger. One was dressed like a Raggedy Anne doll. She wore a layered, long skirt and faded t-shirt. Her red hair was pulled into two braids. The other girl wore a fur-collared coat that reminded Taylor of Penny Lane in *Almost Famous*.

Taylor nudged Josh, who cleared his throat and said, "Are you looking for tickets?"

"Yes! We have this to trade," the Raggedy Anne chick said, holding up a generous, resinous bud. Taylor leaned over to inspect it. When Josh didn't offer the tickets, Taylor pushed his hand.

"I have two tickets," Josh said. "I mean, miracles. Would you like them?"

The girls screamed and jumped up and down, their faces radiating excitement and joy. When Josh passed off the tickets, Taylor accepted the bud in return, and then the girls threw their arms around Josh's neck to hug him, exclaiming, "Thank you, brother. Oh, you kind man. Thank you." He laughed in response. Taylor beamed when he laughed.

The girls dragged them back to the theater to get into the line forming to enter the show. They held their tickets above their heads, waving them back and forth like the prize they won. Taylor tucked the bud into the secret pocket of her small patchwork bag for future use.

Their seats were in the second row, all the way toward the aisle, which delighted Taylor. Even when people weren't standing to dance, Taylor could dance in the aisles without blocking anyone. Not that she could block anyone much anyway, standing at just five feet tall, but that wasn't the point. There was plenty of space to move and to dance. The girls took their seats next to them, and a moment later, Trey walked out on the stage, picked up a guitar, and launched into "Free." By the time he moved into "Winter Queen," Taylor had taken the aisle to dance, tears streaming down her face in joy.

World Gone Mad

In between songs, much like Taylor expected, Trey told stories and engaged directly with the audience in a way that Taylor had never experienced seeing Phish. It was the most intimate show she had attended, and she felt an uprising of love and joy for Trey. Josh seemed to enjoy it, too. He stood for most of the show, laughed at Trey's jokes, and swayed slightly.

A woman dressed in a red kimono, holding books in her hand, stood next to Taylor at the encore's beginning. She smiled at Taylor, who smiled in return, wondering what the woman was doing. Before she could ask, the woman leaned to Taylor and said, "I just want to give my books to Trey. I will stay out of your way, honey. I don't mean to intrude."

Taylor said, "You aren't intruding. It's fine."

She watched as the woman in the red kimono walked right up the steps onto the stage. She waited at the side, outside of the spotlight, almost at the wings, as Trey took his bows. Then, he noticed her, lit up in a way that only Trey can, and approached the woman. She held the stack of books out to him. As he accepted them, he reached out to shake her hand. The woman did not linger. She turned away to walk back down the steps; her hands pressed together in prayer. A silver-haired man Taylor assumed to be the woman's husband was snapping pictures of the whole scene.

He said, "Thank you. My wife is a poet. She just wanted to share her books with Trey. Thanks for being so cool."

"Of course," Taylor said as she watched the couple hug before they retreated to exit the theater. She turned to Josh and said, "Did you hear that? She's a poet, too."

Josh said, "That was pretty cool. I can't believe there was no security and that she could get on stage like that."

"It wouldn't have happened at a Phish show, that's for sure," Taylor said. "But did you like it?"

"Yes and no," Josh said, as they reached their parked car. "I liked the energy of the crowd. You all know, like, every lyric. That was cool. Seeing that poet on stage was cool. I'm just not sure I understand the music."

Before they had left Dayton's city limits and merged back onto I-75, a police car flashed its lights. Josh looked down at the speedometer. He wasn't speeding, but he pulled over diligently under bright streetlights in front of a lit gas station, opened all of the windows, turned off the ignition, and placed both hands on the steering wheel. He turned to Taylor and hissed, "Get your hands on the dashboard now. Hands up."

She nodded without protest. Her heart was beating out of her chest; she was so scared. Josh mentally reviewed the rules Judge had hammered into his brain forever. Windows open, ignition off. Should he toss the keys on the road? His mother always said she would toss the keys and then put her hands out the window. Josh was too afraid to reach for the keys now that his hands were at ten and two. Best to leave them where they were, he thought as the police car behind them beamed its lights on high.

Meanwhile, Taylor had pulled her license and her phone from her small bag and opened the camera. She hit record and then dropped the phone on the car floor and clutched her driver's license in her hand while she used her feet to push her bag deep under her seat. Taylor had to conceal her bag. If they searched it, they would find the bud she accepted for the tickets. Just the idea of being arrested almost made Taylor hyperventilate. She focused on taking a few deep breaths to steady herself. She was trembling at the thought of handcuffs.

"What are you doing?" Josh asked.

"I'm recording," Taylor said, her voice unsteady.

"Put it away, Taylor. I'm serious."

"No," Taylor refused while carefully placing her hands on the dashboard. "Did you never read *The Hate U Give*? I'm not taking any chances."

Josh said, "Remember, our goal is to get home safely. Do not speak. Anything we say can be used against us. And whatever you do, don't talk back. We just need to get out of this situation alive."

When Taylor didn't answer, he said, "Do you hear me, Taylor?"

"Yes, of course," Taylor said. "Of course."

Two officers exited their car and, with their hands on their guns, approached Josh's Lexus. One officer on each side.

Josh said, "Good evening, officer."

"License and registration," the officer barked.

"May I take my hands from the wheel? I am going to reach for my registration. It is here," Josh said, using his chin to indicate the glove box. "My license is in my wallet. It's in my pocket. I'm going to reach for it now, sir."

Josh kept his eyes on the officer's face while he handed over the registration and his license, and the police officer instructed, "Get out of the vehicle now, boy. Whose Lexus is this?"

"It's mine, sir. It's a hand-me-down from my father, Judge Gentry," Josh said as he opened the car door. He didn't turn back to Taylor but instead kept his gaze steady yet respectfully on the officer.

"Get on your knees now," the officer barked. When Josh obliged, he said, "Now face down on the ground."

Josh lay his body on the asphalt, his cheek raised inches from the ground. Meanwhile, the other officer instructed Taylor to exit the car and sit on the side of the road. She slowly opened the door, hands shaking. She kept her eyes averted, only glancing up briefly to try to read the officer's badge before her pounding panic caused her to focus on the break between his ugly uniform and where it met his black shoes.

Tears streamed down her face as she watched Josh lying helplessly like a criminal. She handed the officer her license and wished she hadn't left her cell phone in the car. What if it wasn't recording? What if they were too far away to pick up sound? It never occurred to Taylor the police would order them to step out of the vehicle. This had never happened to her before, so she merely used the rules her parents had drilled into her. A second police car pulled up, lights flashing, as one of the officers returned to his vehicle to check the license and registration.

World Gone Mad

The officer returned and nodded to the other officer who had been standing over Josh and watching Taylor. He ordered Josh to stand and handed Josh back his license and registration.

"Looks like you have a long drive back to Maywood," he said, emphasizing *Maywood* and looking pointedly at Taylor as he returned her license and ordered her back to the car. She had never been grateful to be associated with her hometown until that moment.

"You failed to stop completely at a stop sign, son. I'm going to issue a warning because I see you have a clean record. But pay attention, do you hear me, boy? Pay attention."

"Yes, sir," Josh said. "Thank you, sir. I will. I promise."

"Boy," Taylor mumbled.

Josh gave her a death stare, and the officer said, "Excuse me, miss? What did you say?"

"Nothing, sir. I'm sorry," Taylor said.

The officer frowned, shook his head, exhaled, and said, "I want you kids to get home safely. Let this be a warning."

The officer waited until Taylor and Josh settled back into the car and pulled on their seatbelts before he retreated, the second officer following.

Josh turned on the ignition, signaled the blinker, and gradually pulled back onto the street. They drove in silence until the entrance ramp for I-75. Josh sighed loudly and said, "You realize we just got stopped for driving while black, right?"

"I know. I've just never had that happen to me before. It was scary," Taylor said.

Josh didn't reply to her. Instead, he pushed the Bluetooth voice command button and spoke the phrase, "Call Dad."

As it dialed, Taylor asked, "Why are you calling your dad now?"

"Because I just got stopped," Josh said. "It's a family rule. Not that I have ever had to call before. It is the first time it's happened to me, too."

When his dad picked up, Taylor stayed silent while Josh explained the situation. Judge did not sound happy, but he ended the call, warning them to follow the speed limit and reminding his son he loved him.

"Love you, too, Dad," Josh said as they disconnected.

Taylor felt an unexpected shot of relief mingled ironically with sheer terror and dread, tears streaming down her face. She was terrified by what happened. She fought a wave of nausea when she remembered the bud that was still in her bag. What if the cop had searched them? She and Josh wouldn't be going home with just a warning, that's for sure. She felt dread in the pit of her stomach, just thinking about the risk she put them in. She just hoped Josh wouldn't remember or ask about it, and he didn't. The lovely evening dissipated into a spiral of shame and left an aftertaste of fear Taylor had never experienced before. The silence loomed as Josh drove the forty minutes back to Maywood. As they turned the street into her neighborhood, Josh broke the silence and said, "You realize you almost got me killed back there, right?"

Taylor nodded but couldn't speak. It was like ice in her veins; the horror was so intense. Once Josh had parked in Taylor's driveway, he walked around to open her door, always a gentleman. Taylor looked directly into his eyes, hoping he would say something, worrying this was going to be the end of their relationship when they had just gotten started. Josh remained silent, but he reached for her hand, intertwining his fingers with hers, and walked her to the door.

He leaned over, kissed her lightly, and said, "Good night."

Taylor felt the tears form as she watched him retreat to his car, open the door, turn on the engine, and slowly back out of her driveway. Hopefully, not away from her forever, but after tonight, Taylor would not be surprised.

She dreaded breakfast, knowing what her father would say in response. She pictured him frowning at her, saying, "This is exactly the reason you need to attend an HBCU. I'm proud that Mom and I chose to raise a family in Maywood, but you have been sheltered from your own blackness. It is your only chance to be among people who look like us before you have to compete in a white world for the rest of your life."

Then, her mother will agree with her dad while trying to keep the peace by reminding him that Taylor was her own person and able to make her own decisions and that Dad shouldn't attempt to live vicariously through his children just because he didn't go to an HBCU. Wait until he finds out Judge went to Central State. He'll be damn near planning the wedding if he learns that bit of information, a thought that made Taylor sigh.

16
step

Sam was startled out of sleep by hands that shook his shoulders before he was dragged out of his bed to see Haynes and Winston laughing before they placed a sleep mask over his eyes, which completely blinded him.

"Come on, Sam," Haynes said. "The moon is waxing. All points face left. Toth himself summons your presence." It was almost midnight the night before Halloween. Because it was a school night, Sam had fallen to sleep two hours before, so he was completely disoriented by this abrupt intrusion.

Winston interrupted, "Wait, Haynes. Let me find his shoes, bruh."

Sam could feel Winston push his right leg to put on one shoe and then the other, a gesture which Sam appreciated after they walked him out of the dorms and through campus in the fall evening. He had no idea where they were leading him, even as he heard the creak of a door opening into an unknown building on campus. Luckily, Sam trusted Haynes, especially Winston, who guided his blind walk, flanking him on each side, so Sam didn't trip and fall on his face. He stumbled as they descended stairs, grateful again for Winston's support, even as he felt dread at what Sam imagined he was being dragged into unwillingly.

Sam had no interest in super-secret societies of any kind. He'd much prefer the easy camaraderie at a Phish show. Still, no one was interested in what he wanted, so he just sighed and allowed Winston and Haynes to lead him into what Sam assumed to be the basement of one of the buildings on campus if he recognized the musty, mushroom smell correctly.

When they removed the sleep mask, Sam saw several guys, including Max Donegan, Archer Bates, and Tate Hughes, all dressed in black gowns with what looked like hieroglyphics painted in white all over the satin fabric. Each of the boys was holding a large black feather in their upheld left hand. Sam squinted to see they had drawn black eyeliner around their eyes, ending in swoops underneath, across their cheekbones.

Candles lit the cavernous basement. Sam spied four tall brass candelabras they must have swiped from the formal hall of the Headmaster's building. The candlelight reflected the metallic stars and moons suspended with fishing line from the low ceiling. In each of the four corners stood large paper-mache sculptures of what Sam assumed to depict Toth himself, a man's body dressed in a toga with a bird head. An ibis, Sam wondered.

Suddenly, Reid Yates, wearing the same white scrawled hieroglyphics gown with a paper-mache head mask of an ibis with a crescent moon on the top, emerged and walked, holding a staff in one hand and a black feather in the other. He took center stage as the rest of the QTs made a circle. Sam and six other initiates remained silent as Reid approached them and declared himself as the leader.

"Tonight, the moon begins to wax, and all points face left," Reid proclaimed. "You have been chosen for initiation to a society that sprouts from ancient times and continues in tradition as a student of St. Philips. You will make an oath of secrecy that will never be revealed until your death. Toth himself wrote *The Egyptian Book of the Dead*. Self-begotten, Toth represents the strength of the independent man. Are you an independent man?"

The society members pumped their feathers in their fists and chanted in unison, "We are independent men."

Reid asked Sam and the initiates, "Are you independent men?"

The initiates repeated, "We are independent men."

Reid continued his speech. "Toth was the master of moral law, ruled by science. Without his knowledge, the universe would not exist. Are you a moral man?"

The society members again pumped their feathers in their fists and chanted in unison, "We are moral men."

Reid didn't have to repeat himself. When he faced the initiates, Sam and the others automatically chanted, "We are moral men."

As Reid continued describing all the credits the Egyptians bestow upon Toth, including inventing astrology, medicine, mathematics, writing, philosophy, magic, and more, Sam focused his attention on the mention of *The Egyptian Book of the Dead*. He wondered how it connected to the Grateful Dead. He knew there had to be a connection, but he couldn't remember.

Haynes stepped forward and said, "Time is both linear and eternal, as found with Osiris in the Netherworld. It is also cyclical in its daily reincarnations each time Re rises. To attain eternal life, the deceased must become Re in the moment of reunification with the corpse of Osiris. All roads travel through the Neverland for Re to reach Osiris. There is only one key to resurrection, and what is that key?"

The members of the society chanted, "Knowledge."

Haynes repeated, "What is the key?"

The initiates said, "Knowledge."

"We will not wait for our coffins to be lined with *The Book of Two Ways*. Instead, we will commit our lives to the pursuit of wisdom. Learning to live is the key to eternal life because time is both linear and cyclical, and, in that spirit, we pledge our loyalty to each other, brothers in the pursuit of knowledge."

Reid chanted, "We lift the quill in honor of Toth," and the members and initiates all repeated it in unison, repeating the phrase several times.

When they had finished chanting, members walked to an individual initiate and handed him the feather, saying, "Celebrate the Moon with us."

Haynes approached Sam, who accepted the feather from him because he didn't feel he had any other choice, the way Haynes was looking at him. Thus far, it appeared reasonably harmless, a few candles and paper-mache, feathers, and cheap star decorations in a dark basement.

He liked the part about the concept of time, something that he, Chris, Alex, Claire, and Taylor liked to discuss. The physics of an electron's ability to spin both clockwise and counterclockwise at the same time was as engrossing as the debate of Schrodinger's cat and the question of existence versus reality. Psychedelic experiences opened portals to realities perceived in new ways; even if the immediate hallucination was not trusted, its presence was worth reflecting. Not that you could always remember. That was the hard part about tripping, the inability to express, let alone capture insights, visions, and perceptions at the moment because it flashed too quickly. Perhaps participation with Quill and Toth would lead him to new ideas to ponder, and that in itself may be worth the rest.

17
help

The Thursday evening of Halloween, Claire and Taylor sat in the kitchen watching Chris finish cooking chili while munching on the roasted pumpkin seeds he baked earlier that afternoon. Coltrane and Miles Davis's strains filled the kitchen because Chris believed he cooked better to jazz than any other music. A bowl of candy perched on the table in the foyer, ready for the trick-or-treaters who would descend in droves for the two hours Maywood reserved for this mischief, ringing the doorbells of decorated houses, demanding treats, and running wild through the neighborhood in the dusk. Claire smirked, thinking about all the years she, Taylor, and Chris donned costumes and tasted the sweet mixture of chocolate and limited freedom on their tongues. What she didn't know then was that she would feel that same heady combination of anticipation, freedom, and joy at Phish shows years later, a fact she reminded herself as images of that dead girl, Twizzler, came to mind. That wasn't a Phish show. That was just dark and twisty. Claire wished she could erase it from her mind.

"My five-star chili is almost ready," Chris said, interrupting her thoughts.

"You mean five-alarm?" Claire asked.

Chris looked startled. "What do you mean, five-alarm? You mean five stars, right?"

Claire and Taylor looked at each other and cracked up.

"It's traditionally referred to as five-alarm because of the peppers and the heat, I think," Taylor said. "But, I'm sure your chili is five stars."

Chris didn't reply. Instead, he reached for his phone to research, so Claire turned back to Taylor and asked, "So you've only texted with Josh since Dayton? You haven't talked? It's been two weeks."

"I don't know if he ever wants to see me again after what I did," Taylor said, looking miserable. "Even my parents were furious with me, and I didn't even confess that I had talked back to the cop. But he kept repeating 'boy,' and I was completely terrified when Josh was lying face down on the asphalt. Facedown. Like a criminal or something, and he didn't even do anything wrong. They stopped us because we were two black kids in a Lexus. They stopped us because we were driving while black. Not because Josh didn't stop at a stop sign. I don't even remember a stop sign."

"It sounds horrifying. The whole thing," Claire said. "I would never have expected them to force you out of the car. It was because you were driving while black. That has never happened to me."

"Me neither. And that's the point. I changed my applications to early action from early decision on Kenyon," Taylor said.

"What does that mean?" Claire asked. She had applied for regular decision for her schools. Of course, Parsons was her first choice, but she wasn't confident enough to apply for *early* anything.

"It means that I'm seriously considering HBCUs now. I am," Taylor said. "Maybe what my dad has been trying to hammer home is right. Maybe I don't understand what it truly means to be black. And if anybody knew that I had a bud in my bag? I can't even think about it."

"Josh hasn't mentioned it?" Claire asked, rising to get the pitcher of iced tea from the refrigerator. "Are you thirsty?"

"Yes, thank you. I mean, please pour me a glass of tea. And no. Josh hasn't mentioned it, and I certainly haven't brought it up. Maybe he didn't realize that girl traded me the bud for the tickets when I think about it. It was all pretty subtle. We were in front of the theater. In public. That's another example of me not understanding I don't have the privilege to pretend life is a Phish show. It's not. I'm black."

Claire laughed before she saw how stricken Taylor looked. She set the two glasses of tea on the table and said, "Of course, you're black."

Taylor said, "You don't know. That cop looked directly at me and implied that it was because my home address is in Maywood that they were even going to let us go back home. Like, maybe I'm black, but I'm the right kind of black or something."

"Or maybe it was because they recognized Josh's name. His father is a judge, right?"

Taylor smiled. "No. His father is called Judge Gentry, but he's not a judge. He is a lawyer in Lima. And I guess Josh and I are a special kind of black. Bougie black or whatever. The kind of black forced to lie on the ground, but okay to just get a warning as if being terrorized wasn't enough. I guess it's enough that we got out of there alive."

They were interrupted by the doorbell and, for the next two hours, doled out candy to the costumed children who approached the front porch as their parents stood in the streets, greeting neighbors and corralling the smaller kids from house to house. TJ and Tristan, both dressed in Black Panther costumes, enjoyed their freedom. Being eight and ten, their parents deemed them old enough to trick-or-treat without their parents for the first time. Claire chuckled at Tristan's chocolate-smudged face. He appeared to be eating the candy as fast as he received it.

Before she could ask, Taylor said, "They both insisted on Black Panther. Neither would concede, so even though TJ isn't happy to be dressed like his brother, Mom decided it wasn't worth the fighting and gave in."

World Gone Mad

As her brothers turned away, Taylor grabbed TJ's bag and said, "Wait a minute, kid," and then unearthed a bottle of shaving cream and a roll of toilet paper from the bottom.

"Come on, Tay," TJ protested. "It's not eggs. Just a little harmless fun. You know, like daddy talks about. Mischief Night. We're just trying to make a little mischief. Don't act like such a bitch."

"First of all, who do you think you're calling bitch? Secondly, if you don't get your little behind out of here, I'm calling Mom now. Mischief Night. Whatcha all know about mischief anyway," Taylor said. "Tristan, do I have to search your bag, too?"

"I ain't got nothing," Tristan said, opening his bag in response.

Taylor said, "That's because you're eating it as soon as you get it. You better stop before you get sick. Leave some in the bag for later."

Chris approached them, waving his phone in the air. He said, "Heads up. Alex just texted. Drake's in trouble. They're on their way here now."

"What kind of trouble?" Claire asked. For the third time, Taylor replenished the hand-painted ceramic bowl with jumbo-sized bags of candy. The Cutlers couldn't possibly hand out candy from a pedestrian package. It was not elegant enough with the elaborate decorations festooning the front porch, including Cinderella pumpkins, gourds, corn stalks, battery-operated candles in lanterns that lined the walkway, and even a circle of ghosts appearing to dance in the front yard. Tomorrow morning, before noon even, Boots would carefully remove the Halloween touches, leaving the rest of the autumn décor for Thanksgiving until she transformed the house into a winter wonderland for December. The pattern was predictable, planned, and executed with perfect taste year after year, photographed and archived in Boot's blog and Instagram. Apparently, thousands of other homemakers in America tried to imitate her designs.

"Not sure," Chris said. "That's all Alex texted. Come in and eat a bowl of chili before they get here."

Claire, Taylor, and Chris sat at the table together. Not only did Chris prepare his five-star chili, but he had also baked cornbread with corn kernels and fresh dill. Claire thought it was delicious and complimented him, and Taylor agreed. They finished eating just as Alex texted they had arrived. Chris directed them to pull in front of the garage, the plan being to corral Drake into *Suby Greenberg* without potential parental involvement.

Alex had to drag Drake out of the passenger seat; he was so wasted. Chris hurried over to help.

"What the fuck? He stinks," Chris said.

"He puked everywhere, man," Alex said as Claire entered the keypad to open the garage door. They managed to haul Drake, who was mumbling incoherently, into *Suby* and lay him out on the bed in the back.

"Turn him to his side," Claire said as she reached for the trashcan to place next to Drake. "We don't want him to choke if he pukes again."

"What happened?" Taylor asked, sitting on the bench around the table. Claire and Chris joined her.

World Gone Mad

Alex leaned against the cabinet and said, "Apparently, he drank too much. I'm not quite sure. His texts made no sense at all, and the restaurant was busy. It's Day of the Dead weekend. Serious business for Mexicans. I don't have time for this shit, but what else could I do?"

"Where was he?" Claire asked before Alex turned to leave.

"At the trestle," Alex said. "I'm sorry, guys, but I have to get back. I don't even have time to clean out my car. I handed my tables to my sister and told her I'd be back in a minute. That was almost an hour now."

Claire reached into her pocket for her car keys, handed them to Alex, and said, "Take my car. Leave yours here, and I will clean it. We can switch back tomorrow."

Alex leaned over and kissed Claire on the cheek as he accepted her keys. "Thank you."

After he left, Chris said, "I'll stay here and watch out for him if you two want to start on the car. It isn't the first time we've seen our buddy lose his shit. Won't be the last. That's what happens when you put a leash on your kid and don't let him do anything. He has no sense of boundaries."

"You're one to talk," Claire said. "Weren't you a hot mess this summer? If I remember correctly, you did quite a number on that Lyft driver's car in St. Louis. Or was it Boston? I can't remember."

"And I got my shit together," Chris said. "I screwed up. Yes. But I stopped drinking and, besides smoking a little weed, have kept it together ever since. Drake has been pulling these benders for years. I wouldn't be surprised if he gets alcohol poisoning or something."

"You sound so judgmental, Chris. What's going on with you?" Taylor said.

"Oh," Chris looked surprised. "I'm not judging. I'm worried. Bruh is all splayed out like that time and again. He could really fuck himself up, is all I'm saying."

Claire and Taylor retrieved cleaning supplies, a roll of paper towels, a garbage bag and got to work. Together, it didn't take long to clean up the vomit, so Claire returned to the garage for a vacuum.

"Might as well detail it a bit more as a treat for Alex being such a good friend, don't you think?"

"Absolutely," Taylor agreed as she started to Windex the windows inside and out.

Once they finished, Taylor said good night and returned to her own home while Claire stopped for a couple of sodas from the garage fridge before opening the door to *Suby Greenberg*, where Chris watched videos on his phone. He looked up when she handed him a can and sat across from her brother.

"What are you watching?" she asked. "More Gordon Ramsay?"

"The guys from Yes Theory. Seek Discomfort. This time, they flew to the happiest country in the world, Bhutan."

"I love those guys," Claire said.

"Me too," Chris said.

"As much as you love Grant?" Claire asked, trying to look innocent, taking a swig of her soda.

Chris stared at her for a moment and then said, "I do not love Grant. Let's just start there. I wouldn't call it love."

"Then what would you call it?"

"I'm not quite sure. I'm not quite sure I even like him," Chris said. "That's a terrible thing to say, but it's true. Before you say anything, hear me out. It's just, he has the worst grammar. Like cringe-y. He hasn't read a book in his entire life. He doesn't like to talk about anything we talk about, yet..."

"Yet, you still see him?" Claire finished for him. "You're still attracted to him?"

Chris sighed. "Yes. That's the problem. I'm very attracted to him, but we have absolutely nothing in common. We don't spend much time talking. I know that sounds bad, but it's true. It's different because Taylor and I could talk forever. We always had something to say, but—"

"But sexually?" Claire prodded.

"Sexually, nothing," Chris said and then rose from the table to check on Drake. When he returned, Claire took a deep breath and blurted out, "So do you think you are gay?"

"I don't know what I am," Chris said. "Fucked up, I guess. Drake's all fucked up because his parents keep him on a short rein. I have no idea what I'm doing with Grant. Taylor is questioning her entire life goal of going to Kenyon after what happened in Dayton, and you've been struggling to be okay without Sam. You are okay, aren't you?"

Claire knew what he was asking, and she didn't want to worry him needlessly, so she just said, "Yes, I am okay. You don't have to worry about me, Chris. Just focus on what you want in terms of Grant and follow your heart. It will lead you."

"Instead of my dick?" Chris joked.

"Right. Don't be a dick. Don't follow your dick," Claire said, rising from the bench. "And with that, I bid you good-night. You going to be okay alone here with him?"

"I'm fine. I'll crash in the upper bunk in a while. Get some rest."

Claire turned around, walked back to Chris, and gave him a quick peck on the cheek. She murmured, "Love you," and then exited *Suby*, pulling the door closed behind her.

18
long time

Sam could not have been more surprised to find a driver at his dorm room Friday, November first. He had just returned from classes when the driver knocked on his door, announcing that his dad had sent him to take Sam into the city. His dad scored tickets at Madison Square Garden to see Dead and Company that evening, so Sam quickly changed out of his school uniform into his favorite "Read Icculus" t-shirt and jeans before pulling on his red hunting hat. In the car, he texted Claire what was happening. She said she was jealous of seeing Dead and Company since she had yet to see them, but she was excited Sam and his dad would catch a show together. The driver let him off right in front of the venue, directing Sam into the food court area on the arena's first floor.

When he walked in, he saw his dad right away. He was wearing a gray hooded sweatshirt with a steal-your-face that read, "Yes, I May Be Old, But I Saw The Grateful Dead On Stage," and jeans, which both stunned and humored Sam. They hugged hello, and his dad directed him to get food from the different booths while he got a beer for himself and a soda for Sam. While they ate, they caught up about school and the common apps. When he told his dad he applied to NYU, Columbia, UVA, Kenyon, and Yale, his dad seemed pleased even though he was a Harvard grad. Then, Sam followed his dad to the entrance of the Garden. Their tickets were club seats, of course. These were corporate tickets his dad got from work.

Waiting in line to enter the venue, Sam paid attention to the crowd. Not so dissimilar from Phish, in that they were all hippies, but that's where the similarities ended. He was one of the youngest people there. Most of the crowd were old white guys who looked like any other dads, which made sense to Sam since he was with his dad. Men outnumbered the women in the jam band scene. There was no doubt. Sam wondered if Deadhead women had a group like Phish Chicks. If they didn't, they should. Claire and Taylor always felt connected to their community of women at shows.

They settled into the club seats, which accessed the 360 Club and Bar and Grille. Dad ordered two beers, slipping one to Sam. They sipped beers and chatted until the band took the stage.

"Why is Bob Weir wearing a kilt?" he asked his dad.

"Because Robert Hunter just died," he said. "I'll explain more at set break."

World Gone Mad

Although the tempo was slower than what Sam was used to listening to old Grateful Dead shows, the first set was incredible, especially "Bird Song," driven with a funky beat by the keyboardist Jeff Chimenti. A woman Sam did not know named Maggie Rogers took the stage to add her vocals to "Friend of the Devil," one of Aunt Karen's favorite songs. And although Sam wouldn't say his dad danced, he swayed a bit as he stayed on his feet for the whole set.

Second set was better for Sam as he loved almost every song and knew the lyrics by heart. His dad threw down for "The Weight," which cracked Sam up. Who knew the old guy had it in him? When they closed the show with "Brokedown Palace," Sam had tears in his eyes, thinking about Claire, reminding him of her love for when earth touched the water. Sam consoled himself, thinking that they would be together in this same venue in just a few short weeks.

His dad arranged for a driver to pick them up after the show, asking him to stop to pick up a pie from Rico's on the way home. His dad opened a couple more beers, and they sat together, eating pizza, drinking beer, and talking well into the night. He told Sam about Robert Hunter, who Sam did not know was a descendent of Robert Burns. He shared stories about the shows he and Mom attended and talked about his fraternity and college experience, hoping Sam would choose to pledge next year. He even told Sam stories about pranks he pulled when his dad boarded at St. Philips and about the summer he and Mom backpacked around Europe, staying at youth hostels and traveling with their Eurail passes.

When he couldn't hold himself up a minute longer, Sam rose and said, "Dad, this was the best night I could have ever asked for. Thank you."

"Thank you," his dad said, pulling Sam into a hug. "I feel like something has reconnected between you and me, of course, but also to my younger self, as well. I forgot how much I enjoyed going to shows with your Mom. I'm glad you guided me back, son."

Sam finally collapsed in his old room and slept in until the late afternoon. He and his dad spent Saturday walking the Hudson after breakfast at their corner spot in the neighborhood. That evening, they ordered in Thai and watched movies, both of them with their feet kicked up on the sofa. By Sunday afternoon, Sam was back at his dorm studying for a history exam and texting with Claire all about the show. He realized he had forgotten to ask his dad about Quill and Toth.

19
lost it

The week before Thanksgiving was always rough at school. For whatever reason, most of the main projects and longer research papers were due just before the boys left boarding school for the holiday, so when Sam woke up with a ferocious hangover Friday morning, he was confused. He could only remember pieces of the night before. As he rose to brush his teeth and splash cold water on his face, hoping to clear the cobwebs, he struggled to piece together what had happened to cause him to feel so groggy. He clearly remembered being awakened at midnight by Winston and Haynes, who said, "Bruh, Toth calls. Let's go."

Sam wasn't happy, but he was relieved not to be blind-folded this time. Instead, the boys had walked him away from campus into the woods. Sam had explored the woods before, of course. Just not at midnight. And not in November when the New Hampshire winter was threatening to descend with more than just frost on the proverbial pumpkin. Sam shivered under his fleece, grateful he had at least grabbed that on his way out, regretting not reaching for his trusty red hunting hat. In hindsight, Sam was thankful he had not worn the hat. Most likely, it would have been lost because he could not remember how he returned to his dorm room at all.

They stopped when they reached the clearing, where a bonfire blazed inside a fire pit created with a rock circle. Aside from the fire and the flashlights on the boys' phones, it was pitch dark. Sam heard an owl hoot. He remembered everyone celebrating, slapping each other's backs, yelling, and joking with each other, which felt casual and not as formal as the initiation ceremony. Sam relaxed when he saw guys smoking and hitting the cart. Although they called the evening The Night of the Feast, there was no food at all.

Sam clearly remembered accepting a bottle of what he assumed to be vodka or tequila from Archer Bates. One swig and Sam's throat felt like it was on fire. It tasted like lighter fluid. Bates snorted and explained it was Everclear, not that Sam even knew what that was. After that, things became hazy until Sam knew he could not remember more than pieces, a fact that frustrated him as he walked to eat breakfast before getting to his one class of the day to turn in his project before he planned to pack up and catch the train back into New York for the holiday. One shot should not have caused Sam to blackout. He did not remember drinking any more than that first swig, but maybe he did. He felt so badly, he wouldn't be surprised to learn he drank the whole bottle, yet that seemed very unlikely. Sam had never been much of a drinker. It was all very strange, and he felt disoriented, not remembering the rest of the night.

After he had popped two pieces of bread into the toaster and poured himself a cup of coffee, his roommate Winston approached him, holding a tray piled with eggs and bacon. Just the smell was enough to turn Sam's stomach. How much of that Everclear did he drink?

"Everyone feels awful after the Night of the Feast," Winston said. "Come over to our table after your toast is burned."

Sam nodded. He grabbed an apple, a banana, and his toast. Sitting at the table with Winston were Haynes and Reid. Sam mumbled good-morning and tried to choke down a corner of his toast.

"Feeling rough around the edges, huh?" Haynes joked. "How is your hand?"

"My hand?" Sam asked. He looked down, and sure enough, his right hand was bruised. How had he not noticed this before? "My memory seems a little foggy. Anyone care to fill me in on what happened last night and why I can't seem to remember anything?"

Reid barked a laugh. "You don't remember knocking Bates on his ass? Bruh, it was epic."

"Seriously, bruh. He was asking for it. And who would have thought the douche would go down in one punch?" Haynes said.

"I hit Bates?" Sam said. "I don't remember a thing."

"How could you not remember?" Reid said. "Bates was acting like an asshole, walking around, insisting everyone call him Master. You laughed and said, 'Master Bates' and everyone cracked up."

"I don't think he thought that all through," Haynes said. "So, it was hilarious when you called him out."

"Until he started in on Winston," Reid said. "Then, you went ballistic. You seriously don't remember this?"

Sam shook his head and took another sip of the weak coffee, and asked, "How much Everclear did I drink?"

"Everclear?" Haynes said. "I didn't drink any Everclear. Did you, Reid?"

"No, bruh. I stuck with the Jaegermeister. Who gave you Everclear?" Reid asked Sam.

"I don't remember. Bates, maybe. It tasted like lighter fluid," Sam said. "But listen, I'm not much of a drinker, and I can promise you, I've never blacked out like I did last night. This is crazy. How did I get back to my room? I don't remember shit. I especially wish I could remember punching that douche. He's had it coming since that day at the lake."

Winston finished eating the rest of his eggs and stood, holding his tray. He said, "Whether you remember or not, I won't forget. Thank you. See you guys after break."

"I've got to get to class. And so do you. Let's go. We've got five minutes before Mr. O'Donnell loses his shit," Reid said, rising from the table. Haynes and Sam followed.

World Gone Mad

Later, back at the dorm room, Winston was sitting on his bed, waiting for Sam, his packed duffel bags near the door.

"I think he drugged you," Winston said as a greeting.

"He, who? Bates?" Sam asked. He began loading the rest of his things into his bags.

"Yes, Bates. I just don't think he expected you to be able to move as quickly as you did. But the reason I think he drugged you is that you passed out almost immediately. If Bates had even gotten one punch in, we would have thought you had gotten hurt. But it was crazy. You suddenly jumped up, roared once, and landed a punch square in his face. Almost all of the QTs were cheering you, but then, you sat on a log and almost immediately passed out. At breakfast, when you said you drank Everclear, it occurred to me. I think Bates roofied you. Or gave you fentanyl or ketamine or something. Haynes, Reid, and I had to drag you back here and pull you into bed. I stayed up most of the night to make sure you were still breathing."

"Thank you, bruh. Thanks for watching out for me," Sam said. "Why would he do that?"

"Because you always defend me," Winston said. "I shouldn't tell you this, but I don't care about Quill and Toth right now. Bates didn't even want you to be initiated, but he had no veto power against Haynes. And the fact that he was outvoted by everyone else. We like you, Sam. Bates is a bully and always has been. He's made my life hell until this year when you stepped in. So, thank you. Listen, I'll wait for you. We can take the same shuttle to the train station, cool?"

"Bet," Sam said, grabbing his copy of Michael Imperioli's book, *The Perfume Burned His Eyes*, his red hunting hat, and the rest of his clothes. "Let's go. A week away from this place is exactly what we need now."

20
part

Taylor bit one of her nails as she refreshed the screen for what felt like the millionth time. Since it was Sunday afternoon, she should have been finishing her homework, but there was no way she could concentrate on anything other than the decision that Kenyon should have already posted by now. Instead of staying up until midnight the night before, Taylor forced herself to bed, even though she didn't sleep a wink. She reasoned that if she imposed this sort of discipline on herself, she would be rewarded with the acceptance update she had yet to see, and it was almost three o'clock. Of course, the colleges say they will notify you around December fifteenth, but everyone she knew who applied for early action or early decision was wasting their Sunday refreshing their screens in between grumbling on social media about the misery of the wait. She debated texting Josh but remembered he was busy volunteering at Sunshine House for his mother. Ever since Thanksgiving, they were back on track and even more serious in their relationship, a fact that filled Taylor with more love than she felt possible.

To distract herself, she bypassed Billie Eilish for her favorite childhood artist, Joni Mitchell. She needed to hear *Blue* from beginning to end, so she abandoned her laptop and flung herself onto her bed, volume as loud as possible in her headphones. She let Joni's voice soothe her jagged nerves and allowed her mind to drift back to Thanksgiving when she and Josh had finally made amends and declared themselves officially a couple.

Because Mrs. Gentry served dinner at Sunshine House, she hosted her own family Thanksgiving the following day. Consequently, Josh was able to come to Taylor's family dinner after they had volunteered that morning. She and Josh put paper tablecloths on the tables, loaded pans of food into the ovens, and then served when the shelter's doors opened at noon. Taylor and Josh's brother, Jason, found an easy banter, ganging up on Josh in jest.

Taylor's mom never served dinner before evening because Uncle Joe, Aunt Connie, and their kids always picked up Grandma and drove to Maywood from Dayton. When Taylor and Josh walked into the door that afternoon, the Thompson Family Thanksgiving was well underway. The house smelled of turkey, cloves, cinnamon, wood smoke from the fireplace, and Vivaldi's "Four Seasons" played in the background. Taylor's cousins chased her brothers, screaming in delight from their happiness in playing together, which only happened on holidays and the summer family reunion until finally, Aunt Connie corralled them into the playroom to stream Disney.

"We're home," Taylor said, holding Josh's hand. "Mom, Dad, this is Josh. Josh, these are my parents."

"Very nice to meet you, Dr. Thompson," Josh said, shaking her father's hand.

Taylor's dad said, "Call me Dr. Tony."

Taylor rolled her eyes as Josh said, "Okay, Dr. Tony."

Josh turned to Taylor's mom, shook her hand, and said, "Thank you for including me at your table today, Mrs. Thompson."

"You are very welcome, Josh," Taylor's mom said. "Please, come in. May I get you something to drink?"

"Water would be nice. Thank you," Josh said. Taylor kissed her grandmother, aunt, and uncle and introduced them to Josh. They all took turns shaking hands as Josh smiled in a charming way that revealed his dimples.

"How was it this morning?" Taylor's dad asked. He turned to his brother, Uncle Joe, and explained, "The kids volunteered at a homeless shelter in Lima today."

Uncle Joe said, "That's good. You live in Lima?"

"We do," Josh said. "My mother is the director of Sunshine House, so my brother and I volunteer there all the time. We kind of grew up in and out of there."

"Oh, dear," Grandma said. "You were homeless? Your whole family was homeless? Where are your people, dear?"

B. Elizabeth Beck

Josh looked confused. "No. We weren't homeless. I meant that my brother and I kind of grew up there because it's not just a job for my mom. It's kind of her whole life, outside of raising us. She's the director now, but she's worked there my entire life practically."

"Grandma," Taylor said. "Josh's dad is a lawyer. His name is Judge Gentry."

"Your father's a judge?" Uncle Joe asked.

Taylor turned to Josh, raised her eyebrows, and asked, "What is going on? Are we not speaking English or something?"

Taylor's dad said, "I've heard of your dad. No, Joe. He's not a judge. That's his name. He's a strong voice in the civil rights community, if I'm not mistaken."

"That's true, sir," Josh said. "Dad does a lot of pro bono work and is outspoken in the black community. At least in Ohio. He attended Central State and then UC Law. He's been practicing law in Lima for twenty years."

Taylor groaned when she saw her dad's eyes light up. She knew what was coming next and was right when he asked, "Are you following your father's footsteps to Central State?"

"Wilberforce, sir," Josh said. "Central State. Kentucky State. Those are my top three choices, but I feel confident I'll get into Wilberforce."

"That's a good man," her dad said, slapping Josh on the back. "Did you hear that, Joe? Wilberforce man in the making right here."

"You just will never let that go," Uncle Joe said. "Your big regret. Indiana over Wilberforce. Good thing you had kids to live through. Taylor, what's it going to be for you, pumpkin? Which HBCU for you?"

"I applied to Kenyon, Uncle Joe," Taylor said.

"Kenyon! That ain't no HBCU," Uncle Joe said, frowning. "What's she talking about, Kenyon?"

"She's also applied to Howard, Spelman, and Wilberforce," Taylor's dad stepped in. "But for whatever reason, she's bound and determined for Kenyon. Just wait a few years until your kids are grown and applying to schools. They've got their own ideas and their own minds."

Taylor's mom interrupted the conversation to call them to dinner. Aunt Connie yelled down for the children, which created a frenzy as everyone loaded their plates and settled at the table to eat. Taylor's mom spent all day basting a roasted turkey. There were also mashed potatoes, cranberry sauce, cornbread, sweet potatoes, deviled eggs, macaroni and cheese, collard greens Aunt Connie cooked with ham hocks, green beans, and Grandma's famous rolls. It was much the same fare the next day at the Gentry house; only they also served chitterlings, a soul food Taylor could not bring herself to embrace. Even Mrs. Gentry admitted preparing the dish stank so much; she cooked in the Sunshine House kitchen the day before carrying the pot home for her family, leaving a considerable portion for her employees and volunteers.

Jason doused his plate with hot sauce and dangled a chitterling in her face. "What's wrong, Taylor? Too ghetto for your tastes?" he teased.

"Stop that, Son," Mrs. Gentry chided. "Chitlins ain't for everyone. Leave her be. She's a guest. Besides, I haven't even gotten the potato outta the pot before you're digging in. Where are your manners anyway?"

"I don't even eat that stuff," Josh said, putting his arm around Taylor. He turned to Jason and said, "You're the only weirdo of our generation who does, bruh."

"Important to carry on tradition," Jason said between bites. "Know your history."

"Not every tradition needs to be carried," Josh quipped back.

Their easy banter at the table fueled Taylor with serenity. Both families were familiar and casual with their love for one another, everyone talking over each other, teasing, laughing, eating, and then cleaning up together. Taylor felt more at ease than she had in weeks, leaning back into the security of family. Their casual approach to holidays was in direct contrast to what she knew was going on at the Cutler's household to celebrate Thanksgiving.

Not one to cook, Boots had dinner catered every year. The most work she did was transfer the food into bone china and sterling silver chafing dishes. This year, Chris insisted on cooking. After practicing three different corn puddings and two stuffing dishes, including exotic ingredients like oysters, pine nuts, and fennel, he gained his mother's permission.

Claire complained every year about the linen tablecloth and napkins, and the elaborate tablescapes Boots ordered and snapped pictures of for her blog, and the boring guests who expected different wines for different courses. What Thanksgiving was served in courses? At both Taylor's and Josh's houses, the food was laid out at the same time and heaped onto one large plate. Except for dessert. Okay, perhaps black families served in two courses. Still, certainly, no hired help walked around with canapes on silver platters, cleared dirty plates between courses, and washed every dish before pocketing the generous tips Dr. Cutler doled out at the end. Taylor knew when she grew up, she wanted her family Thanksgivings to be like the one's she enjoyed all her life with her family. No matter how rich and famous she became from her writing, she would never hire help and order food that wasn't prepared by herself in her kitchen.

"I don't know," Josh said when she explained this to him on their drive to Maywood after dinner. "I think it would be great not to have to slave over dishes after spending days cooking. Maybe we could even hire staff to serve at Sunshine House. I think the homeless folks would dig being served by waiters with white gloves. What do you think?"

Taylor laughed. "Okay, yes. If I ever have that kind of money, I'll pay for waiters at Sunshine House before I have them in my own house, okay?"

"Are you sure you're going to study writing and not social work or law?" Josh said. "I think I hear the makings of a civil rights activist in your voice. And remember, at Kenyon, you're bound to meet all sorts of people who live like your friends in Maywood."

Taylor thought about that statement as she rose from the bed to refresh one more time. This time, the wheel stopped spinning, and when the acceptance to Kenyon College blazed on the screen of the computer, Taylor wondered how she would feel joining the twenty percent of the student body who identified as domestic students of color. Before now, she had never considered the other eighty percent.

21
together

Taylor arrived early the day after Christmas to help Claire load her installation piece into the individual bags and into the Range Rover they borrowed from Boots to drive to New York the next day. Unfortunately, Alex canceled at the last minute, so it was just the three of them preparing for the ten-hour drive to spend New Year's Eve weekend with Sam at his apartment at Gramercy Park. If Claire had any worries about how well Taylor and Chris would get along, they were assuaged within the first hour of driving. They acted like siblings, teasing each other and then ganging up on Claire, who was so relieved there would be no tension between them, she took their joking in stride. They listened to Grateful Dead, Billy Strings, and moe. on the drive, eating sandwiches and snacks Chris had prepared so they wouldn't have to stop for anything other than gas and to use the restrooms. When they finally arrived at the front of Sam's building, Claire's heart leaped when she ran into his arms.

"Welcome to New York," Sam said, his arms spread open wide. After they had hugged hello, they pulled their bags out with the help of Sam's doorman before giving the keys to the valet.

"Fancy," Claire teased Sam. She could not stop touching him, reaching for his arm, his hand, the back of his neck. After Sam showed them around the apartment and guided them to the guest rooms to drop their stuff, Claire stood at the windows in the living room, gazing at the park. Sam held up his key in response.

"Would you like to go now or wait until tomorrow when it's daylight?" he asked.

"I can wait," she said. "I want to see everything."

"You will," Sam promised. "We have a weekend together. An entire weekend."

Mr. Abernathy arrived home early to meet Claire, Chris, and Taylor. He made reservations for dinner, so they followed him the few blocks to his favorite restaurant, an Italian place where you ordered several dishes to share family-style, which delighted Claire, of course.

"I'd like to make a toast," Chris said, holding up his water glass. Everyone held theirs in return.

"Congratulations to Taylor, who just received early-acceptance to Kenyon," he said. They clinked glasses and echoed their congratulations to her.

World Gone Mad

"That's fantastic, Taylor. Wow. Early acceptance," Sam said. "You threw it all in, didn't you?"

"What does that mean?" Mr. Abernathy asked.

"When you apply for early acceptance, you are saying it's your first and only choice. If they accept you, that's where you go without negotiations for grants and scholarships and whatever," Sam explained. "But it was Taylor's first choice, so it all worked out."

Taylor kept her mouth shut, smiling at Sam's explanation until Mr. Abernathy said, "That was very brave of you, Taylor. Well done."

"Thank you, sir," Taylor said. She was a bit flushed from the attention. Before she could take a breath to explain that her decision wasn't final, Mr. Abernathy said, "Call me, Drew. You may all call me Drew." He rose his glass again. "Welcome to New York."

22
a minute

New York in December is magical, and Claire wanted to experience every moment with Sam, tucking each memory away like postcards to pull out later when they would be separated again. Even riding the subway to Greenwich Village to order cappuccinos from Café Reggio and watching the buskers, the homeless, and the tourists in Washington Square Park delighted Claire. She and Sam held hands as they walked through MoMa. Claire was astounded how large Picasso's painting "Les Demoiselles d'Avignon" was compared to studying it in books. When they arrived in front of the tree at Rockefeller Center, they took turns taking pictures of each other while watching the ice skaters. Chris loved the lights on Broadway, and Taylor insisted they push through tourists on Times Square, holding hands like grade school children to keep from losing each other.

The best part of the day for Claire was when they returned from sightseeing, and Sam held up his key and asked, "Would you like to see Gramercy Park now?"

"Of course," Claire said. "Let me check with Taylor first, though."

Claire found Taylor and Chris sitting on the guest room bed together. She said, "Excuse me. We are going down to Gramercy Park. Are you two okay?"

Taylor said, "Enjoy. I know how much you want to see the park. Go."

"We'll be fine," Chris said. "Right, Taylor?" He waited for Claire to close the door before continuing the conversation he dreaded and Taylor deserved.

"When did you know you were gay?" Taylor asked.

"Maybe always? I don't know. Maybe not until this year when I met Grant?"

"I guess I'm confused. I mean, I knew there was a disconnect between us, but I didn't understand what that was until I met Josh. Does that make sense?" Taylor said.

"Perfect sense," Chris said. "I love you, Taylor. I always have and always will. I never meant to hurt you."

"I know that. I feel like maybe we were just trying ourselves on as a couple. Does that make sense? Like, we're always together. We grew up together. It made logical sense for us to be a couple, but—"

"But we didn't count on me being gay."

"Are you? I mean, just because you're with Grant now doesn't necessarily mean you're gay. I mean, we know lots of kids at school who reject labels. We know kids who are so fluid, their pronouns change even in one day."

"Right," Chris said, laughing. "I don't know. What I know is that I still identify as he. My gender isn't fluid. I feel like a man in a man's body who is attracted to other men, so at least I've got that all worked out. Then, there's the complicated stuff. Like, I'm involved with Grant but feel pressured by him to join the GSA and officially come out, and it's causing a problem with us. Yet I still call him. Still meet up with him."

"That's gotta be hard," Taylor said. "What has Claire said about it all?"

"To follow my heart," Chris groaned, flopping backward on the bed. "Like I'm supposed to listen to Miss Romance. She's so far in with Sam; she thinks love will solve everything."

Taylor giggled and said, "True." Then she rose from the bed and looked out the window, which overlooked Gramercy Park. She spotted Sam and Claire standing in front of the statue of the Shakespearean actor, Edwin Booth. Taylor knew Claire was delighted to walk in the park, which was so exclusive, only homeowners had a key.

"Taylor, are you happy with Josh? Are you in love? Can you forgive me?"

Taylor turned from the window. Chris had propped himself up with his elbows, half-reclining on the bed. She sat at his feet and said, "Yes to all of the above. We were best friends. We are now best friends. What happened this summer was a fluke. An experiment gone awry, of sorts. We are cool."

The next day, Sam's dad surprised them with tickets to see the show that night. "They're not clubhouse tickets like we had for the Dead, but they're free tickets," he said.

When Chris exclaimed, "They're general admission! These are better than clubhouse, Mr. Abernathy. Thank you," Sam's dad laughed the same way Sam laughed when he was bashful.

Claire studied the similarities between Sam and his dad when they stood together. Sam had his dad's eyes and his mother's nose and mouth, Claire knew from the numerous pictures of Sam's mom she had seen at Calico House and here at the apartment. Sam walked with the same assurance as his dad, especially as he led them into Madison Square Garden for the show. As the boys settled in, sitting on the floor, greeting the people around them, Claire and Taylor took off for the restroom.

"Did you and Chris have a good talk?" Claire said as they stood in front of the sinks, using the mirrors to apply more glitter.

"We did," Taylor said. "He told me all about Grant. Of course, everything makes more sense now, in terms of our relationship. I thought it was me or that my idea of romance was unrealistic until—"

"Until you met Josh," Claire said.

The girls stopped to purchase bottles of water before returning to the boys, careful not to step on garbage bags protecting people's coats and purses, which also served as boundaries of people's dancing islands on the floor. Suddenly, a seven-foot woman and her eight-foot man stepped right in front of Taylor and stopped. Taylor waited a few moments for the couple to move on before Taylor tapped the woman's shoulder and said, "Excuse me."

Chris leaned forward and said," Move on, please."

The woman turned around and snarled, "I'll stand where I want. It's a show, for fuck's sake."

"Not in our area," Taylor said, holding her ground. "We've been here for an hour. See, this is our garbage bag. This is our space. Just move a few steps over, please."

"Is this your first show?" the woman said. "You do not get to take all the room on the floor. You don't have to be so rude."

Taylor took a deep breath and spoke in a tone she reserved for scolding her little brothers. "That's right. I'm rude. I'm a fucking bitch, actually. Do you really want to spend your show with a bitch? Because that just doesn't make any sense. I'm a total bitch."

When the mean seven-foot woman and her eight-foot man walked away, Taylor exhaled and released her hands clenched in fists. Her heart was beating fast, and she felt a trickle of sweat down her spine. She didn't realize the exchange was overheard until the group of boys behind them applauded and cheered. Suddenly, the lights lowered, and the band took the stage. "Turtle in the Clouds" was exactly the song Taylor needed to hear at that moment, as she struck a hero pose with Trey and Mike, feeling powerful and much taller than five feet. Dancing on the floor of the Garden felt so intimate, Taylor forgot twenty thousand souls were grooving together under one giant roof.

As they sat back down on the floor at set break, one of the guys behind them leaned forward to get their attention. "Look," he said, pointing backward. On the back of the seven-foot woman who was sitting behind them, someone had slapped a bright orange sticker on her back that read, *Don't Engage Me. I Chomp!!!* They could not stop laughing at the bitch karma could be.

"Guess I wasn't the only person she freaked out on," Taylor said, laughing.

When Sam excused himself at the "Carini" opener to go to the restroom, Claire reached into the garbage bag for her purse. It was missing. She yelled to Taylor, "My bag is gone."

Taylor helped Claire empty the garbage bag, search through the contents, and return everything before she followed Claire back to the concession stand where they had bought waters before first set. Claire approached the worker and said, "I lost my bag. It's a red sequin drawstring bag. It's not here, is it?"

The worker pointed to the left of the counter where, miraculously, Claire's bag was still there.

Claire reached in and retrieved her phone and wallet. After ascertaining nothing was missing, she exhaled. "I can't believe I was this lucky. Everything is here, Tay. Everything."

"I can," Taylor said. "It's a Phish show."

"You don't understand," Claire said. "This is too much like what happened with that Twizzler chick. I'm kind of freaking out."

Taylor put a hand on Claire's arm and said, "I understand. I do. Take a breath. This is not like what happened with Twizzler. She stole from you. This time, you merely forgot your bag and was lucky. Maybe like a balance of the universe kind of thing?"

"Let's not tell Chris and Sam about this, okay? I just don't want this to be a big thing. I mean, I didn't lose anything, and everything's okay. I don't want this to ruin our visit, okay?"

Taylor frowned and said, "I don't think this would ruin our visit, per se, but okay. Whatever you say. It's a show. We can deal with this later. Let's just go back in."

The girls walked back to the group where Sam had already returned. By the time the band launched the first notes of "Harry Hood," Claire had let a momentary wave of relief soothe her soul. Life was strange and people even stranger, but they were at a Phish show, and for a moment, everything else could disappear long enough to tuck into the notes and let them lift Claire's soul to the ceiling of the venue. She felt absurdly joyous, images of the day colliding with Kuroda's light show, mixing into a profound understanding of the balance of the universe as only can be found between notes of a Phish song.

The last song, "Run Like An Antelope," was so invigorating, Taylor and Claire danced their way out of the venue after the show. They skipped behind the boys, following Sam, who led them to Rico's Pizzeria for a couple of slices to go before returning to the apartment and tucking into bed before midnight. Taylor and Claire were glad they shared a room because they talked for hours, a peculiar combination of relief and exhilaration that would inhibit sleep, even though they would need all their energies for the two days ahead.

23
road

Claire was too distracted to appreciate how happy Sam and Chris were when they figured out how to move the *Love* piece. It was less of a logistical nightmare to drive the Range Rover to Hotel Pennsylvania than it would have been to lug it on the subway or a bus. Everyone but Claire was in high spirits in the elevator, each steadying the bags with their hands on a hotel luggage cart. Her friends joked, asking each other if each pole was "wook-worthy" as they taped and secured the stands and the stakes, while Claire obsessed about last night.

How had she been so lucky twice? Even though it wasn't lucky Twizzler stole her bag, it was fortunate that nothing else was stolen aside from cash. Last night was a miracle that her purse was still there.

How many mistakes could Claire make without suffering any real consequences?

What's worse is the guilt Claire felt as she watched Sam's open expression when he greeted Kristin and Tim, the friendly couple from Kentucky they met on summer tour. Sam was such a good person. How could Claire have not confessed her mistake in losing her bag? She felt terrible thinking these were three secrets she kept from Sam. She didn't tell him about Michael, she never told him about being in the hospital, and now she hadn't told him about last night. When Tippy and Plums surprised them, having driven in from New Jersey that afternoon, it wasn't enough to lift Claire's spirits. Instead, guilt segued into a shame spiral. Even the crowds who exclaimed over her *Love* fountain, reaching to touch the toys, and walking under the rainbows couldn't pull Claire from her funk. She felt a bit robotic, faking sincerity, dread settling in the soles of her feet. She watched as Sam wandered away to explore the other booths. Claire hoped he hadn't sensed her distraction and vowed to muster cheerfulness and not ruin these few days together.

She did great until Chris complained as they were lugging the pieces back to the car. "That's one thing about selling art, Claire. You don't have to carry out as much as your load in if you're doing it right."

She felt the shame like waves crashing over her. He was right. What kind of artist did Claire think she was anyway? She hated the *Love* fountain and worried there was no way she'd ever get accepted to Parsons with the portfolio she had submitted. She thought about her Barbie doll exhibit and shuddered. Would there ever be art that

Claire loved after the fact? Was it typical for an artist to hate everything she creates? She conveniently forgot her pride for her *Charlotte's Web* piece, intent instead on the other two exhibits she now felt were failures.

Nobody was in a good mood once they had navigated traffic to park in front of Sam's building, so he suggested finishing the evening by ordering in and hanging out at the apartment to watch movies, which everyone gratefully accepted. Mr. Abernathy left a note on the fridge that he would be out for the evening. Claire feigned delight when Sam pulled out take-out menus from the kitchen drawer even though they would order everything with an app. from Sam's phone.

As soon as Sam ordered the food, Claire grabbed the vodka Sam unearthed from the freezer. She threw back a shot straight from the bottle as Sam organized cranberry juice, limes, ice, and glasses to mix cocktails. After Sam had mixed the drinks, another quick pull from the bottle and Claire felt a dimming of despair and the false courage it would take to sail through the evening.

They ate too much food, drank vodka, and watched *Fast Times at Ridgemont High.* Then, after smoking a joint on the balcony, they had a dance party, blasting Pigeons Playing Ping Pong and STS9 until Mr. Abernathy returned home. He wasn't mad, but he shut down the evening, claiming it was a Monday night at midnight, and they needed to rest up for tomorrow, New Year's Eve. Claire was buzzed enough at that point to pass out, momentarily released from her shame.

24
again

Claire woke with a pounding headache, her mouth feeling like it was full of cotton, and dread descending around her head as she brushed her teeth, trying to avoid looking at herself in the mirror. She heard Chris and Taylor rattling around in the kitchen and paused to listen for Sam's voice. Maybe he was still asleep, she thought as she turned the knob on the shower.

Standing under the hot water, Claire let the tears fall as she shampooed. Then, she took a deep breath and made a decision. She would set aside her feelings of shame and deal with them later. She wasn't going to ruin these last two days with Sam in New York. She did what she knew would work. She stepped out of the shower stream and turned the knob to cold. Then, she put her head under the icy water, rinsing away her hangover. After she turned off the shower, she wrapped up in a towel and used the blow dryer on her hair, feeling relief in a cleared head.

She tucked back into bed just before Sam knocked, entering the bedroom with two cups of coffee. She smiled when she took the first sip, prepared with sugar, precisely the way she liked it. He looked mischievous as he reached into his coat pocket, pulling out a robin blue box.

"Happy New Year," he said, handing it to her.

"What's this?" she asked, smiling with recognition of the box.

"A gift," Sam said. "Open it."

Claire was delighted to find a Paloma Picasso necklace inside. She squealed as she held up the silver necklace that spelled out Love, put it on immediately, and thanked him with a kiss.

"I love it," she said. "Thank you."

"You're welcome," Sam said. "I love you. When I saw your installation yesterday, I knew I had to get this for you, so I went out this morning."

"Just now?" she asked. "How did you even know about this necklace?"

"We still receive Tiffany catalogs, and I saw it. Dad should probably discontinue the junk mail and magazine subscriptions, but he hasn't yet. Maybe never will."

"Because you read everything in sight," she said. "Makes sense."

World Gone Mad

They joined Chris and Taylor in the kitchen and decided to get dressed to get breakfast and some fresh air. They ate, then walked, and window shopped.

"How far is Central Park?" Chris asked.

"About fourteen blocks," Sam said. "Why? Do you want to go?"

Chris looked at Sam and said, "Not today. I just wondered. Maybe next time."

Of course, the girls demanded extra time to get ready for the show. "It's YEMSG!" they insisted.

"Did you tell Sam about losing your bag last night?" Taylor asked as she and Claire did their hair and make-up in the bathroom.

"No. He was so sweet to run to Tiffany this morning. There's no harm. Why chance ruining the fun?"

"I think you underestimate him, Claire," Taylor said. "He obviously adores you."

"I love him, Taylor. We only have this short time together. I will tell him about the bag later, but I don't know if I'll ever tell him about Michael. I still feel like that's my stupid mistake to live with, and since nothing happened and never will, I don't see a reason to tell Sam."

"Except that you're in a relationship," Taylor said. "I thought that meant you tell each other everything."

"Everything? I don't think that's how it works," Claire said. "Hey! Let's forget about this. It's New Year's Eve! It's our year. Our graduating year. 2020 will be epic; I just know it."

Taylor knew she couldn't push Claire any further and agreed that New Year's Eve was special enough to deal with everything later, so she followed her friend to grab Chris and Sam and head to the show.

Their seats were in the 200 section but in the center of the venue, which was perfect. They wouldn't have to worry about seven-foot women harshing their groove. Three sets divided the show, which included "Fluffhead" and "Punch You in the Eye," two of Claire's favorite songs. When the band came out in costume to launch the last set with "Send in the Clones," they freaked out a bit. They were wearing the same four colors Claire had used in *Love*. It was uncanny. The performers, costumed as color-coded clones, danced and sang on stage as the band members got on four individual platforms suspended above the stage. Claire felt a lifting of shame about her art. She recognized the prophetic color choices in her sculpture in relationship to the show. Once again, she understood the alchemy of Phish and her life to be inextricably intertwined.

Claire kissed Sam at midnight, keeping her eyes open to mentally record the memory as balloons in the same four colors descended from the venue's ceiling. Before the band launched into "Drift While You're Sleeping," it became apparent to everyone that Trey was stuck on the platform. Tears streamed down Claire's face as she sang about love, leaning over to kiss Sam repeatedly. When the clones held metal discus to reflect lights through the venue during "What's the Use?" Claire saw Sam wipe a tear.

World Gone Mad

Finally, Trey admitted he was officially stuck on his platform, still suspended above the stage. It was both awesome and awful. The band planned to finish the show with Trey dangling up there. Of course, nobody in the audience left until the Rescue Squad got on Fishman's platform and saved Trey from his. As the platform lowered, Trey picked up the drumsticks and started playing while leading the audience to chant, "Rescue Squad. Rescue Squad," until they safely returned to the main stage. Trey bowed, walked off stage, and a moment later, the house lights went up. Chris, Taylor, Claire, and Sam linked arms and walked into the night together.

25
both sides

January held its gray, dreary darkness, which made getting up for school drudgery until every Ohio kid's wish was fulfilled in the form of a snow day. The blizzard was so intense that school canceled the night before, a rare occasion and cause for celebration. Claire and Taylor organized the group to meet at Mt. Gibson late afternoon for sledding.

"It's better in the afternoon after all the little kids, and their parents are gone. You know children still wake up early, even on snow days," Taylor said, thinking about her little brothers who would surely wake up and demand pancakes, then sledding, before tucking into non-stop video games all afternoon.

"My dad promised to take TJ and Tristan sledding early.

They're lucky the snow day landed on a Thursday, the day Dad doesn't see patients."

"We're lucky. Otherwise, we'd be babysitting," Claire said. "Okay, since we're free, who else should I add to this group chat?"

"Who all do you have on there?" Taylor asked.

"Me, you, Chris, Alex, Drake, Josh, and Sam," Claire said.

"Sam?" Taylor said. "Just because you miss him?"

"Yes, because I miss him and because I thought he might be happy to be included even if he can't actually be here," Claire said, reaching to touch her Love necklace. Nine weeks was a long time until Spring Break, and Claire counted down every moment to Karen and Luke's wedding, scheduled for the first Saturday in March to coincide with Sam's Spring Break. Leaving him after New Year's was worse than when he left Maywood in August, for whatever reason. The past three weeks felt like an eternity. This snow day was a welcome distraction to Claire's heartache, so she threw herself into the plans with gusto.

"I'll grab some Bailey's, and Chris will make up a thermos of hot chocolate. I told everyone to meet at three at the sled hill. Should I include Grant, do you think?"

"No," Taylor said. "He and Chris are no longer talking; I don't think. We had a chance to talk in New York. Like, really talk for the first time in forever. I think that romance has run its course."

Claire and Taylor ended the call, and Claire sent the group message with emojis of snowflakes, mittens, a mug of coffee, and sleds. She snuggled back into her comforter and turned off the bedroom lights so she could better see the fat snowflakes outside her window. Tomorrow would be a winter wonderland, and Claire looked forward to sleeping past her alarm on a Thursday. She would linger over a cup of coffee without hurrying and spend the morning chilling out to random videos or chatting with Chris in the kitchen, where he would surely spend his time learning a new culinary trick.

"You've become obsessed, and I love you for it," Claire said to Chris the next morning, as she nibbled on a corner of his French toast. He refilled her cup of coffee.

"What else do you have on the agenda for today?" Claire asked.

"Besides sledding?" Chris said. "Nothing. After I finish here, I plan to shower and maybe even go back to sleep for a while. I'm like the little kids. I woke up at dawn practically. I was so excited."

"That's funny," Claire said. "Okay, I'll plan to meet you in the garage at two-thirty. Maybe I'll rummage around out there myself to find the Red Dragon. Remember, Christopher?"

Chris grinned. "Of course, I remember. If you find that sled, it will make my entire day."

The Red Dragon was nothing more than a plastic toboggan, but it was the fastest sled, and it held two people, unlike the multiple disc sleds they also owned that only fit one kid at a time. Claire poked around behind *Suby Greenberg*, pulling out discs, sleds, and boxes of hats and scarves in the process. Although Boots prided herself in an orderly household, the garage was a bit of a disorganized mess, especially after Chris parked his RV in there. Now it was more of a boys' clubhouse, and Boots rarely breached the domain. Claire spotted what she thought was the corner of the Red Dragon, so she unearthed plastic totes until she reached the beloved toboggan, feeling its discovery an omen of what would prove to be a memorable day, sledding with her friends. Maybe all seniors felt sentimental like Claire, wanting to recreate childhood memories to tuck into her mind as she prepared to graduate and leave this world behind.

She struggled to stack the totes and boxes back where they belonged when an old cardboard box fell on its side, flaps opening and contents spilling out. At first, Claire just shoved them back into the box. Then, she started paying attention. They were letters. Cards and letters addressed to Claire in blue ink. She plopped herself down on the concrete floor of the garage and started reading. Although they were written in French, Claire knew what they were. Letters from her mother she had never seen before. Letters and notes and cards. Claire had taken French in high school because she didn't want to lose her childhood language. The first few years after her mother left and Dad had met Boots, Claire refused to speak anything but French. She remembered her rebelliousness as a child, pretending not to understand anything Boots said and always replying in French. She almost smiled when she remembered how furious it made Boots.

Claire gathered the letters back into the box and lugged it to her bedroom, closing the door behind her firmly. She was grateful to have learned to read French as she started sifting through the mountain of letters, notes, and cards. How had she never seen these before? Why had her dad hidden them from her? Her heart was pounding with the mixed emotions of joy to have this connection with her estranged mother, combined with mounting anger at her father.

Claire only noticed the absence of envelopes when she had decided to try to organize the letters chronologically. Where were the envelopes? She would have to use the dates her mother had headed on each card and letter to organize them into chronological order, the oldest messages starting when Claire was just a little girl until the newest cards that were sent just last year. How could this be? When she heard Chris rummaging around in their bathroom, she called out to him.

He walked into her bedroom and found her sitting on the floor, the letters scattered from the open box.

"What's up? Did you find the Red Dragon?" Chris asked. He tilted his head in confusion. "What is all this?"

Claire held up a stack in her hand. "Letters from my mother. Have you ever seen these before?"

"No. What do you mean, letters from your mother? Where did you find these?"

"In the garage, when I was looking for the stupid toboggan. This box just fell off the shelves at my feet."

Claire suddenly remembered back to August when she and Taylor met Theresa. At the time, she thought Theresa was telling her to write a letter to her mother. Maybe she knew about this box and was trying to tell her? Well, not Theresa exactly, but the ancestors or spirits or whoever it is who speaks to her for fortune-telling. Claire shuddered as tears welled in her eyes. She pulled her comforter from her bed and wrapped it around her as Chris crouched beside her.

"Why are you crying?" Chris asked.

World Gone Mad

"I'm not quite sure. I wasn't expecting this. I'm completely confused, and I feel horribly sad," Claire said. She blew her nose noisily.

"Have you read them all?" Chris said. When she shook her head no, he added, "Do you want me to call Taylor?"

"What time is it?"

"It's almost two."

"What?" Claire jumped up. "How can it be this late?"

"Claire, wait. We can cancel. Let me just call Taylor to come over, and we'll cancel."

"We are not canceling," Claire said, whipping around. She mock-kicked at the box. "These letters have been here for years. They're not going anywhere. We are going. I need to race down a hillside on the Red Dragon and forget about this shit. It's too much. What if I hadn't unearthed them today? Would I leave for college without ever knowing that my mother hadn't abandoned me like Boots made me believe for all these years? Instead, she's been writing me letters not only have I never seen but never replied to. What must she think? That I hate her? That I don't ever want to speak with her?"

Chris was concerned, but he knew there wasn't much to do when Claire got into a frenzy, other than to wait it out.

Alex and Drake met Chris, Claire, and Taylor in the parking lot at the base of Mt. Gibson to help unload the sleds. Claire unearthed the bottle of scotch she had grabbed from her father's liquor cabinet and took a big swig. Bailey's in hot chocolate wasn't going to be enough for her. Everyone turned it down when she offered except Drake.

"I knew I could count on you," she said when he took the bottle and took a healthy shot. The scotch burned, but Claire knew it would do the trick, so she took another drink before they trudged up the hill. Between runs, she and Drake snuck back to the car to drink shots from the bottle. The exhilaration of speeding down the hillside while buzzed, fingertips numb from cold, yet insides warmed with alcohol, and the wan sunshine peeking out from behind more snow clouds made for the perfect afternoon of sledding. Chris caught a fabulous picture of her and Taylor on the Red Dragon, which Claire posted immediately with "#snowdayz #classof2020 #makingmemories" as the caption.

Alex took Drake's keys to drive home. Claire, Chris, and Taylor bid their good-byes, and Chris drove them back to their neighborhood. On the drive home, Taylor ordered pizzas to be delivered and texted her parents she would be spending the night with Claire. They peeled layers of snowy, frozen outerwear they left in the garage, took the pizzas and the box of letters to the basement family room, where they set a fire in the fireplace and streamed *Big Night* because Christopher dreamed of making a timpano, explaining it was the Italian word for "gluttony." As they ate, Claire and Taylor began sifting through the stack.

"There's a party going on tonight," Chris said, showing them his phone. "Drake is heading over there. Alex says he has to work tonight. Are we in or out?"

"Out," Taylor said, checking her friend's sad face. "We're staying here tonight. Right, Claire?"

"You can go, Christopher. It might be fun," Claire said. "Don't worry about me."

"I have no interest in partying. I'm worn out from sledding, and I think the football players might be hitting that, and I have no interest in any of that these days," Chris said. He picked up the remote and started scanning. "Maybe we'll pay for a new stream to watch. Is there anything good that's new?"

Claire knew her brother was less interested in movies and more invested in being supportive, which she appreciated.

"I think you need to talk to your dad," Taylor said quietly, hoping not to upset Claire anymore. "He will be able to give you more insight into all of this, don't you think?"

"I don't know what to think. I'm not sure where to start even," Claire said, as she let a handful slide back into the box. "I guess I want to start by reading them chronologically first to see what I learn. Then, I'll know what to ask Dad. Since he's on-call this weekend, I have time."

"No school tomorrow either," Chris said. "They just called it."

Claire walked to the glass doors that lead to the backyard and flipped on the floodlights to watch the snowfall. She turned to her friends and called, "Snow angels."

They tiptoed upstairs to the garage, giggling and shushing each other as they pulled on their outerwear, and returned to the basement to walk outside, turning off the floodlights on their way. Because it was a new moon and the storm clouds were so heavy, it was pitch dark. The three friends walked to the end of the patio, where the lawn started. A few steps into the heavy snow, they fell backward and began moving their arms and legs to make the snow angels as new flakes fell on their foreheads. It was absolute silence none of them broke with their typical jokes and banter. Instead, it felt almost holy, sacred. Claire let the cold seep into her bones, willing it to cool her hot anger and calm her racing mind full of questions, rocking her very foundation to its core.

  She was the last of the three to stand and return to the warmth of the fire. Chris busied himself adding more logs, and Taylor unearthed more afghans after they had once again stripped back down to their sweatpants and hoodies, leaving their snowy coats, hats, scarves, and boots in the garage. Chris found a movie to watch, and Claire leaned against Taylor under the covers on the sofa, content to leave the box of letters for tomorrow. She watched the flames of the fire until the embers burned bright red, and her eyelids fluttered shut, grateful for the escape sleep afforded.

26
time is done

Claire was startled awake by a moan. She was surprised to find herself still on the sofa, Taylor snuggled at one end, sound asleep. She reached to turn on a lamp when she heard Chris wailing, a sound unlike anything she had ever heard him make before.

"No! Oh, my God. No," he said before dropping his phone and crying.

"What is it?" Claire felt alarmed. "Christopher, what happened? What?"

He didn't look up to meet her eyes. Instead, he handed her the phone as Taylor roused, asking, "What's going on? Why are you awake? It's a snow day, remember?"

Claire looked at the text in horror and then handed it to

Taylor, who said, "I don't have my glasses. What does it say?"

"It's Drake," Claire said, stopping to take a deep breath. "There's been an accident. A car accident. Drake. Drake is—"

"He's dead," Chris said. "Dead. He's dead."

"Wait. What?" Taylor grabbed the phone. She began crying, too.

"It's a text from Alex," Claire said. "We've got to go. He says he's in the hospital. He was with Drake. We've got to go. We've got to get to him. Now."

"What time is it?" Taylor asked.

"Five-thirty," Chris said. "In the morning."

The two followed Claire upstairs, where Claire's dad, George, still wearing his parka over his scrubs, was standing in the kitchen. He said, "Kids, I have some bad news."

Claire burst into tears as Chris put his arm around Taylor and said, "We know. Alex just texted. We were planning to go to the hospital for him now."

"Let's wait for your mother," George said to Taylor. "I just spoke to your parents. Your mom is on her way now, honey."

Mrs. Thompson burst into the door, her pant legs covered in snow. She didn't even stamp them clean in her rush to her daughter, pulling her into her outstretched arms, causing Claire to sob even harder, even as she allowed her dad and Chris to embrace her.

"Let's sit," George said.

"We have to go," Chris insisted.

World Gone Mad

Mrs. Thompson pulled a chair and guided Taylor to sit and then took a seat herself. George walked to the coffee maker, taking the pot to fill with water. Mrs. Thompson indicated for Chris and Claire to join them at the table. They did so reluctantly, confused why they were sitting around, waiting for coffee when they should be rushing to the hospital.

When George finished measuring the grinds, and the scent of the brew wafted in the kitchen, he turned to them and said, "Alex is going to be okay, but they're keeping him for observation. Aside from a few cuts and bruises, he seems to be fine. No apparent head injury, but we want to be safe. I will take you to see him, but it's been an ordeal all night for everyone involved. The police were there to question Alex. Of course, his parents and siblings are there now, and I think I even saw your principal when I left. It's incredibly chaotic and tragic, kids. Fortunately, Alex will be walking away from the accident with a black eye and only minor injuries. I checked on him myself. He's fine."

"But Drake?" Claire asked. She needed to hear it again.

"Drake didn't make it, honey," Mrs. Thompson said, reaching to hold Claire's cold hand.

George said, "Drake was driving. Not Alex. Alex was the passenger."

"What happened?" Chris asked. "Were there other cars involved? Is anyone else—"

"Nobody else was involved," her dad interrupted. He brought the pot of coffee, mugs, sugar, and milk to the table. "Evidently, their car hit some black ice. Drake lost control of the car, taking a turn.

They spun off the road and smacked right into a tree, going way too fast. The chances of a driver hitting on his side are slim, but since they were spinning out of control at a dangerously high speed, after hitting a patch of ice, it happened."

"A tree?" Chris asked.

"At school of all places. Your school. The catalpa tree in the front of the building," Mrs. Thompson said, referring to the hundred-year-old tree where every senior class traditionally posed in August to have their picture taken to launch their final year of high school. Tears formed at the corner of her eyes, so she stood to retrieve a box of tissues. "Oh, it's all just so horrible. His poor parents. His poor, poor parents."

Claire turned to Chris and said, "Okay, so wait. Drake went to that party last night, but did you know Alex was going?"

"Alex had to work. I knew Drake was going. He told me that while we were sledding, we decided to eat pizza and watch movies. Let me check," Chris said, scrolling on his phone. "Nothing. Just the texts between Drake and me before sledding, and then nothing until the text from Alex about the accident."

Taylor, who had been scrolling her phone, held it out and said, "Look."

Her feed was filled with party pictures. Kids were holding red solo cups, beer bongs, and blunts. They stopped on the post of Drake, obviously drunk, flashing a peace sign with one hand, a bottle of whiskey in the other.

World Gone Mad

"What is this account?" Mrs. Thompson asked, frowning into the screen. Taylor didn't respond. Now was not the time to get into explaining the difference between a rinsta and a finsta account to her mother.

"Why wasn't Alex driving?" Chris said. "I don't understand. Alex even took the keys after sledding because Drake was drunk."

"Drake was drunk at sledding?" Mrs. Thompson asked, frowning. She turned to Taylor. "You were drinking in the middle of the day while sledding?"

"Not me, Mama. I swear," Taylor said. "Drake may have brought something. I don't know. It wasn't us."

Claire took a deep breath. She appreciated her best friend covering for her, but now was not the time to not be entirely truthful, so she confessed, "It was me. I'm sorry. I swiped a bottle of your scotch, Daddy, and we drank it today. We, meaning Drake and me."

Her dad said, "We will address that later," before he turned to Chris and raised an eyebrow as an unspoken question.

Chris answered, "I was driving, not drinking. We know better. We know not to drink and drive. We know the rules."

"But Drake didn't?" George asked.

"Not always," Chris confessed. "But that's what's so confusing. Alex always shows up for Drake. Always drives when Drake is messed up. What could have happened?"

"So, Drake messes up a lot? I mean, messed up. Oh, this is so horrible," Mrs. Thompson said. "Today wasn't the first day he was drinking and driving?"

"Not the first," Claire said, thinking about the time just this fall when Alex brought him here to sleep it off in *Suby* after he vomited all over Alex's car. "He's been a bit off the rails this school year, I think. Worse than normal. Maybe it's because he wasn't allowed to come with us this summer on tour?"

"What do you mean?" George said. "I'm not following your logic."

"It's just, Drake's parents never let him do anything. They keep him on too short a leash, so he feels like he needs to go all out in response. It doesn't make sense, I know, but it's how it is. If maybe he had a chance to just be free once in a while, maybe he wouldn't take it so far," Claire explained.

"Little too late for that to happen now," Chris said bitterly. When Claire began crying again, he muttered, "Sorry. Fuck. Oh, sorry again. I don't know what I'm doing."

"It's alright," Mrs. Thompson said. "We're all upset right now. It's understandable."

"We still don't know the whole story," Taylor said. "We don't know why Drake was driving. Why Alex was with him, I thought he was working last night?"

"He was working. It wouldn't be the first time Alex left the restaurant for Drake." Chris said. He turned to George and said, "When can we go to the hospital and see him? Obviously, we need more answers."

World Gone Mad

Taylor held her phone up again. "It's already all over social media. People are starting to post pictures and RIPs. I can't believe this. I just can't believe he's gone."

Boots entered the kitchen, dressed in her yoga clothes. She stopped short when she saw them all in her kitchen this early in the morning and asked, "What's going on? Good morning, Ivy. What's wrong?"

Mrs. Thompson rose from the table and walked to Boots. They bowed their heads as Mrs. Thompson filled Boots in, which caused Boots to crumble. Claire had never seen her stepmother cry before this moment, and it wasn't pretty. For a moment, Claire felt a pang of empathy for her, until a new wave of horror and grief washed over her, and she put her head down on the table and let the sobs wrack her body, picturing Drake as he looked when he was a little kid in Sunday school. She thought about their random lunch together and wished she had more moments alone with him. Why hadn't anyone taken the time to stop and talk with Drake about his mounting recklessness until it was too late? It was too late for anything now. Too late for him to graduate. Too late for him to blaze his path, to study engineering in college, and go on to have a career, maybe even get married and raise a family. She thought about his cold, dead body and pictured what the car must have looked like, smashed against the tree. The thoughts turned her stomach. She barely made it to the bathroom before vomiting. Taylor followed her to hold her hair, provide her a cold washcloth and a cup of water to rinse her mouth before leading her back into the kitchen.

George held Boots in his arm. He looked up and said, "Why don't you kids all take showers and get dressed now. We will make a little breakfast and then take you to the hospital to see Alex. You aren't going to settle down until you've seen your friend and gotten the answers to your questions."

Boots pulled Chris into a hug and then gestured to Claire, who moved into her stepmother's embrace for the first time in years. Claire appreciated the moment of comfort more than she would have expected until she suddenly remembered the box of letters. Anger surged more quickly than Claire could handle, so she pulled away and turned her head not to meet Boots' eye. Mrs. Thompson began to rummage in the refrigerator, stacking juice, a carton of eggs, butter, and the Vermont maple syrup Boots special orders on the table. She turned to Boots and said, "Shall we make pancakes, maybe?"

Claire walked downstairs to retrieve the box of letters while Chris and Taylor trudged upstairs. She was able to slip past the adults in the kitchen and make her way to her bedroom unseen, where she stored it under her bed for the time being.

Taking turns in the shower, they scrolled through their feeds and yelled to each other when a new post about Drake appeared. Not one moment of brushing their teeth, standing under the shower stream, and changing into clothes, felt normal. Instead, they felt like zombies, stuck in a hazy mental space of grief and trauma. After they clamored back down the steps and ate a few bites of pancakes, George and Mrs. Thompson loaded them into the SUV and drove them to the hospital while Boots stayed behind to clean up. She also wanted to call the florist and write a list to start a meal chain for the Whitaker's. Although the Cutlers didn't attend church, Boots remained active with the community enough to start the work mothers do in crisis times. Claire had never remembered seeing Boots act with such compassion.

Claire returned to the kitchen to grab a box of tissues for the ride. A fresh wave of grief overcame her to see Boots, her back turned, shoulders shaking from the sobs she could no longer restrain in empathy for a mother facing her worst nightmare and for the loss of a life taken too soon in such a violent manner. Claire quietly left her, unsure how to interrupt this private moment, feeling dread and sorrow of her own, mixed with lingering anger and resentment that Boots had hidden those letters from her mother her entire life. Nothing was the same anymore. In one day, life had radically changed in ways Claire could never have predicted. Drake no longer existed in this world, while Claire's mother had unexpectedly emerged as more than just a faded memory.

27
end

    Although Claire hadn't been to the hospital with her father in several years, everything felt familiar. The antiseptic stinging odor mingled with overheated coffee, the incessant chirps of monitors, and the greenish-yellow cast of overhead florescent lighting remained the same. She was grateful to follow blindly as her father assuredly hurried them through the corridors to Alex's room. In the hallway was the entire Dominguez family, who rushed to hug first her father and then each of them in turn before ushering them into the room where Alex lay on the bed, his back turned to them. Chris and Taylor hung back as Claire sat on the corner of the bed, touched his back, and whispered, "Alex, honey. We're here. Alex?"

    When he rolled over, Claire began crying when she saw the

bandage on his forehead and his left eye swollen shut, blackened from the accident. He sat up to hug her. Chris and Taylor joined them, wrapping their arms around them in a group hug while they all cried together. When they regained composure, Chris took a chair and pulled Taylor onto his lap while Claire stayed perched on the bed with Alex.

His voice cracked when Chris asked Alex, "What happened?"

"I don't know what I was thinking," Alex said. "I don't know. The whole thing—"

When he sobbed, Claire poured a cup of water from the plastic pitcher on the swinging hospital table. Alex took a few sips and then continued.

"I thought he'd sleep it off. I really did. I took his keys and drove his car from the hill. The whole way, he was scrolling and talking about the party. He asked me to drop him off at Scott's house. He was drunk, and I was in a hurry. My shift was starting, and to be honest, I was pissed at him. I was mad, you guys. Seems like every other moment of my life is dealing with Drake, and I knew my dad would be furious if I were late, so I just dropped him off at Scott's house because it was closer than driving out to Drake's house, and he was so drunk, there was no way his parents could see him like that. How was I supposed to get back to the restaurant on time? It was convenient for me to leave him at Scott's. For me."

Alex broke into fresh tears. Then he took a breath and started again. "At the time, I felt like I was doing the right thing, you know. I thought I was protecting him. At the end of my shift, I started getting those weird texts. I had finished my shift and had just mopped the floors, so I walked from the restaurant to Scott's house."

Scott Warton was a junior at Maywood High School. His family's historic home was in Maywood's old part, only a few minutes' walk from the restaurant. Whenever his parents were at their house on the lake, Scott threw notorious parties and never got caught. At least until now, that is.

"What weird texts?" Chris asked.

Alex handed him his phone. Aside from the same pictures of the party they had already seen, the rest of the texts were a jumble of letters, a few random words, but not even complete sentences or anything understandable.

"When I got to the party, my focus was on getting Drake out of there and getting his ass home. The house was packed. Not like other nights. Tons more people, kids I hadn't even seen before. It was loud, the music was blasting, and I had a feeling the police were going to descend any minute. Looking around, I panicked. I just panicked. There was no way I was going to be caught there, the only Mexican kid over eighteen with a bunch of white, underaged, drunk kids, you know?" He looked at Claire and said, "Sorry. No offense."

She said, "None taken. I get it. Did the police arrive?"

"Yes. I'm trying to explain why I was in such a hurry. Why it was important I get Drake the hell out of there and be far away. Why I panicked and made the mistake."

"What mistake?" Chris asked. "Sounds to me like you were just trying to help."

World Gone Mad

A nurse entered the room, interrupting to take his temperature, check his blood pressure, and ask him if he was in any pain, to which he shook his head no. Claire's dad followed behind, lifting Alex's chart and peering through his glasses to read the notes.

He said, "We need to let Alex rest now, kids."

"One minute, please, Daddy?" Claire asked. He looked at their faces and said, "Just one minute, and then it's time to leave, okay?"

When he left, Alex continued. "The mistake I made was to let him drive. I begged him for his keys, but he was belligerent. I guess I thought that if I got into the car with him that I could keep him safe or something. Like, I honestly thought being in the car with him would be enough to save him. Fucking stupid. Stupid—" Alex broke off, looked away, took a breath, and started again.

"Before I could think it all through, the first cop car pulled up, lights flashing. So, that's when Drake and I freaked out. We jumped into his car and pulled away. I thought I could convince him to pull over and let me drive. I was sure once we had turned onto Oak Street, he would come to his senses. I stupidly thought that if I was at least in the passenger seat, I could keep him safe. I just wanted to keep him safe—" Sobs wracked his body, his face in his hands.

After he composed himself, he said, "Not only was I yelling for him to pull over, we fought about the music. The stupid music."

He paused, shook his head, and continued. "The music was blasting while I kept reaching to turn it down as he was literally slapping my hands. It was crazy. Chaos. I kept yelling, 'Pull over. Drake, pull over. Stop,' which made him accelerate even more. We hit the patch of ice just as we approached school, and the car spun completely out of control. At that point, we were both screaming, and the last thing I saw was Drake take his hands from the wheel and cover his head as we hit. I must have blacked out or passed out or something because the next thing I remember was waking up in the back of the ambulance, screaming for Drake. I think they gave me a sedative or something to calm me down. I don't know. The whole thing has been a blur. Even talking to the police. I don't even know if I made any sense, and I don't even care. He's dead. Drake's dead, and it's my fault."

    They were all silent as Alex laid his head back on the pillow, exhausted from reliving the ordeal. He closed his eyes when Claire said, "It's not your fault."

    He winced when Chris said, "I'm just glad you're alive."

    Taylor hugged Alex as the three quietly exited his room. Mrs. Thompson drove them home, as Claire's dad decided to stay at the hospital. They were all silent. Once they arrived home, they all hugged before Mrs. Thompson put her arm around Taylor and guided her home. Claire and Chris entered an empty house. Boots had used their group text to explain she was running errands for the Whitakers. Claire retreated to her room. She was dreading the call she had to make, but somebody needed to tell Sam and that somebody was her.

    Chris retreated to the privacy of his bedroom, leaned against the closed door, and let the tears stream down his cheeks. So many feelings overwhelmed him as memories swirled. He thought about how impatient he always was that Drake's parents never let him do anything. Last summer, he rolled his eyes when Drake couldn't go on Phish tour with them. Like it was Drake's fault. Chris felt guilty about that and felt even worse, remembering how angry he felt when Drake would get so wasted, everyone else had to take care of him. Why was he so impatient with Drake? They had been friends since elementary school. Chris always saved a spot for him in line and at the cafeteria table. He picked Drake for every team in gym class, but he took for granted Drake's very existence. Since that was no longer a fact anymore, Chris felt a sense of panic. How could he be dead? The shock and horror that Drake was truly dead were staggering. There was no do-over. No undoing what had been done.

28
clouds

Sam hung up the phone in disbelief and horror. How could Drake be dead? Although he didn't know the dude very well, he was part of their phamily, and to hear Claire so upset was awful. Sam's heart broke for her, and he wished he could fly to Ohio to be with her for the funeral, but he knew that wouldn't be possible. His school schedule was demanding, and his father wasn't even in New York to ask permission. He was in China again and not always available when Sam reached out due to the time change and his father's hectic schedule. Although Claire assured Sam she would be fine, he felt guilty.

Winston returned from class. When he saw Sam lying on the bed, he asked, "What's up, bruh? You okay?"

World Gone Mad

Sam explained the situation, pulling up pictures of Drake on his phone to show his roommate, who said, "Man, that's rough. Beyond rough. I'm sorry."

"I feel more at home in Maywood than I ever have here, and I was only there for two months, yet I've been at St. Philips for four years. This year has already seemed like purgatory to me, biding my time until I can go home and be with my real friends again." Sam saw Winston wince, so he apologized. "I don't mean you aren't my real friend. You are, Winston. And maybe Haynes, too, but the rest?"

"I know Bates is a douche bag, but he's been facing some hot water after he pulled that shit drugging you."

"Hot water with whom?" Sam asked.

"The elders, bruh," Winston said. "Listen, Quill and Toth have been in existence for years. You didn't think there weren't adults involved in our activities, did you? I mean, they don't show up, but what happens is reported back, and from what I understand, Bates has been called to a tribunal of sorts to determine whether he will even be allowed to continue. I don't think I've ever heard of anyone being kicked out of QTs, but I guess it could happen. Bates was complaining about it just the other day. I hate even to mention this now, but you need to watch your back. He's going to be gunning for you."

"This is ridiculous," Sam said. He was so angry at this juvenile situation in light of the real tragedy of losing Drake. "If he so much as comes near me, I'm going to jack him up. In fact, how do I get in touch with this tribunal? I want out. I didn't choose to be tapped. I don't even like the idea of fraternities, let alone secret societies. How did I even get involved, to begin with?"

"Your father, maybe?" Winston said.

"My father?" Sam repeated. "How is he involved?"

"He's St. Philips alumnus, right? There aren't many legacies, but every dude I know whose father graduated from here is also a QT. Think about it."

It had never occurred to him that his dad was a QT. He never mentioned a word about it, even when Sam thought they had started connecting again. Sam thought back to the Dead and Company show his dad surprised him with. His dad never mentioned a word about QTs at the show, and Sam forgot to ask about it. Nor did he say anything at Thanksgiving or over winter break. Although Sam remembered, he didn't mention anything about it to his dad, either. He picked up the phone to call. If what Winston said was true, maybe his dad could get Sam out of the QTs forever now. There had to be a way out.

29
ghosts

Taylor pulled her one black dress over her head, adjusted her black tights, slipped into tall, black boots, and reached for a strand of amber beads to wrap around her neck. Unfortunately, she had to forgo mascara as she could not stop crying and didn't want make-up to melt off her face for what would be the first funeral of her life.

Tristan opened her bedroom door without knocking and asked, "Why you crying, Tay? Are you still sad? Can you help me with my tie?"

Taylor smiled through her tears as she kneeled in front of her baby brother to help him. The Thompsons were attending the funeral together as a family. Dad canceled his appointments, and Mom cleared her calendar. TJ and Tristan wore ties and real shoes, enduring their mother's repeated shushes and reprimands to stop squirming on the wooden pews, which was a welcome distraction for Taylor. The church packed so fully, crowds stood in the lobbies around the sanctuary and even outside in the cold. The forced heat, combined with the stench of too many lilies, made Taylor dizzy as she stared at the poster-sized picture of Drake next to his closed coffin while listening to the minister lead the congregation in prayer. Tristan began to cry as he pricked his finger on the straight pin that held the green ribbon included with the paper program that featured the same picture of Drake on the cover with his birth and death dates. Taylor unconsciously rolled it into a scroll, causing it to be a bit damp with sweat from her palms.

She wished Josh was there to hold her hand, but he had two exams he could not miss and promised to drive to Maywood to meet Taylor after the funeral. For comfort, to steady her nerves, she focused on the back of Chris and Claire's heads, next to Boots and Dr. Cutler, in the row directly in front of the Thompsons. The school choir joined with the church choir to sing hymns. Their principal, Mrs. Lee, spoke a few words before the final prayers when everyone followed the coffin held by the pallbearers, including both Chris and Alex, into the cold, January afternoon. Although it was no longer snowing, the dirty-gray banks piled high framed the plowed streets, sidewalks, and parking lot, making the landscape look bleak under a white-washed pale blue sky overhead.

The procession to the gravesite was a short drive to the Maywood Cemetery. The minister said more prayers before ushers distributed flowers to lay on the casket. Taylor's mom gasped when Drake's little sister fell to her knees, sobbing. Taylor held both of her brothers' hands tightly in her own as her dad put his arm around their mother. Claire leaned against Taylor and tilted her head on her head. She and Chris were holding hands. Alex stood with his own family across from them, his black eye shielded by sunglasses.

At the Whitaker's house, the dining room table groaned with platters of food where people were busy piling their plates high as if they had never eaten before. No matter. Boots had organized enough food to replenish the platters with endless rounds brought out by the other church moms from the kitchen. Sam's aunt Karen and her fiancée Luke approached Taylor, Claire, and Chris, who were clustered in the living room to pull them into a comforting hug.

Karen said, "I know Sam is distraught not to be here with you. I spoke with him last night."

Alex approached them, pulling his tie, and said, "Dad said I could spend time with you today. He and Mom had to go back to the restaurant to set up for dinner service, but they send their love. Where are we going after?"

Karen said, "Why don't you all come to Calico House? You are more than welcome, and we would love for you to be with us. We'll light a fire in the living room. I set a pot of chicken and dumplings before I left. There is always plenty."

They all agreed immediately, relieved to have such a comforting place to go. Calico House was where they could retreat to begin the long process of healing from the horror they all felt in the face of their tragedy. Chris, Alex, Claire, and Taylor piled into one car and followed Karen and Luke on the short drive to her home, where she brewed a pot of tea while Luke set the fire. Grateful Dead streamed from the strategically placed speakers around the house's rooms, and Claire settled back into a sofa and pulled a quilt on her lap. Taylor dropped next to her, texting Josh the directions so he could join them.

When he arrived, Taylor introduced him to Luke and Karen, who made Josh a bowl of chicken and dumplings. Even though he protested he had already eaten, when he politely dug in, complimenting Karen on the taste, Taylor fell even more in love with him.

"May we change the music?" Chris asked. Claire frowned at what she thought was a rude request until he explained. "If we could listen to 'Ghosts of the Forest' right now, it would be good. Would that be okay?"

"Of course," Karen said. "I was thinking about 'Brokedown Palace,' but Phish it is."

Claire was relieved Chris didn't correct Karen. 'Ghosts of the Forest' wasn't Phish; it was Trey Anastasio's project, but to say anything would be rude, the silent message she sent Chris with a scowl. Chris saw her and bowed his head as the music began. They listened silently, everyone crying except Josh, who held Taylor's hand tightly in his own. When Trey sang the last lines to "Brief Time," Claire felt her heart break all over again. She paused the music before the last track, 'Beneath a Sea of Stars,' and said, "Maybe we should go outside for this last song? I know it's cold, but I feel like we should at least be looking at the sacred elm or something."

Karen said, "I have something planned for you, and it is outside. Get your coats and meet me on the porch. Now is the perfect time."

When they met on the porch, it was dark except for strings of lights around the eaves of the porch roof. The moon was waxing, and the stars glimmered in the night sky now that the storm clouds had passed. Claire could see her breath in the crisp, cold air. Luke helped Karen unearth white paper sky lanterns she bought for tonight, which they lined up on the porch.

She said, "Everyone, choose a lantern. You may say a prayer or make a wish or send your love to Drake, whatever serves you best. Whatever feels right. Then, we'll launch them into the sky."

As each approached, Luke assisted, steadying the little candle basket upright before they stepped off the porch into the snow on the lawn. Karen cued up the song on the outdoor speakers as each of them took turns lighting their lanterns and sending them into the sky. As they watched them float, Chris leaned to Karen to choose the last song for the ceremony that felt more final than the funeral at the church, especially as they all joined in the last refrain of "Dirt."

30
love

"I cannot believe how angry everyone is getting about the catalpa tree," Claire said.

She and Taylor sat across from each other in the cafeteria for a rare lunch together. Most days, their schedules didn't align, and since the accident, Claire had been avoiding the cafeteria altogether because she didn't know what she'd say to Mrs. Whitaker. Claire was ashamed she hadn't seen Drake's mom since the day of the funeral, but she still didn't go through the line today. She just didn't know what to say. She knew she would burst into tears, and that was something she didn't want to happen at school. Instead, she chose to keep her tears for the privacy of her bedroom.

"I can't believe Valentine's Day is Friday. I haven't done a thing yet for Josh," Taylor whined.

She looked at Claire, who was so distracted, she didn't even seem to hear the comment about Valentine's Day, so Taylor said, "I agree with you about the catalpa tree. They should just cut it down."

"What? No," Claire said, looking at her friend finally. "I don't agree with that at all. Cut it down? What are you talking about? They can't cut it down. Wait a minute. We're not on the same side on this?"

"What side?" Taylor asked.

"I'm shocked you haven't heard the drama. One side is demanding to remove the tree because it's too traumatizing and because it's become a memorial of sorts," Claire said, referring to the flowers, notes, stuffed animals, and candles people had stacked at the base of the tree. "The other side wants the tree to remain, saying that it's over a hundred years old, and although it's hard for our graduating class, that's not a good enough reason to cut it down. I agree with them. It's like the sacred elm tree at Karen's house. Sam and I fell in love under that tree. We spent all our time together under that elm, never knowing his mother's ashes were scattered there. Knowing that didn't ruin the tree for us. It made it more special. It has history deeper than just what's going on now. That's important. The catalpa tree must stand."

Taylor knew better than to argue with Claire when she was passionate about something, even if she disagreed. Taylor hadn't thought much about it. Walking past the memorial and the damaged tree every morning as she entered school had become part of the bleak winter emotional landscape of life. Wanting to distract Claire,

Taylor asked, "And what do you want to do for our birthdays this year? Eighteen is a big one. What should we do?"

Claire shrugged, crumpled her empty bag of pretzels, rose from the cafeteria table, and said, "Whatever you like, Tay." Then, she looked at her friend, stopped, and said, "You know what? You're right. Let's plan. Eighteen is significant, but I don't want a party. Just us, okay? Let's just you and I do something special."

Taylor was relieved to be able to distract Claire from her grief. From her own grief, as well. Taylor's kiss with Drake at prom last year was an err in judgment, but it had been sweet. She felt haunted by his death. Birthdays were always a big deal to both her and Claire since they landed seven days apart from each other. They had always celebrated together.

When they were little, Taylor's mom made them silver crowns using poster board and aluminum foil with their names written in glitter glue, which Claire insisted they wore with matching pink party dresses. When they turned eight, they celebrated by roller skating. They had a lavish party at the country club Boots insisted on for their sweet sixteen, which even Claire would admit did turn out to be a cool event. Not that Taylor wanted to plan something that elaborate, of course. Not all of their birthdays were formal. Her favorite memories were of them just celebrating together with their families and with each other. Taylor was determined to do something special. First, she needed to consider the poem she was writing for Josh as a Valentine's gift. She didn't know what else to give him that would be more meaningful than her words, but since they hadn't spoken the L-word aloud yet, she had to watch how she constructed her language. Taylor considered this to be a big step in their relationship.

Taylor printed the final draft minutes before Josh arrived at the house for their date, an arrangement of white roses and purple irises in hand. It was the most elegant bouquet she had ever received. Much lovelier than boring red roses, for sure.

"Thank you," Taylor said. He smelled so good, Taylor wanted to do more than politely kiss his cheek, but both of her parents hurried into the foyer to say hello.

"I hear congratulations are in order," Taylor's dad said as he shook Josh's hand. "Wilberforce is damn lucky to have you."

"Thank you, Dr. Tony," Josh said, beaming.

He had just received acceptances into every school he applied, Wilberforce being his top choice. Taylor had yet to tell her parents she received the same acceptance into Wilberforce. She was waiting for Howard and Spelman before she decided to change her decision from Kenyon. If she decided to change. Because she was still undecided, Taylor knew it best to keep her parents out of the conversation. Maybe she would discuss it with Josh tonight.

"Where are we going?" Taylor asked as Josh opened the car door for her. "I hope I'm dressed okay." She looked down at her favorite pair of tan suede boots, tucked into winter white leggings over which she wore a beige tunic with her amber beads around her neck. Josh looked handsome in a brown leather jacket over a gray sweater.

"It's a surprise. Happy Valentine's Day," Josh said, driving in the direction of the Maywood branch of Ohio State, where they had met in a writing workshop in August.

B. Elizabeth Beck

He parked in the circle driveway in front of the old building at the center of the small campus situated in the center of Maywood, north of the county courthouse building. The school, an all-girls college in the 1800s, became a satellite branch of Ohio State in the 1970s. Taylor had never known it as anything but the college many kids attended right after high school if their grades weren't good enough for the main campus or if they were pursuing an associate's degree and wanted to stay home. She had taken workshops and classes there her entire life and felt comfortable walking the cobblestone pathway through campus, past the library, to a building at the back of the city block of ivy-covered red brick buildings that made up the campus. Josh opened the heavy oak door that creaked on its hinges. She followed him through the corridor. Before he opened the next door, he leaned down and kissed Taylor. She closed her eyes and fell into the kiss, almost dropping the scroll she had tied with a ribbon for his gift.

"Ready?" Josh whispered when the kiss ended. Taylor had no idea what she was ready for but nodded.

When he opened the door, a string of white globe lanterns illuminated a greenhouse overflowing with plants. The walls and ceiling were glass panes. Lined across the tile floor were troughs and containers overflowing with blooms. Hanging from the top were ferns of every shape and kind. On the floor at the end of the room, Josh had laid a red plaid blanket on which a picnic basket rested, its lid open. Criss-crossed suspended from the bottom of the hanging plants were white paper heart-shaped garlands making a canopy of sorts over the blanket. Taylor reached to touch one of the hearts, which read, "I love you." She moved to the next and then the next, reading the phrases, "I adore you," and "You make me happy."

"What is all this?" Taylor asked, overwhelmed.

"You've never been here? I'm surprised. The Maywood Horticulture Society uses this building."

"The *what* society?" Taylor asked.

Josh laughed and pulled her down with him on the blanket. He unearthed chocolate-covered strawberries, a wedge of brie, a plate of crackers, and a seltzer bottle from the basket.

"The Horticultural Society," Josh said as he poured the seltzer into plastic cups. "Petra Kirk is a member. She brought me here once, and since I thought it was so special, I called her for this favor. I asked her if we could use it for tonight. Do you like it?"

"Very much," Taylor said. Even though she frowned at the name Petra Kirk, she didn't want to spoil this moment, so she mustered a better smile. "Thank you. I love it."

"I love you, Taylor," Josh said, looking directly into her eyes.

"I love you, too," Taylor whispered, her heart pounding. It was the first time they had exchanged the words, and Taylor felt joy warm her. She remembered her gift and handed Josh the scroll, who untied it and read the poem, his smile response enough.

If the universe a blanket
let it be woven, my life
a thread knotted
to your life, a thread
strengthened, together
wrapped in memories
we unravel the meaning
of life one afternoon,
sitting on the grass
at the edge of the lake
ignoring invitation
in our quest to know
each other, each blade
Whitman's understanding
of truth cannot survive
in a vacuum, existentialism
questioned and answered
even as pizzas fly, a diet coke
introduces ideas about chocolate
but not really chocolate,
and judges who don't really judge,
my heart belongs to you
a key to the lock
an answer to the question
I love you.

31
focus

Alex begged to have off work Friday, even though Valentine's Day meant huge tips. He asked his mother, who had a soft spot for her eldest son, telling her the truth about his plans.

"Chris, Claire, and I are going to hang out if you'll let me off," Alex asked. "I would like to be with my friends tonight, please."

Although his sister, Fernanda, bitched about having to pick up the shift, there wasn't much rancor in her complaints. The entire family worried about Alex, who was still in such grief and felt such deep guilt; they paid extra consideration to him. Even his father, who was generally a stoic man who believed men should take it in the chin and keep working, regardless of the circumstances, was concerned.

His mother did what Mexican mothers do. She lit candles for

him at Mass Wednesdays and Sundays, lamented to her priest, and stuffed him as full of enchiladas, tacos, and tamales as possible.

"I'm just going to have to beg Miss Elva to let me come watch the next time she makes tamales," Chris said, stuffing his face with the food Alex brought.

They settled in the basement family room on the sofas, afghans wrapped around them, a fire burning, and streamed *Little Fires Everywhere*. Claire brought the box of marzipan Sam had mailed to her to share, although she had to whack Chris in the arm after he reached for more than one. She tacked the card Sam sent on her bulletin board with the other cards, notes, and pictures collected there and hoped he received the gift she remembered to mail him.

It was a marker drawing of song lyrics, a new series Claire was exploring. She was tired of leaves and flowers and enjoyed the vibrant colors the markers produced. It was a new medium for her to study while listening to music, her favorite thing to do in life. She had several Phish songs illustrated and had delved into the rich tradition of the Grateful Dead. It served as an excellent distraction to the chaos of life these days. If it wasn't enough to be grieving their classmate, the student body had to divide into a war about the fate of the tree.

"Alex, I have a question to ask you," Claire said. "It's about the catalpa tree."

"What's up?" Alex said.

"Do you think they should cut the tree down or leave it be? It's important I know where you stand," Claire said.

"Where I stand?" Alex repeated. "I don't know if I stand anywhere, per se."

"There are people who are adamant the catalpa tree needs to be cut down. Other people think the tree should be left to heal, and I just need to know what you think. I have an opinion, but it doesn't matter. It doesn't matter what anybody thinks except you and maybe Drake's family. You are my friend. I want to do what's best for you," Claire said.

"Cutting the tree down isn't going to help anybody. It's not going to help me. I haven't even driven by school since that night, and I still have nightmares. Cutting the tree down isn't going to make that magically disappear. It's not going to bring Drake back," Alex said. He took a swig of soda and continued. "This town is too small. Everything reminds me of him. It's haunted for me now: the trestle, the restaurant even. Everything. The only thing I can do is get the hell out of here as soon as possible, and that's what I'm planning. I got in. I got the acceptance last week. Come August; I'm out of here."

"That's great, man. I got my acceptance, too. Ohio State, here we come. We're Buckeyes, bruh," Chris said as they bumped fists. "Onward and upward, as they say."

Claire said, "Congratulations, Alex. It's what you wanted. Everything you worked for. Meanwhile, I'm over here in purgatory."

"That's not true. You know you're going to hear from Parsons soon," Chris said. "And in the meanwhile, you've gotten into every one of your back up schools."

"Every school?" Alex said. "Claire, that's good news. You should be celebrating."

Claire said, "I should, but it's hard. If I don't get into Parsons, I don't know what I'm going to do. It's not like I'm going to be happy at any of the other schools if I can't be with Sam. Lately, with everything going on, I'm with you, Alex. I can't wait to get the hell out of Maywood. I'm ready for my childhood to be a footnote to the rest of my life."

"A footnote?" Chris said. "That's harsh."

"I mean it, Chris. I do. Losing Drake the same day I found the letters from my mother has been a lot to deal with all at once. What's even stranger? Forget it. I don't even want to tell you. You'll think I'm a horrible person," Claire said. She looked at Chris and Alex, took a deep breath, and continued. "I'm not even sure how to explain this, but you know I'd been fighting depression again this fall."

"I've been worried," Chris said. "I wasn't sure what to say, but I knew."

"Well, it's illogical. Something about the day of the accident shook it loose. Don't get me wrong; I'm still grieving. I'm hurting. I think about Drake every day, and I still cry. I don't know how to explain this, but I'm no longer depressed. I'm sad about Drake. I'm angry at Dad and Boots about my mom, but the gray cloud that pushes down on me is gone. It's just gone. When I feel depressed, I can't feel anything. It's like a numbing haze that makes me just want to sleep. The past few weeks? I feel, I mean, I really feel everything. Does that make any sense, or am I a monster?" Claire leaned back on the sofa and wrapped an afghan tightly around her.

World Gone Mad

Alex spoke first. "I think it makes sense. Death has a way of bringing a new sense of perspective to life, I think."

"That's part of it, for sure. I mean, compared to dying, I feel stupid about being depressed. I mean, I'm alive. You're alive. There's a reason for that," Claire said, relieved to be understood.

"You can't feel stupid for something you can't control," Chris said. "It's not like you choose to be depressed."

"See, that's what's so mystifying. I can't control feeling happy either. What I mean is that when I'm depressed, I don't feel that natural spark of joy just to wake up or whatever. To see a pretty leaf or eat a special meal. None of it makes any difference. So how does it just disappear all of a sudden?"

"Trauma, maybe?" Alex said. "Maybe you're still traumatized, and it's tricked your brain into thinking that you're not depressed? Like, maybe you're running on adrenaline now, but when that wears off, what happens then?"

"Maybe," Claire said, feeling worried. What if Alex was right? What if this wears off, and she ends up back where she started? That never occurred to her.

"I still feel trauma. I still feel that shock-y feeling you get watching a horror movie or whatever. And I still have nightmares, too, and I wasn't even in the accident," Chris said and then turned to Claire and asked, "What about the letters? Have you read them yet?"

"Yes," Claire said. "I don't know what to think. Of course, the first letters she wrote were for a little girl, so they don't explain anything. It's more her sending me love and telling me she misses me. As the years passed, they dwindle to an annual birthday card. You can be sure I'll be hovering over the mailbox next week. I haven't had time to think about talking to Dad. I guess I'm not sure if it is a conspiracy between him and Boots or if it was her decision. I don't know what to think other than being pissed off they lied to me my entire life. They're hypocrites. They betrayed me. Goddamn phonies. I haven't figured it all out, obviously."

"Listen, I know my mom can be a bitch, but she's not a monster, Claire," Chris said. "She wouldn't have hidden those cards for all these years without George knowing. I'm just not sure what they were thinking, though. It is bullshit. Have you decided what to write to her?"

"I haven't even decided to write to her," Claire said. "I don't even know what I would say. Like, thanks for abandoning me when I was a baby? Or why did you send cards to a child and not question why you never heard a response? That's shady as fuck as it is, right? Or what the hell did you do, to begin with, that you didn't think you could fight for visitation, even?"

"I never even considered that," Chris said. "That's deep. You think she did something?"

"I think you need to talk with your dad, Claire," Alex interjected. "He is a nice man. He was great to me in the hospital. Maybe if you talk with him, you'll get all the answers you need. And if you do think you're feeling stronger, no longer depressed, maybe it's time you can handle the truth and know what to do from there."

Claire rose to stoke the fire. She added two new logs before closing the glass doors and returning to the sofa. Chris rose to refill everyone's drinks. For once, nobody was drinking alcohol. Alex excused himself to go to the bathroom. When they all returned, Claire said, "It's funny. Taylor and I truly believed in omnia paratus. We weren't ready for all things. We were nowhere near."

"And now?" Alex asked.

"I still don't think we are. Probably less so than ever. Losing Drake proved to me that you could never truly prepare for life. No matter how much work you do," she said, thinking about the three enormously complicated installment pieces she devoted her life to creating in the last year. "Or however much you mess up, life will lift you up and hurl you through the universe regardless. Do you ever wonder about Twizzler, guys? I mean, ever wonder if she lived? If she's okay?"

"She was going to be fine," Alex said. "We sent the police to save her. They probably hit her with Narcan. Claire, you can't worry about her. She stole your bag, remember? She and Bones were on the take, and we are not responsible for what happened to her."

"Her gray face does plague my nightmares, though. I've never seen anyone OD," Claire confessed. "I keep picturing that girl in that Shel Silverstein poem. Remember, Chris? The girl who wanted to fly, so she grew her hair long enough to sail over the world? That's how I feel. Like I'm hurtling through space, catapulted before I was ready for anything, let alone all things. I never expected to fall in love with Sam. I surely didn't plan to feel so depressed all fall that I kissed Michael. I never expected—"

"Wait a minute," Chris said. "When did you kiss Michael? Does Sam know?"

"No," Claire said. "And you better not breathe a word to him when he comes home in two weeks for the wedding. Do you hear me, Christopher? It was stupid. I saw Michael at school for Career Day. He gave me a ride home; only he stopped at the trestle. I knew he wanted to hook up, and I should not have let him drive me there, but I did. But, when he kissed me, I stopped him. I did. I stopped the whole thing right there and made him drive me home. I feel horrible. I do."

"So why did you do it?" Chris asked.

"I don't know. Maybe I wanted him to still think I was pretty? Maybe I wanted to feel something because I was already so depressed? Maybe because I'm a masochist who will do anything to self-sabotage? Why does anyone do anything, really?"

"Because you're human," Alex said. "Human. Not a monster. And Claire, it was only a kiss, right? You said you stopped it. I don't know if a random kiss is enough to consider cheating on Sam, technically. It was just one kiss."

Claire looked at Chris, who was glaring at her. "I already feel bad enough. I don't need your judgment."

"I'm not judging. I'm not. I just wished you hadn't kissed that asshole."

"Well, me neither, and I've been suffering ever since. This has been the worst school year. Senior year sucks."

"Good thing it's only the beginning of 2020," Alex said. "Who knows? Maybe this is the worst. I mean, what more could possibly happen?"

32
everyone

Luke met Sam at the luggage carousel at the airport. After they hugged, Sam spotted his second duffle bag and pulled it down next to his first bag, his backpack already strapped on his back.

"Packed for a month, maybe?" Luke teased him as he grabbed the bags and hauled them into the back of his truck.

"I don't know," Sam said. "When Dad called, he told me to pack everything from my room as if I wasn't coming back. Something about the coronavirus in China?"

"I know. He called us, too. He isn't coming for the wedding," Luke said.

"I think he's overreacting," Sam said. "Is Aunt Karen upset?"

"She agrees with your dad. In fact, she's been glued to the

news and has been stockpiling in response."

"Stockpiling *what*?" Sam asked.

"Toilet paper, hand sanitizer, rubbing alcohol to start. But also dry goods like flour, sugar, you name it. Wait until you see the basement. It looks like a storage facility or something. Karen bought metal shelves I assembled to store all the stuff. She's convinced the virus is going to hit the US, and we're going to be in quarantine," Luke said. "That's what your father is doing now. Because he's been in and out of China, as you know, he is now in quarantine for two weeks in New York. He's concerned he's been exposed, so that's why he isn't coming for the wedding. He doesn't want to chance it. He's anxious about you, so we said you could stay until this all blows over. How long could it be? A few weeks, maybe?"

Sam said, "I know it's bad to say in light of a potential pandemic, but I'm so grateful to be back in Maywood. I can't wait to see Claire."

"I'm just grateful Karen didn't cancel the wedding altogether," Luke said. "At least we didn't book a traditional honeymoon. We plan to go to Italy in August. Karen has a friend who owns a home in the wine country, and since I've never been to Europe, we plan to take a month."

"I'm sure by August, this will all pass," Sam said before he picked up his phone to text Claire he had landed safely and was en route to Maywood. She replied she was already at Calico House, helping Karen decorate and waiting for his arrival.

World Gone Mad

Sam sighed when Luke took the turn down the country road to Calico House. He was delighted to be back in Maywood. Calico House was like no other in the world. Aunt Karen had grown up in the same house, almost her whole life. Sam's grandparents settled there with his mom, who was Aunt Karen's older sister when the girls were in middle school after living on tour with the Grateful Dead and in a commune called Willow Grove, a piece of history Sam had just learned about over the summer. A few years ago, Aunt Karen was inspired to transform the formerly white Dutch colonial by painting it in ways no one else would ever think to do.

She divided sections of the house and painted the siding in rainbow colors defined with black. Part of the stripes ran vertically; other areas ran horizontally. The chimney, painted red and white, resembled a Cat-in-the-Hat. It was an artist's house for sure, and Sam loved it. A porch ran around the exterior, and the house faced a pond. Between the house and the pond was the sacred elm tree Sam had spent his summer under when he wasn't on Phish tour with his friends. Aunt Karen had a separate building that operated as her art studio painted blue with a black door and shutters detailed with crisp white trim. The chicken house was painted bright yellow. Next to the detached garage was a large barn Luke said he was converting into his studio after the wedding. He was a furniture maker and carpenter. Helping Aunt Karen transform Calico House brought them together as a couple. They would live there together, which meant Sam could continue to consider it his home.

The moment Luke parked the truck, Claire ran out of the house and into his arms, saying, "You're here. You're here. You're finally here."

Aunt Karen trailed behind, laughing. Sam pulled away from Claire for a moment to hug his aunt, who said, "Welcome home, sweetheart."

Luke hauled the duffle bags from the truck. He and Sam each grabbed one to bring inside.

"It's crazy your Spring Break is so early," Claire said, as they walked through the house and upstairs to Sam's room. "Is it always this early? Maywood's Spring Break isn't until the end of the month, meaning next week while you're lounging in bed, I'll be at school, which sucks."

Sam laughed. "It sucks? It sucks that I'm here? Come on, Claire. It is going to be great. We have at least nine entire days together. Let's look at the positive. Did you receive the gift I sent for your birthday?"

"I did, and I love it," Claire said, referring to the snow globe of a miniature New York skyline.

"And what did you and Taylor do to celebrate? You never told me what you decided."

"We kept it simple this year," Claire said. "Taylor's mom baked us a cake. Chris cooked, and we all had a combined family dinner. Very quiet. Just what I wanted. Did you receive my Valentine's gift in time?"

"Of course," Sam said.

World Gone Mad

He reached into his backpack, where he had carefully scrolled the picture into a cardboard tube he borrowed from the art teacher at St. Philips to keep it from crumpling on the plane. He considered it one of his most valuable possessions. Both Sam and Claire loved the rendition of "Strawberry Letter 23" that Phish covers, so Claire had created a visual representation of the song, including rainbows and waterfalls, orange birds, blue flowers, and a cherry cloud. Taylor had collaborated by scrawling in calligraphy, their favorite line in the corner.

"I love it. Claire, I've never seen this style from you before. Is it new?" Sam said.

"It is. It started as a doodle of sorts. I got this new set of markers I wanted to play with. It is one of the first songs I've drawn."

"You draw songs?" Sam asked. "Do you have more?"

Before Claire could reply, Aunt Karen called them down for dinner. When they walked into the kitchen, Crosby, Stills, Nash, and Young played through the speakers. The kitchen smelled of garlic and basil, and Luke had set the table. Aunt Karen insisted they sit as Luke poured wine, and she served them bowls of pasta, saying, "Fresh marinara just made today." She reached in the oven to retrieve a loaf of garlic bread she sliced before setting it into a basket for the table.

"I shouldn't eat a bite of this bread if I want to look good in my dress tomorrow, but this wild garlic is just so good."

"Everything tastes good. Thank you, Aunt Karen. It's been months since I've eaten homemade food," Sam said, twirling pasta on his fork.

Luke asked, "Cafeteria food isn't the greatest?"

Sam smiled. "Not like this."

After they had finished eating, Sam and Claire insisted on doing the dishes. At the same time, Luke and Aunt Karen sat at the table, discussing the list of things still to do before the ceremony, scheduled at four-thirty tomorrow afternoon. Claire sang along to "Our House" as they cleaned.

Aunt Karen said, "He wrote that song for Joni Mitchell, you know? Stephen Stills? He and Joni Mitchell were living together in California when he wrote that song."

"It wasn't Stills," Luke said. "It was Graham Nash."

Aunt Karen said, "Nash, Young, Stills, Crosby, no matter. It's still a romantic song."

She and Claire finished the refrain together as Sam hung the towels to dry. He was just so damn happy to be back home.

"So what's with this coronavirus?" Sam asked his aunt as she rose to put a plate of cookies on the table for dessert. "Is it something we should be worried about? I know when I'm at school, it can seem a little isolated, but how did I not hear anything about this until Dad called last night?"

"Do you watch the news?" Aunt Karen asked.

"Apparently, not as much as I should," Sam confessed. "The only thing anyone is talking about at school is our college acceptances. It's a dicey time of year, for sure."

"Dicey, how?" Aunt Karen asked.

"College is everything at boarding school. It's our whole reason for being, which is sad but true. Every year, when guys are declined from their top choices, it becomes a huge drama. Like, they have counselors on campus and group meetings. Hugely overblown, but that's how it is," Sam explained, reaching for a chocolate chip cookie.

"It's not so bad now as it will be after Spring Break when the ivies send out their decisions. Makes for a rough end to the semester," Sam said before he turned his attention to Claire and asked, "Have you heard anything yet?"

Claire said, "Yes. I've been accepted to DAAP, the art program at the University of Cincinnati, as well as to Miami University, Ohio University, and Denison."

"That's great," Aunt Karen said.

"No Parsons yet?" Sam asked.

"No Parsons," Claire said. "Not yet. You?"

"I'm still waiting," Sam said. "But I've heard from Denison and the University of Chicago already. Both accepted me."

"Why didn't I think of a school in Chicago?" Claire mused.

"You don't need to worry about a school in Chicago, Claire," Sam assured her. "You will get into Parsons. I just know it."

"What schools are you waiting for, Sam?" Aunt Karen asked.

"Columbia and Yale," Sam said.

"Yale?" Claire said. "And Columbia? I thought you were applying to NYU."

"Columbia has a better writing program. And even though Dad went to Harvard for undergrad, he supports my application to Yale. It's my reach school, Claire."

Luke asked, "Why have you heard from some schools and not others?"

Sam said, "Schools reply as early as January or February. Except for ivy league, they make you wait until March, April, for whatever reason. I don't know why that is, except that it makes for a long winter at boarding school—anyway, enough school talk. Let's talk about tomorrow. What do you need us to do?"

The evening ended with the four of them sitting together in the sunroom while Aunt Karen poised over her list. The living room was already decorated, as the ceremony would take place there under a trellis Luke had made before the food would be set out in the dining room. Luke had rented heaters for the porch for people to spill out there and stay warm on the winter day. Because it was an intimate affair, it seemed as if everything would run smoothly.

Karen didn't seem a bit nervous, and Luke acted like the perfect groom. He was very solicitous of his bride, holding her hand, refilling her tea, and giving her small kisses. Sam was pleased he and Claire could run errands to pick up the flowers and the cake. The caterers would bring the rest of the food, and Alex volunteered to bartend, which pleased Sam, who hadn't seen his friend since August, even though he had sent texts and emails after the accident, of course.

Thinking of the accident made Sam feel a flash of grief. His mind jumped around. He felt anxiety when he thought about the QTs. In their phone conversation last night, Sam's dad was too hurried to discuss the issue with Quill and Toth in his haste to direct Sam in packing and explaining the virus, which he was certain would spread from Asia to the states. Sam took a deep breath to stop the swirl of worries, relaxed back into the sofa and pulled Claire against him. He wasn't going to fixate on college acceptances, the QTs, or a deadly virus. Not tonight. Not when he was exactly where he wanted to be with the people he loved the most in the world. The rest could wait.

33
stay

Although the March day was cold, the sun was shining bright with promise for the wedding day. After Claire and Sam had finished their errands, directed the caterers, and greeted Alex, who arrived early to organize the makeshift bar, they retreated to get ready for the ceremony. Not that it was formal, but Sam chose to wear a coat and tie. Claire slipped into her dress and knocked quietly at Karen's door.

When she entered, Karen was fully dressed and sitting at her dressing table. She planned to wear a wreath of baby's breath instead of a veil. When she stood, Claire gasped at the beauty of the dress, which was a floor-length, simple champagne-colored silk shift with an overlay of antique lace, that skimmed Karen's trim figure.

Karen turned around and hugged Claire, who wore a pink silk

dress with spaghetti straps. She had pulled her hair into a messy topknot revealing tiny diamond studs in her ears. Karen wore simple pearls that looked elegant with the dress.

"My question is about my hair," Karen said. "Up or down?"

"With that dress? Up, of course," Claire said, reaching for the hairbrush to start. "I think a simple twist or a loose, low bun. I can do either."

As Claire set to work, they heard a quiet knock on the door before Taylor peeked in, stretching out a tray of champagne flutes.

"Happy wedding day. May I come in?" Taylor said. She wore a purple silk dress and had woven matching metallic strands into her braids.

"Of course, darling," Karen said, reaching to kiss Taylor after she set the tray down and handed each of them a glass.

"It looks so festive downstairs," Taylor said. "The trellis is beautiful. You're going to be happy with how it turned out."

Because it was an indoor ceremony, Luke used simple grapevines to construct a light trellis Karen's friends had decorated with baby's breath, white roses, and white hydrangea, using the same flowers in Karen's small nosegay bouquet. The trellis stood in front of the fireplace in the living room. Magnolia leaves, baby's breath, and white candles adorned the mantle of the fireplace. Earlier in the day, Sam, Claire, and Luke had pushed the upholstered furniture against the walls to make room. Sam even helped Luke lug some of the pieces, including the dining room chairs, to the garage to clear space. They arranged the rented heaters around the wraparound covered porch where Karen's friends had strung white lights and garlands of flowers around the eaves. Calico House was adorned for the event, and guests who were arriving deposited gifts and accepted cocktails from Alex as they waited patiently for the ceremony to begin.

"I hope I'm this serene on my wedding day," Claire complimented Karen.

"Well, I'm older, honey," Karen said. "Luke and I know what we're doing. At least, I hope we do. Seriously, though. We're best friends. I'm in love with him and feel grateful I met such a special person to share my life with."

Claire raised her glass and said, "To Luke."

"To Luke," Karen toasted.

"And to you, Karen, the most beautiful bride in the world," Taylor added as Sam knocked to tell them it was time.

Claire reached to adjust Karen's wreath and gave her a quick kiss before she and Taylor descended the stairs to join the guests. Luke looked handsome in his suit and not a bit nervous either. Maybe getting married when you were older was the way to go if it meant you knew what you were doing, Claire thought. Taylor's father began the familiar strains of Pachelbel's Canon on his violin, accompanied by Taylor's mother on cello, their wedding gift to the couple. Karen descended the stairs on Sam's arm. Claire began crying when she saw Luke's face light up when he saw his bride. Taylor handed Claire a tissue. Taylor reached for Josh's hand and squeezed as Sam hugged Luke and retreated to stand next to Claire.

The officiant, a woman Claire recognized as one of Karen's friends, began the ceremony.

"Friends, loved ones, welcome. We are joined together to witness the sacred vows Karen and Luke will exchange to join their lives together in marriage."

Claire held Karen's bouquet as they exchanged rings and said their vows to each other. The crowd erupted into applause when the officiant announced them husband and wife, and Luke cradled Karen's head as they kissed. They cheered when Luke lifted Karen's hand in his and exclaimed, "Let's get this party started. We're married!"

In the corner of the outside porch, a band set up. Mason, the banjo-playing French translator, Josh, the yogi who plays guitar, and Dave, Luke's carpentry buddy on drums, began playing as people mingled, balancing plates on the railing. Alex was in his element, cracking jokes while mixing cocktails and pouring glasses of wine and champagne. Just after Karen and Luke cut the cake, feeding pieces to each other without smashing them into each other's faces, which Karen had commented the night before was a tradition best served for younger couples, Taylor's parents bid them farewell.

"We have to pick up TJ and Tristan, but you kids stay and enjoy the party," Mrs. Thompson said as she kissed the girls goodbye. Claire's dad and Boots had not attended the wedding. They sent a wedding gift along with their best wishes with Chris.

Chris walked into the house and ushered everyone outside for the first dance. Claire and Taylor nudged each other as Theresa, the fortune teller, took her place with Mason and the musicians and began singing "Shining Star."

"A singing fortune-teller?" Taylor joked to Claire. "Now, I've seen it all."

"She does have a pretty voice, but it is bizarre," Claire said as the two giggled.

Sam reached his hand and asked, "May I have this dance?" He and Claire held each other close and rocked slowly in each other's arms, his breath in her ear, sending shivers down her spine.

Alex left the bar in the dining room to join his friends. Everyone applauded when the song ended. Theresa took a small bow, and then the musicians launched back into bluegrass, this time with everyone on the porch dancing.

"I wish Drake were here for this," Claire said, leaning to hug Alex, who pulled away.

"Cut the bullshit. Drake didn't give a shit about any of this. He would have been wasted by now, and it would have been me taking care of his ass," Alex snarled and then stormed off the porch toward the elm tree. Claire was shocked by his outburst, as Alex was usually so mild-mannered and seemed completely fine just moments before, tending bar. She immediately followed Chris, Taylor, Josh, and Sam, who took off to follow Alex.

"Alex!" Claire called. "Alex. Wait."

Alex turned around, tears streaming down his face, and said, "I just can't take it anymore. I can't. It's hard enough without revisionist history. Everyone acts like Drake was this big victim, and it's just not true. He did this. He killed himself. Hell, he almost killed me in the process when all I ever did was try to look out for that kid. Fuck him. Fuck him anyway."

"Alex," Claire said. "It's okay. It is. You have every right to be angry. We understand. We're your friends."

"I'm a terrible person. I am. I shouldn't have said that. It's awful," Alex said.

"You are not a terrible person. You went through a horrible tragedy none of us could possibly understand, and you're right," Taylor said. When she looked at her friends' expression, she continued, "What? It's true. Drake was out of control, and you know it. What happened was inevitable. Maybe not that he was going to die, but he was an accident waiting to happen, and you can't deny that. I just hate that you had to suffer, Alex. I do."

"You guys didn't know him like we did," Claire said, referring to herself and Chris. "We went to Sunday school together when we were little. He wasn't always out of control. He was a sweet kid who didn't deserve to die."

"Of course, he didn't deserve to die," Alex wailed. "That's what I'm trying to tell you. It's my fault. It's my fucking fault. All of it, and I can't help it. I'm pissed at him. Pissed he wouldn't listen to me. Pissed at myself for even trying to help him."

"Anger always comes with death," Sam said quietly. "It's part of the process of grief. What you have to remember is that you aren't responsible for what happened. And when someone spirals so far out of control in a self-destructive path, everyone else feels responsible when it's not their fault at all. At least, that's what I learned last summer when I processed my mother's suicide, being here with Aunt

Karen at Calico House and with you on tour. What you feel is what I felt, which is survivor's guilt, which's completely natural. I still feel it sometimes, but Alex, you did everything you possibly could. It's okay, man. We love you."

At that, everyone murmured they loved Alex as they wrapped him in a group hug until the inevitable giggles started and the moment had passed. Together, they walked back to Calico House, lit by lanterns and love.

34
microscope

Sam felt disoriented for a moment when he opened his eyes in the guest room at Claire's house. He was dreaming about school and woke to a pounding heart, images of Quill and Toth vivid. He still needed to talk to his dad about this. There had to be a way out.

He glanced at his phone, where he found several texts from Alex even though it was only eight o'clock on Sunday morning. Alex needed to drive to Cincinnati Monday and wondered if Sam would ride with him. Since everyone else would be at school, he immediately replied since Sam had never been to Cincinnati.

Sam spotted Claire's bra tangled in the sheets when he rose to find a bathroom. Claire had snuck out of the guest room sometime in the middle of the night, saying that her dad and Boots would not appreciate them sleeping together, even though they were both over eighteen. The only reason they returned to the Cutler's was to give Aunt Karen and Luke Calico House to themselves on their wedding night. They were supposed to stay in a honeymoon suite at a hotel, but Aunt Karen was too frightened of the coronavirus; she canceled everything but the actual wedding, which is also why there were so few guests invited. Even less than her regular gatherings, now that Sam thought about it.

Chris was at the stove cooking when Sam walked into the kitchen. He said, "Good morning. There's coffee if you like."

"Thank you," Sam said, pouring himself a cup. "Where's Claire?"

"Sleeping, I think," Chris said. "Sit. I'm making breakfast. Are you hungry?"

"Sure," Sam said. "Sounds great. When did you start cooking?"

"This year. It's been sort of an obsession of sorts, and I've learned a lot, but I still have a way to go," Chris said, serving Sam an omelet filled with cheese, ham, and apples. "I'm considering trying out for *Master Chef.* Do you know that show?"

"Gordon Ramsey, right?" Sam said. "I haven't watched the show, but I've been to his restaurant in New York."

"Of course you have," Chris muttered, pouring himself a cup of coffee.

"This is good. I've never had an omelet with apples," Sam said.

World Gone Mad

"Good morning," Claire said as she walked into the kitchen. She looked adorable with her hair pulled up in a scrunchie, wearing her pajama pants with a tank top. Sam could see her nipples, as she wasn't wearing a bra, and fought the urge to touch them as she reached to kiss his cheek. "Sleep well?" she murmured.

"Almost. Until you left," Sam said, then turned to Chris again. "So, if you audition for the show, what about college?"

"I will take a deferment or something," Chris said. "Or maybe I just won't go. Maybe I'll apply to culinary school instead. First, I have to nail the audition and get onto the show. One step at a time."

Boots hurried into the kitchen, weighted down with boxes Chris hurried to take from his mom's arms. "What is all this?" he asked.

"This is just the beginning. I need you all to help, please. The Range Rover is packed, and I still have more to organize," Boots said.

Then she turned to Sam. "How nice to see you again, Sam. How are you? How was the wedding?"

"It was wonderful. Thank you, Mrs. Cutler. I'm happy to help," Sam said, rising from the table to put his plate in the sink. "What can I do?"

Although Luke had warned Sam that Aunt Karen had stockpiled in the basement, he hadn't gone down there in a rush to help with the wedding, so he was jaw-dropped to walk into the Cutler's storage room. It looked like a warehouse; it was stocked so full.

"Mom," Chris whined. "Are you serious? How much more shit do we need?"

"This is no joke, Christopher," Boots reprimanded. "Put those over there so I can start organizing everything."

She held a clipboard and pen in her rubber-gloved hands. The mask she wore into the store was hanging around her neck. Although she dressed in yoga pants, Boots was still imposing, lipstick in place, hair pulled into a severe ponytail, and diamond earrings secured. Knowing not to argue any further, Chris and Sam retreated to the vehicle and carried box after box down the stairs to the basement. Once they had completed the task, Boots dismissed them, saying she needed to organize everything on the shelves. Sam asked Claire for a ride back to Calico House.

Aunt Karen and Luke were grateful Sam and Claire had arrived to help, especially moving the furniture back in place in the house. They all worked steadily until late afternoon when Aunt Karen brewed tea and requested everyone join her in the living room for a well-deserved break.

"You two are angels," Aunt Karen said, handing each of them a mug. Luke walked in, carrying plates of wedding cake.

"This cake is still so good," Sam said, after taking a bite.

"It is good," Aunt Karen agreed. "Yesterday was such a flurry; I barely tasted anything."

"May I drive with Alex to Cincinnati tomorrow?" Sam asked permission. "He needs to bring supplies to his aunt or someone. I'm not sure who, but he asked me to go with him. And since Claire and everyone will be at school, I thought it would be a good idea."

World Gone Mad

"I'm so worried about him," Claire said, and she explained what happened yesterday at the elm tree. "He's taking on the responsibility for the accident, and it wasn't his fault. Not at all. Maybe you can get him to talk, Sam. He'll open up to you."

"I feel a little nervous letting you go to Cincinnati because of the virus," Aunt Karen said. "Kids, this is looking like it's going to be bad. Schools are already closing. I won't be surprised if this is your last week, Claire. And Sam, I doubt you will be returning to school just like your dad predicted. We may have to hunker down until this thing passes, however long that may take."

"So, you don't want me to go?" Sam asked.

"No," Aunt Karen said. "But I will let you. As long as you drive directly to his family's house, unload the supplies, and return directly to Maywood. No running around the city, okay? Just there and back."

"Except for Skyline," Alex said the next morning when he picked Sam up. "I mean, your aunt didn't mean we couldn't stop for lunch, right? It's the whole reason for going. That, and Graeter's after. It's the world's best ice cream."

"I have never eaten Skyline chili. You're right. Aunt Karen would want us to eat lunch before we drive home. She wouldn't want us famished," Sam said, joking.

"Exactly," Alex said. "Seriously, though. We are merely dropping these supplies off to my aunt, who lives in Clifton, where the Skyline is. She is a nurse. And a single mom. A busy lady, that's for sure."

Alex neglected to tell Sam his aunt's apartment was on the fifth floor of a walk-up building. It took several trips to unload the truck. Although Alex's aunt was grateful, she briskly informed them she was late for work before slipping a twenty in Alex's hand and dismissing them.

"That was easy," Sam said as they pulled into the parking lot behind the restaurant on Ludlow Avenue. Because Sam had never been, Alex said he would order for them both.

"Two large three-ways, juicy. Four coneys, no mustard, no onions," Alex ordered without consulting the menu. "Trust me."

They snacked on oyster crackers doused in hot sauce as they waited for their food. The restaurant was bustling with lunch traffic, yet the food arrived within minutes.

"Is that cinnamon?" Sam asked after the first few bites.

"And chocolate, I think," Alex said. "It's Greek originally. Do you like it?"

Sam took a bite of one of the coneys and said, "It's good. Strange, but good."

Suddenly, Sam stopped eating, tilted his head, and asked, "Hey, bruh. I thought you were vegan?"

"You have a good memory," Alex said. "I stuck with the vegan route for almost six months until I was dizzy all the time. You know how much I hike and swim. I couldn't get enough protein in my body, not to mention being tired of fighting with my mother all the time about how thin I was. Working in a Mexican Restaurant is not a good fit for a vegan, and I'll be honest, I missed my mother's tamales."

Sam laughed. "That I understand."

After they paid, Alex handed Sam a York peppermint patty he bought at the register.

"I thought we were going for ice cream," Sam said, unwrapping the foil and popping the mint into his mouth.

"We are," Alex said, leading the way to cross the street. "It's tradition to have a mint, but that doesn't preclude ice cream, does it?"

Driving home, Sam groaned. "I'm so full. How can you eat so much? That was so good."

"And you only had a single scoop, lightweight," Alex said. He had eaten two scoops; chocolate-chocolate chip and mocha chip. Sam chose raspberry chip.

"Aunt Karen said this would be my last road trip for a while. She says we need to hunker down to wait out this virus."

"My parents are worried about the restaurant," Alex said. "If schools close, restaurants, bars, barbershops, and salons are all going to close, too. Stores are already running out of everything, which is why we had to drive this stuff down to my aunt. She works too many hours while raising two kids. I wish you could have met my little cousins. They're the best. Anyway, I guess she couldn't even find toilet paper in Cincinnati. She waited too long or something."

"Do your parents have a stockpile, too?" Sam asked.

Although Aunt Karen's basement wasn't as large as the Cutler's, it was packed full of supplies.

"We have the restaurant for storage," Alex said. "Enough toilet paper for a lifetime, cans of tomatoes, bags of beans, and pounds and pounds of rice. That kind of thing."

"My dad has been in and out of China for the past year," Sam said. "I'm worried he has the virus."

"Is he ill?" Alex asked.

"No. Not yet, anyway. He's at the apartment in the city now," Sam said. "He says he's in quarantine, which I guess means he's working digitally from home or whatever. Of course, it's New York, so you can order in whatever you want whenever you want it."

"I'm sure he'll be okay," Alex said. "So, you'll stay in Maywood until this blows over? That's awesome."

"That part is awesome," Sam said. "I hated not being at the funeral, Alex. I'm sorry."

"Man, I shouldn't have lost my shit at the wedding. I feel terrible about that."

"You shouldn't feel terrible about that. We're your friends. We're here for you. It's totally understandable. There are no rules to grief."

"There are no rules at all," Alex said. "I've been thinking about that a lot lately, how the rule is supposed to be that the natural order of the universe is that children bury their parents, not the other way around. It breaks the rules for a parent to bury their child because Drake broke the rule. The no-drinking-and-driving rule. He reached out for help. I showed. He broke the rules. I broke the rules. I knew better than to get into that car," Alex said.

"Why did you?" Sam asked.

"I don't know. I freaked out because the police were arriving. You know I'm twenty, Sam. A twenty-year-old Mexican in a house full of underaged drunk kids does not make for a pretty picture. I panicked. And I had this dumb notion that if I were at least in the passenger seat, that would be enough to keep him safe. I could not have been more wrong."

Sam said, "The rule is there are no fucking rules. Just life. Random shit and life. I don't know how natural the order of the universe is that I had to bury my mom. Not that we buried her. She was cremated, but same difference. It didn't feel natural to me; I can tell you that. I'm not sure about the rules, but it feels like a rule is broken when you lose your mom." He took a deep breath and continued. "What I know is that grief cycles, and it takes time. You've got to take it easier on yourself, bruh. Nobody blames you. You know that, right?"

"Maybe Drake's mom," Alex said. "She blames me."

"Did she say that?"

"No, but it was the way she wouldn't look at me at the funeral."

"I promise you, that was grief, Alex. I mean, I don't know Drake's parents, but he was driving. Not you. Him. It's a miracle that you are alive."

Alex said, "Thanks for being a friend."

"It is a miracle," Sam repeated. "Now, the question is: what are you going to do with it?"

"Here's another thing I keep thinking about. Dreams. It occurs to me the only difference between being alive and being dead is dreams. If existence is beyond the physical, and I'm sure it is spiritual, then the only thing that separates life and death is dreams. All sentient beings dream. Dogs dream. Cats dream, right?"

Sam nodded but stayed silent to follow Alex's theory as they drove I-75 North to Maywood.

Alex continued. "Think about dreams for humans. They're more than just REM cycles other mammals experience. Humans have sleep dreams, daydreams, goals and vision dreams, premonitions, although I think mammals get premonitions, too, right? Like when a herd suddenly stampedes, knowing a lion is approaching or just before an earthquake? Are those premonitions or pure animal instinct based upon senses? Anyway, back to what I was saying. Dreams. Failed dreams, unrealized dreams, broken dreams. Have you ever seen that old Robin Williams movie, *What Dreams May Come*?"

When Sam shook his head, Alex continued. "It's a great film. The theory of reality in that film is based upon reincarnation. Do you believe in reincarnation?"

"Yes and no," Sam said. "I believe our souls are energy, and when we die, our energy leaves the body and combines with the energy of the universe, like dissolving sugar into water. Each granule still exists but is no longer contained. Therefore, I don't believe that the entire essence of me, of Sam, will enter into a new body after I die. I don't think the soul is that tangible. Like, as much as I'd like to believe, I don't think my mother's soul will be reincarnated as my daughter. And even if she did, it still wouldn't be my mother because our existence is more than our spirit; it is the culmination of our experiences in life as well."

World Gone Mad

"Have you had a chance to talk to Taylor's dude, Josh, yet? He's into philosophy and would love to be in on this conversation."

"He seems nice. Do you think Chris cares that Taylor and Josh are a couple?"

Alex glanced over to Sam, grinned, and said, "I think our buddy has his own new romance going. Have you met Grant, the football player?"

"Wait; what?" Sam asked. "Was he at the wedding?"

"No, but I'm sure you will meet him soon. Chris hasn't said anything to me directly, but the energy is there. If he's happy, I'm happy."

Sam repeated, "If he's happy, I'm happy. Does Claire know?"

"I have no doubt Claire is quite aware of everything that's going on. You know our girl," Alex said as he pulled into the driveway of Calico House. "Thanks again for driving with me, buddy. It made the whole trip better having you with me, bruh."

"Bet," Sam said, climbing out of the truck. "I've got you."

35
mask

Chris knew not to respond to Grant's text, but he couldn't help himself. They met in the garage to retreat to *Suby Greenberg* for privacy, as was their routine. Grant even parked his car a few houses down, not that it fooled anyone who was looking. But nobody seemed to be looking. Chris still wasn't proud of his behavior and tried to use willpower to ignore Grant as much as possible, but every few weeks, it seemed, he broke down and replied. The routine was predictable and shameful. Chris would burn with self-hatred for days after, but his desire proved to be stronger than his self-esteem. Or lack thereof. As soon as Grant opened the RV door, Chris greeted him with a kiss, but Grant had other ideas.

"Let's talk," Grant said, sitting at the table instead of retreating to the bed in the back. "I told you how I felt back when we started, whatever this is. I feel like I've been patient with you, especially the past few months since the accident, but it's been since August, and nothing has changed."

Chris didn't say anything. He didn't know what to say. If Grant broke up with him, Chris deserved it. He had no business hooking up with somebody he was ashamed to date. However, another rule from the Courtly Rules of Love is that love either increases or diminishes with time. Chris felt dread knowing the truth. His passion for Grant had increased, not diminished if you could label what they had as love.

"I remember how hard it was for me to come out," Grant said. "So, I've been patient with you, but you haven't seemed to make any progress. You refuse to come to the GSA meetings at school. You still ignore me completely in the hallways. I don't know what to tell my friends who ask about you. I call you my mystery man and refuse to name you. I do this because I care about you, but I'm starting to feel like this relationship is not good for me. Not at all. I don't deserve to be treated like this, and honestly, you don't deserve me. I'm a good person, yet you still use me and discard me."

"I don't discard you," Chris said, feeling his face blaze. "And I'm just not in the process of coming out. That's why I don't go to the meetings. I don't belong there."

"Wow," Grant said, rising from the table. "You are so far into denial; you can't even see it, can you? What do you mean you're not in the process of coming out? What the hell do you think this is? We're gay. Together. And often. Gay, Chris. Gay."

"I don't buy into labels," Chris insisted.

"Bullshit. You claim Phish. You call yourself a phan. That's a label. You're a chef. You're a son. A brother. A friend. There are many labels you claim. Be honest. It's me you don't want to claim."

Chris remained silent. Grant was right. Chris knew he was gay, especially after being with Grant this year. He couldn't even imagine being with a girl again. But does everything have to be labeled and part of a drawn-out process of coming out or whatever? It exhausted Chris just to think about it.

"I want to go to prom with you," Grant said. "I'm giving you a month to work this out. If you choose to go with me to prom, as my date openly, we can talk. Otherwise, I'm done. I want you, Chris. You. But you need to want to be with me for this to continue."

"I do want to be with you," Chris said. He rose and pulled Grant into a hug.

Grant pulled away and said, "Then prove it."

He exited the RV and let himself out of the garage door. Chris stayed behind. He needed to process everything. It was only Wednesday night, yet the week was already crazy without this drama. One of the reasons Chris texted Grant was to escape reality. Everyone was freaking out about the coronavirus.

Rumor had it, school would close on Friday. Of course, it would be Friday the thirteenth, the only part of this that made any sense with its inherent doom. Although prom wasn't until May, promposals began as early as April, each one a bit more elaborate than the last, meaning that after a couple of weeks for the virus to pass, they'd be returning to school in time to begin this crazy tradition. Chris and Grant wouldn't be the first gay couple to attend a Maywood prom, though. It's not like Claire and Taylor didn't already know, so what was the big deal about telling everyone else?

36
loneliness

"So, it's rules you're worried about?" Claire asked Chris, who woke early to roll out pasta, his newest culinary obsession. Since school closed the day before, there was nothing but empty hours to fill.

"How do you even remember the Courtly Rules of Love anyway?" she asked, scrolling on her phone to find them.

"I do remember some things from school, Claire. I'm not a total idiot. But I'm not just talking about those rules. I'm talking about all of the rules. Which make sense? Which to discard?" Chris hung the individual strands of pasta on the back of the wood lattice kitchen stools to dry.

"I like this one," Claire said. "*Love can deny nothing to the one he loves.* And listen to this one. *Good character alone is quality enough for any man worthy of love.* But some of these rules contradict each other, Chris. Like one says, *No law, natural or moral, forbids one woman from being loved by two men or one man by two women,* and then another says, *a double love can never bind anyone.* There are a lot of rules about jealousy, though. Huh. According to these rules, jealousy is evidence of true love and good to fuel passion in love. Or are you talking about this rule? *When love is made public, it rarely endures.*"

"Yes, but more that when love is made public, the lover is ashamed of that love, and therefore it is unseemly to continue that relationship," Chris confessed. He felt relieved to say the words aloud to someone finally, and Claire was the only person he could trust. "I'm thinking about all of the rules. Like the rules of society or the rules of parenting. The rules of grammar and the rules of cooking."

"Holy shit," Claire said. "That just gave me the best idea."

When Chris saw the expression on her face, he knew inspiration had distracted her far beyond the conversation about Grant, so he sighed and asked for an explanation as he fed more dough through the roller for the next batch of pasta. It took so much more pasta than one would ever have thought to feed four people. Chris knew he'd be rolling forever.

"The Helping Friendly Book, of course," Claire declared. "The rules of the Phish world. The most important rules to follow. It makes sense now, of course. All these song illustrations I've done? They're studies. Rough drafts. It's perfect now that I think about it. The most peace I feel is listening to music and creating images of the lyrics. I could do that for the entire Gamehendge. I could illustrate each of the songs. I mean, nobody has actually written the book, right? It's just a myth. I mean, everyone goes around saying, *read the fucking book*, but nobody's literally written it."

"So, you're going to write it?" Chris asked.

"Why not?" Claire said. "I'll do the illustrations, and Taylor can help with the text. What else do we have to do? I mean, we're probably going to be out of school for a few weeks, at least."

The closure of school was suddenly announced on Friday, March thirteenth. Over the PA, the principal instructed the students to clear out their lockers as best they could, reminding them to bring their laptops, musical instruments, and any other equipment they may need for the coming weeks. There was a bit of a scramble for the agriculture students to find homes for the baby chicks they had hatched. The underclassmen lamented how they could possibly empty a year's worth of stuff gathered in their overly decorated lockers, as their parents clogged the school parking lot, so their precious babies didn't have to lug everything on the yellow buses. The seniors, however, walked out with barely a glance back. Nothing counted at this point of the year. The college decisions had either been received and were on their way.

Boots entered the kitchen, took one look at the pasta drying over the backs of her barstools, and sighed. "I assume these strands won't leave marks on the wood, Chris?"

"No, ma'am. They never have before. When you taste what I'm making, you'll forget all about your chairs, which are just fine, for the record," Chris said. He was always so calm with his mother, unlike Claire, who had to grit her teeth with every conversation.

"I'm going to Calico House," Claire said, rising from the kitchen table.

"Oh no, you are not, young lady," Boots said. "They canceled school for a reason. No one is safe. We are all going to stay here for at least two weeks. Nobody goes anywhere, and nobody is to come over."

"You cannot be serious," Claire growled. "Sam is there. You are not going to tell me I can't be with Sam."

"For two weeks," Boots said. "Those are the rules."

Claire's dad entered the kitchen from the garage, looking exhausted.

"Daddy," Claire said. "Tell Boots she's crazy. She says I can't see Sam for two weeks."

"Hello, Claire. Chris, this looks delicious. Is it for dinner?" George said.

He leaned over to Boots to kiss her. He pulled out a kitchen chair and sat at the table, gestured Claire and Boots to join him, and said, "Boots is right, Claire. Don't blame her. They are the rules. We don't know how this virus is spread, but we do know it is rampant. This quarantine is no joke. You've seen how much work Boots has done to stock up the house. I understand that this will be hard for all of us, but we are going to lock down the house for two weeks. If Sam is not showing any symptoms, as I'm sure he won't, and if we are all still well, we can talk about how we will live from there. Sam isn't going back to school either, is he?"

"No," Claire said. "His school announced before ours. And his dad is following the two-week quarantine as well. That's why he didn't fly for the wedding. He's in New York. It's just; he thought Sam would be safer in Maywood, which is why he is here. I'm well. He's well. We were together for the wedding, so what difference does it make now?"

"That's exactly it, Claire. You attended a wedding Saturday, March seventh. You continued going to school until Friday, March thirteenth. We stay in quarantine until Saturday, March twenty-eight, and that way, we'll know nobody spread the virus to anyone else who was at the wedding or who was at school. This includes everybody, even Taylor. I'm not going to discuss this any longer, and I don't want to receive texts that you disobeyed these rules. Do you both understand me?" Her dad said, looking stern.

"What do you mean, texts?" Claire asked.

"I'm going back to the hospital, honey. It's a madhouse there now, and I'm not going to risk my family in the process. I'm home to retrieve what I will need, see you all, and then I'm going back. I've checked into the Maywood Inn, where I'll sleep between shifts. You can reach me whenever you need, but this is the decision we've made, and I need to be able to trust you to do the right thing."

Claire and Chris agreed immediately, stunned by the harsh reality of the situation. Until this moment, getting out of school early seemed like getting a free pass. They didn't consider the cost of what could happen if their family got sick.

37
stands still

"There's no way they're going to allow us," Claire said to Taylor on the phone. "If we ask to stream the show together before our two weeks is over, they're going to say no. Boots has been on a cleaning rampage. It's been crazy."

"My mother is bug crazy again," Taylor complained.

"*There ain't no bugs on me,*" Claire teased, quoting the title of a Jerry Garcia song the girls would sing to Mrs. Thompson when she freaked out over bugs in the house.

In response, Mrs. Thompson would always say, "This is no joke. You two weren't raised with bugs as I suffered. You have no idea what poverty looks like, and I hope you never do. Now, go get the bug spray and stop talking back."

"It looks like they're planning to stream every week," Taylor said, reading from the announcement on Jambase.com. Phish had announced they plan to stream old shows every week in a series called "Dinner and a Movie" for the phans during the quarantine, beginning March twenty-fourth.

"There's a recipe for Trey and Sue's vegetarian chili. Think Chris is up for making it?"

"Of course," Claire said. "All he's done for the past two weeks is cook. I guess we'll have to wait until the following week, but we need a plan of action. We need to get our parents together, I think. We can state our case to be together, so we don't all lose our minds."

"I would love to see Josh. I miss him so much," Taylor said. "How are the drawings coming along?"

Claire positioned her phone to show Taylor her progress on The Helping Friendly Book series. "I guess I can hand these to the mailman to deliver to you, maybe?" Claire joked.

"Very funny. Just put them into a folder and walk them over. You can ring the bell, and I'll wait until you step back to open the door," Taylor said.

"This is ridiculous. They're acting like we're those idiots who are posting pictures of corona parties. Have you seen them?"

"Those kids have no sense. The numbers are already growing. People are dying," Taylor said.

"Since the accident, Scott Warton hasn't had any parties, that's for sure. Our senior year has spiraled from bad to worse. I thought grieving Drake was hard. Now we are all isolated at home with our parents? I thought it would be better with Sam in Maywood, but it's almost worse to have him here and not to be able to touch him. I'm calling my dad."

Although Claire passionately pleaded her case, her father didn't budge. He arranged for a video conference call with the Thompsons and Karen to discuss the situation for the kids after the two weeks ended and not a day before. They decided as long as everyone agreed not to go anywhere but to see each other, they could become what Claire's dad called an "isolation group," which included Chris, Claire, Taylor, and Sam. Nobody mentioned Alex, and Taylor was furious Josh wasn't yet included. Because his mother runs Sunshine House, the parents didn't think he's safe. Taylor argued they were elitist, but the parents countered that they were cautious. Taylor's dad defended their stance because he had closed his dental practice for the time being. The governor was closing restaurants, salons, and retail stores in the state.

"My dad said he would call Mr. Gentry soon," Taylor said. "It's not like Josh works at Sunshine House. He's just been lying around, doing nothing like the rest of us."

"Aunt Karen pled our case by saying the parents should all be grateful we weren't attending corona parties or wanting to go out, but that we needed to be together for emotional support. It was cool," Sam said the following Tuesday, March thirty-first, when they were permitted to stream the show together at the Cutler's house.

Chris had spent the day making Mike Gordon's recipes of beans on toast and mushrooms on toast and had also prepared chicken marsala.

"I've never eaten anything on toast but butter," Chris said. "So, these were fun to make, but as an appetizer. Don't worry. The chicken will fill you up."

"I think these toast points are tasty," Sam said, stuffing another into his mouth. Claire retrieved drinks from the refrigerator as she, Taylor, and Chris carried trays of food to the basement family room to stream the show.

Claire was startled when she heard someone knock on the basement door. Chris jumped when he saw it was Grant.

"Hey, guys," Grant said as he followed Chris into the house.

"Hi, Grant," Claire and Taylor said.

Chris handed him a toast point while Claire offered to get Grant a soda. As Grant settled on the sofa, Claire hoped her dad and Boots wouldn't come downstairs. They hadn't approved Grant in their isolation group, of course. Chris hadn't even asked.

Taylor followed Claire to the bar and hissed, "But Josh can't be here?"

"I know," Claire whispered. "I promise you; Grant is not here by permission."

Taylor frowned in response. The girls returned to the sofa. Claire handed Grant a cold soda.

"What did you think of that 'Carini' last week?" Chris teased Sam, who notoriously hated the song.

"Still not converted, but the jams were great. Looks like we're in for a Tweezer fest tonight," Sam said.

World Gone Mad

"You looked up the setlist?" Claire said in mock outrage. "What's the fun in that?"

Unlike an actual Phish show, the stream started precisely on time. "The Curtain With" into "46 Days" seemed almost prophetic in light of the pandemic. At set break, they decided to step outside to smoke a joint.

"I got into Spelman and Howard finally," Taylor said. "Now, it's time to make a decision."

"Have you told your parents yet?" Claire asked.

"Not yet. I want to sit with it alone for a while. I need time to think," Taylor said. Then she turned to Grant to include him. "My parents are hung up on me attending an HBCU."

Grant shook his head and asked, "What is an HBCU?"

"Historically black college. Like Wilberforce," Chris jumped in to explain.

"If I don't hear from Parsons soon, I don't know what," Claire said. "The waiting is killing me. More because we're stuck at home. At least we'll be launching digital instruction next week, whatever that means."

"I've had time to read," Sam said. "Being holed up in Aunt Karen's house with her library has its benefits, that's for sure. I found a book you have to read, Chris. It just may replace your love for *Growing Up Dead*, it's that good."

Chris guffawed. "There will never be a replacement for *GUD*."

"Okay, but this one is really good. It's called *Beautiful Music* by this dude named Michael Zoo-something," Sam said.

"Zadoorian," Taylor interjected. "Michael Zadoorian. It's a brilliant book. We studied it at the Reynolds Writing Program for his prose. The way he evokes song lyrics in the reader's head."

"Phenomenal," Sam said. "I didn't know all of the songs, but yes. That's it."

"Claire, you would relate to the way the character's life was saved by music," Taylor said.

Sam turned to Claire and said, "And you will be happy to learn I just read *Oryx and Crake*. I felt bad for never reading Margaret Atwood, so I did."

"How did you like it?" Claire asked.

"I loved it. You know there's a second book? It's called *Year of the Flood*."

"We read Atwood in English class. Which book did we read again?" Chris said, looking at Grant, who kept his eyes down and mouth shut.

"*The Handmaid's Tale*," Claire supplied the title.

"That's right. I didn't like it," Chris said.

Silence lingered. When Grant didn't raise his eyes, Sam continued, "Have you read Patti Smith's memoir? *Just Kids*? Now that was an incredible book. Aunt Karen says it's one of the favorite books of her life. If only I could write like that. I mean--"

"I rarely read memoir," Taylor said. "If it's not poetry, I read fiction except Jessica Topper. I love her books. But she writes like a poet, so that makes sense, I guess."

"That's also because she writes about backstage and about being in love with a rock star. Who doesn't love that?" Claire said.

"I will loan you Karen's copy of Patti Smith's book. It is amazing," Sam offered.

"Did you read the book Taylor lent you? *The Hate U Give?*" Claire asked.

"I read that first, of course," Sam said.

"You and your books," Claire said.

"Well, I needed to do something for two weeks when I couldn't see you. School launches for me next week, as well. I have a feeling I'm going to be here for the duration. At least my dad isn't sick. It's been over two weeks, and no symptoms. That's a relief."

"We can go to prom together," Claire said. She giggled and got down on one knee. "I don't have a planned promposal except this. Will you go to prom with me?"

Sam laughed and reached down to kiss Claire. "Yes, I'll go to prom with you. Now get up. It's time for second set."

Chris stole a look at Grant, who frowned as he watched Claire and Sam kiss before they entered back into the house. Chris let Taylor walk ahead before he grabbed Grant's hand and pulled him back. When Grant turned to him, Chris leaned in to kiss him, but Grant put his hand on Chris's chest.

Grant said, "I'm tired of sneaking around. You need to decide because this is the last time I'm knocking on the basement door."

38
an hour

Quarantine in April's month took on a rhythm revolving around Tuesday nights when everyone gathered to stream the shows. In between, they mostly all stayed at their own homes, half-heartedly participating in digital learning and video calling each other. By April first, the pandemic had reached new heights everyone took seriously. Ten thousand people had died in Italy. Of course, the Italians were caught unaware, and since the country is so small, the virus spread at an alarming rate. CNBC reported a global death toll of 30,982 out of 669,310 reported cases, with the US, China, Spain, and Germany being the highest, which was not an April Fool's Joke. The numbers were staggering. Even more upsetting was the news of the cancellation of prom.

World Gone Mad

"What am I going to do with my dress?" Taylor lamented on a video call with Claire. Taylor and her mother had driven to Cincinnati in late February to buy it.

"Keep it for formals, I suppose," Claire said. "It sucks, though, Tay. It's a cute dress."

"I wonder if they have formals at Howard," Taylor said.

"You decided?" Claire asked.

"I've decided Howard over Spelman. That's a start. I don't want to attend a women-only college, and I don't want to live in Atlanta. It's too hot. I like that Howard is located in D.C. It's still between Kenyon and Howard. Now back to the Helping Friendly Book," Taylor said, in an attempt to distract Claire, who was still waiting to hear from Parsons.

"Really, it's a book of rules, don't you think?"

"Yes, but you keep making illustrations for each of the Gamehendge songs. I'm wondering how to create the text with the rules." The girls had used social media, tapping into the Phish phan groups to accumulate a complete set of what people perceive as The Helping Friendly Book's rules, so they had a list written. Now it was a matter of finding a way to incorporate those lyrics into the illustrations Claire created.

"I think it might be better if I started a new batch of drawings specific to the rules," Claire said. She picked up the sketchbook that was full of completed illustrations. "Let's begin by organizing the rules. Like, we can group rules that I can render illustrations for, which might make more sense."

"So, abandon Gamehendge? All these drawings?" Taylor asked.

"Not abandoned. Maybe I can gather these together as their own collection. But I clearly see that I need to create new drawings for our book. That leaves you, though. I mean, what are you going to do while you're waiting for me to finish the art?"

"Don't worry about me. I have more than enough work to do. I still have to finish editing the final edition of the literary magazine for school. I want to polish my chapbook for submission, and I'm still participating in NaPoWriMo," Taylor said, referring to National Poetry Writing Month, which was always April. The idea was to write a poem a day, every day for the month. Although she had individual poems published in various anthologies and journals, Taylor had yet to publish a book, one of the goals she wanted to accomplish before graduating, so she hoped participating in this disciplined structure would help her complete her manuscript.

"You know what I read?" Claire said. "The plague shut the theaters in London for five years. That's how Shakespeare wrote all of his sonnets and his major plays. He was stuck in Stratford-Upon-Avon without any technology for five years. Shit. Imagine what you could write in five years."

"Everyone always questions whether Shakespeare wrote all of his plays," Taylor said. "This makes sense, right? I mean, five years of seclusion?"

"I also started thinking about 'the roaring twenties.' I mean, in history class, we always talked about the response to prohibition, the beginning of an industrial society, and the stock market. When, in fact, the people were roaring out of the Spanish Influenza. These plagues. We're not the first generation of humans to suffer quarantine. I just never considered what they do to society until we've experienced this. I wonder how we'll roar when we're free to be again? Can you imagine what it will be like when Phish tours again?"

Dead and Company tour, as well as every major music festival, was canceled for the summer. Everyone except Phish, although it was just a matter of time before they followed suit. Prom was scrapped entirely, and parents were already talking about ideas for alternative graduation ceremonies. The high school could not be crowded with commencement as they've historically always done. One parent had proposed using the Maywood Drive-In, and someone was contacting Mr. Kennon, the owner, to see about that idea. Nobody was going to have a graduation party, but the parents were adamant they find some way for their children to cross the stage in cap and gown, whatever stage that may be.

Claire glanced at her laptop and squealed. "I got in! I got in! Tay!"

"Parsons?" Taylor clarified. "That's amazing, Claire. I knew you'd get in. I just knew it."

She was so relieved for her friend. It was a long wait, and Taylor worried about Claire. She knew Claire suffered from depression when Sam left for school in August. The chaos of that Twizzler chick overdosing or whatever at the Louisville show did not help matters in the least. Taylor was so caught up in her drama after she and Josh were stopped driving while black in Dayton. She didn't think she would ever recover from that humiliation and rage at the injustice. Then, they lost Drake. Taylor had been so worried; she hadn't pushed Claire about finding the letters and what Claire decided to do about that. Claire couldn't even handle telling Sam about losing her bag at the Garden, let alone kissing Michael back in the fall.

One of the things she loved most about Claire was her ability to suspend reality. It was also the thing Taylor worried about most for her friend, as well. But she had never seen anyone work as hard as Claire worked on those installment pieces, and that hard work paid off. No matter prom was canceled, and graduation would be one of the most unconventional ceremonies ever. Claire had succeeded in her goal, and her dream of living in New York with Sam would become a reality. The pandemic was hard enough without something to look forward to.

Claire texted Sam, who called back two seconds later. After he congratulated her, he said, "I've got good news and bad on my side."

"Okay," Claire said. "Spill."

"The bad news is I got wait-listed at Yale. The good news is, I got into Columbia." He could not stop laughing at Claire's reaction.

She was as happy as he had seen her since summer tour, which felt like an eternity ago. When they returned to Maywood after the last show, they could never have expected the summer to have been an end of an era. That idyllic moment in time was innocence that no longer existed. Who knew how long it would be before a vaccine was created, and enough people had received it to rejoin society like before? How long until they could go to a Phish show with thousands of other phans again?

Sam cringed, remembering Bates' battle and how much he wanted to find a way out of Quill and Toth. Sam finally found the courage to discuss it with his dad, though. Ironic how insignificant the incident with Bates now seemed in light of everything else. Drake was dead. Sam worried about his dad more than he admitted to Claire. His dad had traveled in and out of China, of all places, the past year. That he had endured the swab testing that poked back to the brain to be sure he was negative was reassuring, of course. Sam could relax knowing his dad was not ill. The relief to receive the college decisions was just the break from all the stress both he and Claire needed. Perhaps things were changing, even in these strange days of quarantine amid a global pandemic. Sam could not predict what was going to happen in this new reality.

"Stay right there," Claire said. "I'm coming to you now. I want Karen and Luke to be the first to hear our news."

Claire knocked on Chris's door on her way out to share the news with him because she had told Taylor. She could tell her dad and Boots later. Right now, she needed to get to Calico House to wrap herself up in Sam's arms.

39
the day

In the studio, Chris found Claire listening to the new Phish album *Sigma Oasis*, working on her designs for The Helping Friendly Book. When Chris turned the music down, she looked up. Chris was counting on the fact she had been in a great mood since her acceptance to Parsons. He rifled through the sketches, which were an explosion of color with whimsical images.

"These are amazing," Chris said. "What will Taylor do with them? They look finished."

"The drawings are finished. Now it's time to lay the text. Taylor and I organized the list of rules. See?" She showed him the pages she and Taylor had printed. "She will use her calligraphy skills to write the phrases onto the drawings. This has been one of the happiest projects I've ever done. I get to tap into my favorite band, work with my best friend, and pour all my love and joy into the drawings. They're fun, don't you think?"

Before he could answer, she said, "Wait. I want you to see this one. At the top, we'll scrawl the lyrics from 'Joy.' Do you see what I did?"

Chris peered closely at the compositional "rooms" on the page. In the bottom corner was an image that looked like Alex inside a deep purple box. Claire had drawn a mountain and colored a yellow sky with a blue sun, which Chris recognized as Grateful Dead lyrics come to life. At the top of the mountain were four figures with arms stretched to the sun.

"Us?" he asked.

"Yes," Claire said. "I plan to frame this original as a gift for Alex."

"That could have just as easily been you in that box of gloom not too long ago, Claire. I know this sounds cringe-y or whatever, but I am checking in with you. Still feeling good, feeling strong?"

"Yup. You don't have to worry about me, brother. What I told you and Alex two months ago seems to still be true for me. I will never understand it completely, but I'm so grateful not to be depressed; I'm not questioning it. Losing Drake shook my depression loose faster than any medications or therapies I've tried. Right now, I'm committed to living fully and well, as a tribute to Drake."

"I'm glad to hear that because I have a favor to ask," Chris said. "It requires a sense of romance and drama I'm counting on you to bring. Are you in?"

Before Chris even explained what he was requesting, Claire said, "I'm in. Of course, I'm in. Now whatcha got?"

Chris took a deep breath and blurted, "I've decided to ask Grant to prom."

Claire frowned and said, "What prom? There is no prom."

"I propose we host a prom for six in our backyard. Maybe more of a dinner dance than a prom since I plan to cook everything, of course."

"Of course," Claire said. "I love this. We can decorate the patio, and everybody can dress up. Oh! Taylor is going to be so happy. She already bought her dress."

"I know Mom will help," Chris said. "She lives for shit like this. But here's where the favor comes in. I need help with the promposal. I've been scrolling for days, trying to think of something original. The main thing is this: I need to make it public. How that will happen in quarantine, I don't know. But it has to be public. There is a scene from that old 80's movie, *Say Anything* Grant loves. The scene where John Cusack holds up a boom box or whatever they called those things outside his girlfriend's window. Grant loves that scene. But where am I going to get a boom box, and what song? Do I use the Peter Gabriel song, 'In Your Eyes'? I don't know what to do. Where would I even find a cassette to play in a boom box if we even found one? What do you think?"

"I've got this," Claire said. "When do you want to propose?"

"After we talk to Mom and Dad. Let's get their permission even to host a prom-for-six before I humiliate myself."

"You are not going to humiliate yourself," Claire said. "I promise. I've got you."

A week later, Chris, Claire, and Taylor drove to Grant's house, prepared to propose. Of course, Boots was delighted with the idea and began making calls immediately to rent tables, chairs, tablecloths, and flower arrangements. Not all of the stores had reopened by May, but Boots prided herself in her connections through her lifestyle blog and assured them the patio would be transformed into "a space not to be forgotten," her words. Claire dropped her illustrations to paint a cardboard box to look like a boom box. Boots had merchandise delivered to their door several times a day. There were always boxes to spare.

They brought a portable speaker with them, the Peter Gabriel song cued up. There was a brief debate about the song, though. Claire suggested they use the new Phish song, "Shade," because she thought the lyrics were romantic, but she was vetoed.

"It has to be the Peter Gabriel song to work," Taylor insisted. "Otherwise, it won't make sense. Besides which, I'm assuming Grant isn't much of a phan, is he?"

"He is not a phan. If I'm doing this, I'm going to do it right," Chris said.

He was dressed for the occasion and wore a trench coat he borrowed from Dad over a white t-shirt, jeans, and sneakers. "I don't have a Clash t-shirt, so I hope this will do, and I don't know what kind of sneakers he wore, so I just wore my Chucks."

"You look perfect. Just lift the collar, so it stands straight up," Claire assured him as they pulled into Grant's driveway. "This is so exciting. You're sure he's home?"

"He's home. His family is home. Everyone is home," Chris grumbled. "Let's get going."

They pulled on masks over their faces, retrieved the cardboard boom box, the real speaker, and the four other posters. One read, *Will you.* The next, *Go to.* The third, *Prom With.* The last, *Me?* Claire and Taylor would hold one in each hand, flanking Chris, who would lift the cardboard boom box over his head while the music played.

Taylor ran to the front door, rang the bell as Claire cued the music. Grant's younger brother opened the door and yelled, "Grant, it's for you. Grant! It's for you!"

Grant looked a bit flustered when he saw them on the driveway until Claire looked over to Taylor to signal. One by one, they revealed the signs as Peter Gabriel sang the chorus. Behind Grant, his mother stepped out to see what was going on.

Grant hesitated, shaking his head in wonder until he reached Chris, who said, "In public."

When Grant said yes, Chris dropped the box, and they hugged as Grant's mother ran down the steps, yelling for them to stop.

"You need a mask! You need a mask!" she cried, waving a mask in her hands. The boys separated quickly. When everyone laughed, she conceded. "It is romantic," she said. "But there is no prom. They canceled prom."

World Gone Mad

Claire handed her the special invitation she crafted in addition to painting the boom box. She was glad she had included the line, *creative formal* as dress code when Grant's mother lamented the tuxedo shops were closed.

"I don't care what I'm going to wear," Grant said. "I can't believe you did this for me."

"Wait a minute," Grant's mother said. "This says Tuesday, May twelfth. That can't be right."

Claire stepped forward and said, "We chose a Tuesday for a special reason. It's not a mistake. And since we don't have school officially and this isn't a prom officially, we decided to make up our own rules."

40
you fly

May first was known as college acceptance day, which was a big deal unless you were Claire and Sam, who had no doubts about their mutual decision to live in New York together to attend college. Alex accepted his admission to Ohio State and couldn't wait to escape to the main campus, presumably to room with Chris in the dorms. Josh had proudly worn a Wilberforce hoodie for weeks, it seemed.

Taylor sat at the kitchen table with her parents, studying the barn wood her mother used as a bulletin board in her kitchen to match the urban farmhouse decor. On it, her mother had pinned the stickers from Kenyon, Denison, Miami University, Wilberforce, Spelman, and Howard; all the schools that accepted Taylor. As her parents talked, Taylor stared at the tiny painting Claire had created as a gift for her mother when they were in middle school. It was a little canvas, no bigger than two by four inches, yet the river's image in a forest seemed large. Taylor marveled at the ability to render a reality that seemed to stretch for miles in such a small composition. It was one of her favorite paintings because it soothed Taylor to follow the river's lines to a vanishing point in the forest.

"Of course, we're so proud of you, honey," her dad began. "All of your dreams have come true, and that's because of the hard work you put into it, Tay."

"Tell us what you're thinking," her mom said. "We want to hear your decision."

Taylor looked at her parents' faces and knew she had to break their hearts, so she took a deep breath. "I've considered this seriously. I've made a decision. I don't want to live in Atlanta. Spelman is too overwhelming when you consider Morehouse, and I hate the idea of living in D.C. to attend Howard. I've never wanted to live in a big city, especially D.C. I'm not political. It's not part of the vision I have for my life. So, I've decided to accept my first choice, Kenyon. I'm sorry if this decision disappoints you."

"We are not disappointed," her mom said.

Her dad said, "I'm not gonna lie. I wanted you to attend an HBCU because it wasn't a choice I had. You know that, Taylor. I had to take the best scholarship opportunity, and that was Indiana. If I had to do it all over..."

"You can," Taylor said bitterly. "You can do it all over with TJ or with Tristan. They can fulfill your dream or whatever."

"Slow down, honey," her dad said, putting his hand over Taylor's. "Having said that, I will repeat: Mom and I are proud of you. We couldn't have asked for more than what you've accomplished, and if Kenyon is still your decision, we support that."

"We do, Taylor. We love you. Honestly, I already knew what you'd decide. The fact that you weighed your options and considered them is all Daddy and I wanted for you. Not for us. You," her mom said, looking pointedly at her husband. "Kenyon is your dream. It always has been. I understand."

"You're just happy your baby is only moving three hours away from home," her dad grumbled.

"Well, that's true," her mom conceded. "There's nothing wrong with wanting to stay close to family, and you know it."

Later that evening, on the phone to Josh, Taylor said, "I'm just grateful they didn't make any snarky remarks about choosing Kenyon so I can be closer to Wilberforce."

"Would they be snarky?" Josh asked. "And wasn't that even a little part of your decision?"

It wasn't, but Taylor lied and said, "Of course. It will be great that we can see each other on weekends and holidays. Now, let's talk about prom. I'm so grateful to be able to wear my dress. Just wait until you see."

When they ended their call, Taylor pulled her Kenyon hoodie over her head and stood in front of the mirror, grinning. She pictured the gothic buildings on campus at the foothills of Mount Gambier and shivered with anticipation. Part of figuring out who she was going to be, was figuring out where she wanted to do that, and the relief in making the decision made Taylor feel lighter than she had in weeks. Although she loved Josh, she was realistic. Not many high school couples made it through college without breaking up. Not everyone was like Claire and Sam. Taylor knew she had to put Josh out of her mind to decide, and she did. The fact she would be closer to him seemed like an immediate bonus more than a long-term goal. Was it wrong to want to launch her life untethered? Not that she wanted to break up with Josh. She just wanted the freedom to allow any possibilities when she was this young. These were things she didn't want to share with Josh. She didn't want to hurt his feelings. She loved him.

41
there

Chris found Boots in the kitchen, making yet another call to pull together *Social-Distance-Prom-for-Six*. She had done so much, he felt bad asking for yet another favor and questioned his decision to identify himself as a flower chef, to begin with. It was an idea formed when he focused on plating techniques while binge-watching all the seasons of *Master Chef* to prepare to audition for the show. He knew he needed a signature of sorts, but trying to locate cilantro flowers, garlic blooms, and chive blossoms were proving to be more arduous than he anticipated. Of course, the ingredients were difficult to obtain amid a global pandemic. He had already altered his menu from quail to braised beef short ribs when Boots put her foot down, explaining there was not a quail to be found in the state of Ohio. He edited his

World Gone Mad

love for truffle oil in response to Gordon Ramsay's disdain of the trend to garnish a dish in the hopes of elevating it. No truffle oil. No quail. And absolutely no microgreens, a mistake he regretted because he could have grown them himself if he had planned ahead. When he sighed, Boots looked up from her laptop.

"I found the Papasan loveseats, and you wouldn't believe what I had to do to hunt them down, but they are on a truck arriving from Cincinnati as we speak," she said.

Chris sat at the kitchen island next to his mom. "Do you think we could find a chocolate fountain, too? I'm so overwhelmed with the first two courses. I would prefer just to cut a bunch of fruit and have the fountain serve as dessert while we watch the show."

"That's easy," Boots said. "Let me make a note, and I'll rent the same as your thirteenth birthday party, okay? Is that what inspired this idea?"

"Yes, and that my date happens to love chocolate," Chris said.

He kept his eyes on his phone while they talked. "Grant can eat all the chocolate he wants because football practice keeps him in shape."

"Oh!" Boots exhaled. Chris waited, but she didn't say anything. He did feel her eyes on him, so he forced himself to face his mother.

"His name is Grant Fields, and he is a graduating senior, too," Chris said. "We started talking this fall, but it's turning into something a bit more. Prom will be our first official date."

"And where does Grant plan to attend next year?" Chris wasn't surprised by this question. College was the most important thing on her mind, which is why he hadn't the courage to confess he planned to defer Ohio State for a year to audition for *Master Chef*. One step at a time. Telling her about Grant was enough for this conversation.

Anticipating her disappointment, he met her eyes and said, "He will attend MBSU," referring to Ohio State University's Maywood branch. "His family doesn't have a lot of money, so he plans to live at home for the first two years and then transfer to main campus."

Boots frowned like Chris knew she would. If only Grant were Ivy League material, Boots would better accept the situation. The irony was Grant's family's economic situation was better than how Boots had grown up. Chris knew the story of how she crawled her way up by attending college and then marrying Chris's dad, who came from a rich family in Cleveland. When she landed George, her second husband, the marriage secured her position in the Junior League and fulfilled her destiny to become a doctor's wife. Chris would never understand his mother's need for social standing.

He never met his grandparents nor saw where his mom had grown up in a Youngstown trailer park. After she left for college, she never went back. He never experienced financial hardship in his life, so he knew he didn't understand his mother's perspective. Although Chris's dad left them before he was three years old, his monthly checks were never late, even if he often forgot to send a card for his son's birthday.

World Gone Mad

"You will like him, Mom," Chris said, patting his mother's shoulder. "He's very handsome."

"I'm sure I will," Boots said. "Have you decided what to wear? Are you sure you don't want me to try to find a tuxedo?"

"I think I'll just wear my dinner jacket, Mom. You've already done enough for me in ordering all the food. I know it's been a pain trying to find all of the flowers, but I appreciate it."

"Speaking of flowers, I found a nursery in Dayton that will ship the pea blossoms," Boots said. "And the florist finally got back to me about the floral centerpieces since I insisted on orchids. They will be able to deliver the four potted trees in time, too. As long as their workers wear masks, and because they won't have to trek through the house, I think this event will finally come together."

"It's going to be amazing," Chris said.

"I just feel so bad for you kids. It's not fair. We ask so much of you. Especially senior year. The common apps, the classes, all the extracurriculars you've done for years, and to not have prom or graduation? It's just not fair. It's not what I pictured for my son for his senior year. And who knows? Maybe my blog will influence other mothers to create a special event during these dark days. God knows we need a little break from the chaos."

As Chris stood to leave the kitchen, Boots put her hand on his arm and asked, "Does Grant make you happy? Is he deserving of my son?"

"He does," Chris said. "I'm just not sure I deserve him, but I plan to try."

42
reprieve

Because the show began promptly at eight-thirty, the group assembled in the backyard at six, a fortuitous number for their *Social-Distance-Prom-For-Six*, who jovially posed for endless pictures in the backyard for the parents and Aunt Karen before they all retreated a bit tearfully. Chris had changed from his chef's clothes to a white dinner jacket over a black dress shirt unbuttoned at the neck, paired with jeans, which complimented Grant, who wore a black suit coat over a white t-shirt. He wore jeans as well, and both guys wore sneakers. Because Taylor wore her formal prom dress, a long silver column gown, Josh dressed formally in a black pinstripe suit, crisp dress shirt replete with cufflinks, and silver silk tie to match Taylor. They looked stunning together.

World Gone Mad

Sam had unearthed his khaki sports coat from the stack of what he now called his *boarding school days* clothes he shoved in the back of his closet at Aunt Karen's house. He chose a white dress shirt, gray trousers, and his trusty red hunting hat firmly in place, which was as creative as he could think for the occasion. Claire suffered searching for a dress until Aunt Karen swooped in and saved the day by inviting Claire to borrow from her. The attic of Calico House stored her mother and sister's clothes. Since Claire had borrowed from Aunt Karen before, she was delighted to rummage through cardboard boxes in the hot, unfinished space. The result was well worth the effort when Claire stepped onto the patio wearing a vibrant pink-and-orange print full-length dress tied behind her neck. She had pulled her hair up to reveal the back, which plunged dangerously low.

"It was your mom's dress," Claire said when Sam complimented her. "I hope you like it."

Boots had outdone herself decorating the patio. She had taken photographs earlier in the day for her lifestyle blog, of course, and would return when the sun had set to capture the canopy round lights strung crisscross between the four enormous potted trees that defined the space. At one end, Claire and Taylor set up the screen, which was flanked by speakers on either side. The patio in front was uncluttered, so the three couples could dance. Claire had retrieved the laser lights Chris used all the time from the garage. Once the show started, they would create a little light show with multi-colored lights reflecting off the trees.

Somehow, and using all of her catering connections, Boots had rented three oversized round wicker Papasan-style love seats with deep cushions, ample room for each couple. A low table in front of each sofa featured a centerpiece of white roses and orchids surrounded by fairy lights. Fairy lights were strung and tucked in too many places to count around the patio, a fact Claire and Taylor could attest to since they worked as Boot's assistants to decorate. The seats were arranged in a semi-circle so the couples could talk to each other. They were also facing the screen if anyone chose to sit during the show, but since it was the 2018 Alpharetta show, Claire didn't anticipate anyone sitting for long. She cheated for once and checked the setlist. It was blazing, and she couldn't wait.

Chris and Sam retreated to the kitchen, returning with two silver platters of hor d'oeuvres. Grant laughed when he saw cheese puffs next to the prosciutto-wrapped melon, figs dipped in honey and rolled in almonds, stuffed mushrooms, and asparagus tips held upright with cucumbers sliced so thin, they were almost transparent.

"Cheese puffs?" Grant smiled at Chris.

"I'm glad you remembered," Chris said and popped one into Grant's mouth.

The second platter featured a charcuterie, including seven types of meats, eight different kinds of cheese, olives, four tapas spreads, and three miniature braided loaves of bread Chris had created from scratch, of course. They placed the platters on a banquet table decorated with a white linen tablecloth, also featuring a rose and orchid centerpiece.

Before anyone could eat, Chris took pictures of the carefully arranged food he had created and then pointed out the edible flowers that garnished the dish. Purple chive blossoms rested next to the delicate white flowers of cilantro. Delicate arugula flowers and purple and white pea flowers completed what Chris said was to be his signature.

"I'm going to be known as the flower chef," he said. "I've been studying different ways to garnish dishes. I have been bingeing all of the seasons, the British and the American versions, of course. You've got to have something to stand out."

"Stand out in what?" Sam asked, reaching for a fig.

"*Master Chef.* The cooking competition. I've decided to defer Ohio State next year and audition for *Master Chef.* If they have auditions, that is. Regardless, I'm going to focus on cooking full-time now."

"Have you told Boots and Dad?" Claire asked.

"Not yet," Chris said. "I wanted to tell you guys first."

"I think it's awesome," Taylor said. "You are going to get on the show if they have auditions and even have a show. This stupid Coronavirus is ruining everything. Have you heard about the decision for graduation? I guess we're going to be the feature at the Maywood Drive-In."

"At least you have a ceremony to attend," Sam complained. "St. Philips is doing a virtual graduation. They don't want anybody back on campus until fall, I guess."

"Our high school is doing a virtual ceremony, too," Josh said.

"Are you ready for the main course?" Chris asked.

"There's more?" Josh said. "This is better than prom any day. This is a feast."

"Of course. We will be right back," Chris said as he and Grant carried the now empty platters back to the kitchen.

"While they're gone, let's take more pictures while it's still light outside," Taylor said.

Claire opened a bottle of champagne and poured glasses while Taylor took pictures of Josh and Sam, and then Sam took photos of Taylor and Josh. Finally, Taylor took pictures of Claire and Sam before they lifted their flutes to toast.

"To quarantine prom," Claire toasted.

"To friends," Taylor added.

Chris and Grant returned with the platters loaded with dinner plates. The group cheered for Chris, who took a bow like any practicing chef. Chris had prepared beef short ribs that fell off the bone and melted like butter that he paired with gnocchi tossed in sage butter with perfect tiny yellow, purple, and red tomatoes cooked until they exploded in the mouth like mini fireworks. A bed of wilted greens tossed in red wine vinegar completed the meal. Chris had scattered pansies and the white flowers of garlic mustard blooms and oregano in an artistic arc on the plate, which enhanced the tomatoes' colors.

"Your plates are like works of art, Christopher," Claire complimented him.

"Thank you, Claire. From you, that is a high compliment. I'm working on my plating skills. See how I smeared the sage butter across the plate? I'm trying."

World Gone Mad

"I'm seriously impressed, bruh," Josh said. "You have a future in this. I'll bet you nail that audition."

"Thanks, man," Chris said.

The group ate dinner at their little tables, each taking turns to take pictures of each other. Claire popped open two more bottles of champagne and refilled everyone's flutes.

"Where did you get all the champagne?" Josh asked as he lifted his flute for Claire to refill.

"From the storage room. Boots has cases and cases of champagne and wine in there. Whatever she needs to entertain. Don't worry. She won't miss it. She has no one to entertain right now," Claire said.

When they had finished eating, Claire and Taylor volunteered to return the platters to the house so they could also retreat to the bathroom and touch up their make-up and hair, excuses they used to be alone for a moment to chat. Dessert would be fruit to dip in a chocolate fountain Chris would set up on the table to snack on throughout the show.

"I already started assembling," Claire said, pointing to the bed, where she had strewn boas of sequins and feathers in several colors, Baba Cool shades, a headband with cactus antenna, and several strands of metallic beads. "Don't forget to grab my grandfather's top hat. It will look great on Josh with his suit. I think it's in the closet."

Taylor poked around, found the top hat, and asked, "Claire, is this the box of letters from your mother? In the closet?"

Claire kept her gaze steady in the mirror and continued to dab the gold glitter on her cheeks, shoulders, and cleavage. "I don't know where the silver glitter is for your dress, Tay. Do you have it?"

"Yes," Taylor said, reaching into her purse. "Do not change the topic, please. What's going on? Have you confronted them yet?"

"No. I plan to sit them down after graduation. I wanted to get through prom first. This means something to me."

"It means something to me, but I don't understand how you could keep this a secret all of these months. Doesn't it bother you? I mean, how are you dealing with Boots? Your dad, even? You just smile and don't say a word? I don't know if I could do that."

"You don't tell your parents every single detail of your life. Did you tell them you've had sex with Chris and that you're having sex with Josh? You're having sex with Josh, aren't you?"

"Yes, as a matter of fact. Since Valentine's Day, if you must know. And I didn't tell my mother I had sex with Chris, but she did make an appointment for me after I told her about Josh so I could go on the pill. I mean, I did go to her, Claire. She knows Josh and I are in a meaningful relationship, and what could she say? I'm eighteen."

"I'm glad, Tay. The pill works great for me. So how is it? With Josh?" Claire said as she wrapped a pink boa around her neck and scooped everything else into a basket to carry downstairs.

"It's wonderful, but come on, Claire. Let's talk about the letters, please," Taylor insisted.

World Gone Mad

Claire paused in the doorway, the basket on her hip. "Taylor, I love you, but this is why I didn't want to confront my parents and let it rain shit on what is an epic night of our lives. Please trust me."

Taylor followed Claire down the stairs, who paused and said, "I mean, shit. If Christopher could stay in the closet, why can't I leave that in the closet for just a while longer? In the scheme of things? Drake is dead. He's dead. He's not here with us tonight. He's under the fucking dirt. Then the coronavirus hit, and now everything else is just blown to hell. Can't tonight and graduation just be two good things? Just two. Then, I'll deal with it, I promise."

Taylor pulled her best friend into a hug. She whispered, "I get it, sister. I get it."

Claire hugged Taylor and said, "Thank you."

When the band took the stage and launched a pounding "First Tube," everyone pumped their arms in the air. Josh wore the top hat while Sam held on to his hunting hat. Chris and Grant donned beads and boas. The laser lights transformed the elegant event into a more psychedelic vibe as the day surrendered to the evening. The celebration intensified when the band sang, "Back on the Train." Sam and Chris hugged, reminiscing about last summer's tour with *Suby Greenberg* that solidified their friendship, securing Sam's position in the phamily they had become.

"I wish Alex were here," Claire said wistfully.

"I invited him for second set. He should be here soon," Chris said. "I figured since we were making our own rules about prom, he should be allowed to join us, right?"

Before Claire could answer, Phish segued into "Free," the song every senior could claim as their anthem. "Martian Monster" confused Josh, who had never heard that song. Claire instructed everyone to get a drink, declaring it time to toast Drake.

"What is with those sirens?" Josh said to Taylor. "You know what that reminds me of."

He excused himself and retreated into the house to use the bathroom. Luckily, the song was only four minutes long, so when he returned, the band had segued into a blazing "Tube."

Alex walked through the lawn to the group and said from behind his mask, "I know I'm early, but I didn't want to miss the chocolate fountain. Where is it?"

"Still in the kitchen. I'll bring it out at set break. Until then, smoke this," Chris said, handing Alex a joint.

"I brought my own glass," Alex said, holding up his pipe. "It may be paranoid, but I don't think I should share saliva."

When the group sat for the last two songs of the set, Taylor said, "'Tube', 'First Tube.' Which came first? Were they written together? How does that work?"

"Don't forget 'Last Tube,'" Claire said.

Consulting his phone, Chris said, "It says 'Tube' came first. It is Fishman's song and debuted in 1990. 'First Tube' debuted in 1999. And 'First Tube' is a TAB song Phish plays, but 'Last Tube' is a TAB song Phish doesn't play. It was last to be written of the three."

"How do you guys keep up with all of this?" Josh said. "Phish has to be one of the most complicated bands I've heard of."

World Gone Mad

At set break, the guys helped Chris carry the chocolate fountain, plug it in, and arrange the fruit platters and cookies for dipping, while Claire and Taylor retreated to the bathroom. They returned to find the guys posing like they were drinking straight from the fountain for pictures they took of each other.

"Don't you dare!" Boots yelled as she approached the patio to take pictures of the setting now that it was dark enough to see the lights.

"We're just kidding, Mom. Relax," Chris said, putting his arm around her.

After taking her pictures, she looked at the champagne's empty bottles, sighed audibly, and raised one eyebrow in her customary Boots' manner.

She said, "I will leave linens, blankets, and pillows in the family room since it appears everyone is spending the night, right?"

"Josh and I will walk home, Mrs. Cutler," Taylor said. "My mom set up the guest room for him already."

Since the Thompsons only lived two doors away, Boots agreed. But she made Alex, Sam, and Grant promise they would stay the night, who agreed immediately, of course.

The second set launched with a "Tweezer" Claire had anticipated. She had forgotten they played "Prince Caspian" and loved when Josh asked Taylor, "Prince Caspian from *The Lion, The Witch, and The Wardrobe*? That Prince Caspian?"

"The very one," Taylor said. "Trey loves C.S. Lewis."

"I was not expecting that," Josh said. "I still don't understand this band."

They all cracked up when Sam yelled, "My song!" at the first notes of "Carini." He notoriously hated the song, an almost sacrilegious sentiment in the Phish community.

The best part of the show for Claire was dancing with Sam to "Winterqueen," one of her favorite songs. Josh exclaimed, "I know this song! Trey played it in Dayton, right?"

Social-Distance-Prom-for-Six closed with the friends singing "More" along at the top of their lungs, tears streaming down all of their faces.

43
things

Sam waited for his dad's arrival at Calico House on the front porch. Exercising caution, his dad drove from New York instead of flying. After six months of practically living inside the apartment, his dad was anxious to get to Ohio to see Sam and to be able to at least take a walk without wearing a mask.

"You mean the joggers in Central Park wear masks?" Sam asked his dad on their last telephone conversation.

"Yes, everyone. Everyone on the streets. Masks," his dad said. "Aren't you wearing masks in Ohio?"

"Of course, Dad. Like, if we go into town or to a store or whatever. But not just to take walks. You know these country roads are deserted. There's plenty of space in Ohio to walk and relax."

"That sounds like just what I need. I'm looking forward to seeing all of you."

Sam wondered if his dad planned to take him back to the city with him and hoped that was not the case. There was no reason to leave Ohio any sooner than necessary. Although their apartment was large by New York standards, it would seem small if he and his dad were confined in that space, especially if Sam was rattling around without Claire for the summer. But after his dad arrived safely and had settled on the porch with a glass of iced tea, he put Sam's fears aside when he sighed, looking at the pond, and said, "I'm so grateful this is where you spend your summers, Sam."

Sam exhaled relief and said, "Me too. There's nowhere else I'd rather be."

"So you're graduation ceremony is on-line? What's that going to be like?"

"Stupid," Sam said. "And pointless. Just as weird as having graduation at a drive-in, though."

His dad chuckled. "Yes, that will be interesting to see. That's tomorrow?"

"Yes," Sam said. "We'll drive with Aunt Karen and Luke in their car. I don't know if we'll even be able to talk with Claire, but at least I'll be able to see her and Chris walk the stage."

Aunt Karen stepped out of the house and joined them on the patio. She said, "Dinner should be ready soon. Sam, why don't you find Luke and tell him your dad arrived?"

World Gone Mad

"Luke has almost finished converting the barn?" Drew knew Luke's plans to use it for his furniture making. "I'd love to see it tomorrow."

"How have you been, Drew?" Karen said. "I'm so glad you made the drive. I hope you can stay. It's almost warm enough to swim in the pond."

"You have no idea how grateful I am Sam has been here, safe with you. New York has been a nightmare. Thank you."

"No thanks necessary. You know we love having him here. It has been rough on everybody. Did he tell you about their *Social-Distance-Prom-for-Six*?" Aunt Karen launched into the details as the sun began its descent over the pond. James Taylor sang about his desire for fire and rain, sweat pooled at the bottom of his iced tea glass, and Drew relaxed for the first time in months.

He took a deep breath and asked Karen, "Is that honeysuckle?"

She said, "Yes, it just bloomed."

After dinner, a feast Karen prepared of roasted chicken, wild rice, and steamed asparagus, Sam lugged his dad's duffle bags from the car, per his request, saying, "I have gifts," as he handed each of them boxes wrapped in heavy white paper tied with white satin ribbon.

Sam unwrapped the paper to reveal a monogrammed leather wallet with his initials, a moleskin journal, and a watch. When he picked up the watch, his dad said, "It was the watch I received from my parents when I graduated from high school. I thought it was appropriate to pass it down to you."

"Thanks, Dad," Sam said, sliding it over his wrist.

Karen opened hers to find a hand-painted porcelain tea set and cups from China. "This is beautiful, Drew. Thank you."

"You are welcome. That is your wedding gift. I also have another gift for you, Karen. Perhaps not so much a gift, but—you'll see."

He handed Karen a cobalt blue silk drawstring bag embroidered with flowers. Her eyes grew wide until she carefully loosened the drawstring, reached in, and retrieved the opal earrings she knew to be within. Then, she closed her eyes, clutching the earrings in a fist to her lips. When she opened them again, she was crying. Sam leaned closer to inspect the large opals set in a halo of diamonds in a filigree gold setting.

His dad said, "I found them in her jewelry box when I was rummaging around to find the watch to pass on to Sam. I've never seen them before, but I recognized the signature stitched to the bottom of the bag. That's your mother's, right?" When Karen nodded, he continued. "I thought you'd like to have them. I still haven't sorted out her jewelry, so if there are other pieces you would like, I'd be more than happy to send them to you."

Karen said, "No. I don't need anything else. Not anymore. Just these. I can't believe. I just can't believe."

Sam couldn't tell if she was happy or not from her mixed reaction, and because she rose to make coffee and serve the pie, he could tell she wouldn't elaborate any further until she was ready. Luke shrugged in a silent communication of solidarity and rose to help his wife. After they had eaten the pie, Karen rose to excuse herself to bed. She walked over to her brother-in-law, kissed him on the cheek, and murmured, "Thank you."

"Good night," Sam said. "I'll take care of these dishes."

After his dad helped him rinse the dishes, they settled on the patio. Sam flicked on the lanterns that provided enough light without distracting from the lightning bugs flashing in the elm tree leaves.

"We never talked about Quill and Toth," his dad said. "And although it's a moot point now, I do want to address it."

"How is it a moot point?" Sam asked.

"You graduated. It's over. You're not going back to St. Philips. From that perspective, it's a moot point. But, Sam, your experience was quite obviously different from my experience."

"You are admitting you are a QT?"

"To you, I am. You are my son, and that is more important than any oath of a secret society. At least, in my book, it is. The only reason I wanted you tapped was that I wanted you to have the kind of friends I had and to have the same fun. Sounds like your experience wasn't very fun."

Although Sam already told his father about the incident with Bates in a telephone call, he didn't realize his father had already been informed by the other QT elders, who responded with an emergency meeting to handle the situation. Before consequences could be meted, the pandemic hit, scattering the students away from campus for the rest of the year.

"However, his reputation will follow Bates wherever he goes to college. If he goes to an ivy, that is. It's how it works. The system. The rules. He displayed a lack of character, which will be a black mark on his reputation forever. No matter how rich and powerful his father may be. But then again, maybe that's not true anymore. Dignity and integrity aren't valued. Look at the president. You couldn't find a more heinous, corrupt, crass individual in your life."

Sam laughed. "Tell me how you really feel."

"Have you decided about college?" his dad said, switching gears. "Tell me everything."

They talked long into the night, neither wanting to leave the comfort of sitting side-by-side on the porch swing. Sam explained although he had finally been accepted to Yale, his heart was in New York. Especially amid a pandemic, Sam would prefer to be closer to his dad even if he moved into the dorms.

"Columbia a great school to study journalism, it's in New York to be with you, and Claire is attending Parsons," Sam listed his reasons as his dad nodded in agreement. He made his dad laugh with his retelling of prom and asked him if he had ever eaten Skyline Chili. Finally, they talked about Drake and how it had affected all of Sam's friends.

"That's something I didn't experience until I was older, losing a friend. How is your friend, Alex? He was driving?"

Sam cleared up the confusion and reflected on them in his retelling to his dad. "I think Claire is stronger, in a strange way, maybe? She confessed she felt depressed this fall after I left. I felt depressed, too. Well, maybe not depressed-depressed," he backpedaled when he saw the alarm on his dad's face. "More like heartsick if that doesn't sound stupid."

When his dad relaxed, Sam continued. "And Chris seems to have found completely new directions in life with his boyfriend and his chef's dreams. Alex is the one who can't wait to escape. The dorms better open in the fall, that's all I'm going to say."

They discussed the possibilities of the dorms not being opened, especially in New York, where the quarantine was strictly observed to keep the infection rates as low as possible. Sam didn't want to consider what would happen if Claire had to stay in Ohio to learn digitally in the fall, and from everything his dad explained, it sounded like it might be a remote possibility. So much was in turmoil, in addition to the upcoming presidential election. Sam was relieved when his dad assured him he would not be traveling for work. Everyone was working digitally from home. The comfortable rhythm Sam and his dad had been slowly establishing in their comfort and trust of each other felt reassuring that as swiftly as life was evolving, they could count on each other.

44
stay the same

Mrs. Lee, principal of Maywood High School, stood on the stage the school had constructed in front of the drive-in movie screen for what had to be the most absurd graduation in Maywood High School history. The lot was full of cars packed with families required to wear masks, stay in their vehicles, and not mingle. Of course, there were always those few who do what they want without regard for anyone else.

The graduates in masks, caps, and gowns lined up to cross the stage without shaking hands and to receive their diplomas. The annual baccalaureate ceremony was hosted the week before at school instead of at the church, where they usually held the non-denominational yet spiritual ceremony, which was more meaningful than this peculiar drive-in graduation.

There were two reasons Mrs. Lee held the baccalaureate at school. The first was because the graduating senior class and parents simply weren't allowed to congregate inside any building, even wearing masks. It was too dangerous. The real reason was the dedication memorial of the catalpa tree garden bench the senior class donated in Drake's honor. The bench circled the enormous tree's trunk. The PTA planted a garden at the base. The bench would protect the garden from trampling students' feet. It was beautiful, a symbol of hope and renewal.

"Graduates, parents, and families," Mrs. Lee began. "We are gathered today to celebrate your achievement, your successful graduation from high school." The crowd cheered and applauded.

"We are also here today to dedicate this memorial to our beloved classmate, Drake Whitaker, who we lost this winter. After much debate, we have decided the hundred-year-old catalpa tree will remain standing. We consulted with the experts, of course. Both Town Branch Tree Company, Maywood's professional arborists, and the Horticultural Society advised us that the catalpa tree will heal; will continue to grow. Much like you will heal and continue to grow. It has stood for over one hundred years and will continue standing. This bench is dedicated to the wonderful memories of our Maywood Cardinal, Drake, who will be memorialized for the bright young man he was and not for the fatal mistake he made. In his honor, this garden will bloom around the trunk base, symbolizing your lives, blooming, and growing from the dirt of tragedy and loss. If we may now all bow our heads and share a moment of silence in honor of Drake Whitaker, please."

Claire didn't wipe away the tears that streamed down her face. Instead, she quietly clasped hands with Chris. They exchanged a look that spoke volumes of their shared grief. He squeezed her hand twice to communicate his love silently, and she squeezed in response.

Mrs. Lee continued, "Thank you, everyone. Graduates, it is time to launch you into the next phase of your life. We've shared your successes, your grief, your loves, your heartbreaks, and your joys for the past four years. And now, it's time to celebrate your commencement. Even a global pandemic wasn't enough to keep the Class of 2020 down." The crowd chuckled from behind their masks, each family unit a cluster that remained a six-foot distance from the next.

The school choir planned to sing until the new research showed that singing was one of the fastest ways to spread the virus. There was a choir where almost every member was infected after one of their rehearsals. Mrs. Lee was so concerned; she wouldn't even allow the orchestra to perform even as a smaller chamber group. Instead, they piped recorded music over the speakers at the end of the ceremony that felt odd anyway, since the families immediately dispersed instead of shaking hands, congratulating each other's graduates, and hugging. There was absolutely no hugging of any kind anywhere. Instead, people crooked their elbows to tap, elbow-to-elbow. Sam's dad declared the pandemic to be the official end of handshakes in western society. The baccalaureate ceremony that usually lasted over an hour with time to socialize was reduced to a short thirty-minute ceremony. Sam, Aunt Karen, and Luke didn't even attend, as they weren't considered immediate family. However, it was still more heartfelt than the graduation at the Maywood Drive-In.

The make-shift stage activity was projected onto the big screen while the families in their cars tuned into the FM channel to hear their graduate's names called.

"I'm sweating under this mask, cap, and gown," Claire complained to Chris. As usual, they stood in line together, Cutler falling alphabetically behind Carter, Chris's last name. "It's gotta be at least a hundred degrees today."

"It's only ninety-two. Don't exaggerate," Chris said. "This whole thing sucks. I should have brushed my teeth before we left. My breath stinks behind this mask."

"At least you don't have to worry about your glasses fogging up," a classmate named Joe Crawley, lined up in front of Chris and Claire, turned around to say. His glasses were fogged, sweat pouring from under his cap. Claire felt terrible for him. For all of them suffering through this graduation just for the benefit of their parents. At least Sam and his dad, and Karen and Luke, were allowed to attend. They had driven their truck and were parked, watching from somewhere in the vast crowd of cars.

It felt eerie to hear her name called without applause. Claire climbed the stairs to the stage and walked across, accepting her diploma. She automatically reached her hand to shake Ms. Lee's, who shook her head and said, "No shaking. I'm sorry. Congratulations," before ushering Claire on.

In the end, the graduates moved their tassels from one side to the other, as instructed. They were strictly forbidden from tossing their caps into the air. Mrs. Lee said the melee from retrieving the fallen caps would violate the social distance rules.

Boots wouldn't allow a social distance graduation party in the backyard, as Chris and Claire requested. "I shouldn't have allowed prom to begin with, but I caved. I feel sorry for you; I do, but no. We are not hosting a graduation party in any way. I'm sorry, but no."

Since George agreed, there was no point in arguing. The four returned home, where Chris and Claire dropped their cap and gown and immediately showered, per Boots' instructions. She even had them leave their shoes outside the house. They gathered in the kitchen, where Chris had prepared a platter of shrimp cocktail and crab cakes to eat while he and George grilled steaks and the potatoes finished baking in the oven.

"I've missed your cooking so much," George said, dipping a crab cake into the mustard sauce Chris created. "These are delicious, Son. Have you found out more information about the *Master Chef* audition? We are behind you one hundred percent."

Chris said, "I've pre-registered and downloaded the application. Saturday, October twenty-sixth, I will be in New York to see you, Claire. Will you come with me to the audition?"

"Of course," Claire said. "How cool is it that the auditions are in New York? That worked out well."

"I chose New York. The auditions are all over the country. Chicago, Los Angeles, Atlanta. This way, I can see you and Sam," he said, standing at the stove, whisking bearnaise sauce in the double-boiler. He turned down the flame, checked the oven, and lifted the platter of steaks. "Ready to grill, Dad?"

Claire and Boots set the table in the dining room. When Chris and George returned with the steaks, the candles were lit, and Bach played in the background.

Boots looked around the table and remarked, "This is the first family dinner we've had in almost a year, I believe. This is nice."

"Senior year has sure been one for the records, that's for sure," her dad agreed. "It's been a whirlwind."

"Are we any closer to getting a vaccine, Daddy?" Claire asked.

"Yes, but even with a vaccine, it's going to take time. Kids, what we're looking at is a paradigm shift—a new normal. Life is not going to be the same for years to come. Not just months, years. What I've seen at the hospital and what I've learned from the epidemiologists is frightening in terms of mutations of the virus and the long-term effects that we won't understand for years. I cannot emphasize how important it is you keep social distancing, wearing masks when you are out in public, and washing your hands thoroughly in between," George said.

As Boots served coffee for the graduation cake, George distributed their gifts. Chris opened his first to find a set of Wüsthof knives and a crisp white chef's apron with his name embroidered across the chest.

"Thank you," Chris said, pulling the apron around his neck and tying it behind his back. "I will wear this for the audition, and you know these are the knives I need."

Claire opened her box next, which revealed a gold charm bracelet. She studied the charms, including a little palette and paintbrush, a miniature New York skyline, a gold apple, a tree, a red enamel cardinal, a star, a moon, a cluster of bezel-set gems, and a fish.

"A fish?" Claire looked at Boots.

"To represent both you as a Pisces and your love for Phish," Boots explained. "They didn't have a Phish logo fish, so I hope this works."

"I love it," Claire said. "Thank you."

"I always wanted to give you a charm bracelet," Boots said. "You know, so you could add to it whenever you travel or have a milestone like graduation. I don't know why it took so long to get you one."

Claire kept her gaze steady on the bracelet she had attached to her wrist, took a deep breath, and said, "Dad, Boots, there's something I need to talk to you about."

Chris stood, put his hand on Claire's shoulder, and said, "I'm going to clean the kitchen. I'll be right there, within earshot, if you need me."

"This sounds serious," her dad said.

"It is," Claire said. "Back in January, when we had the snow day?"

"The day of the accident?" her dad asked, brow furrowed.

"Yes, but before that. I was digging around in the garage for Red Dragon, that old toboggan we loved. Remember? Anyway, when I reached for the sled, I accidentally pulled a box down from the shelves. One of those boxes were the letters," Claire confessed. "I found the letters."

Her dad looked at Boots, but neither of them spoke for a moment. When Claire opened her mouth to speak again, Boots interrupted.

"I told you we should have told her before she found out on her own," she said to her dad and then turned to Claire. "I'm sorry, Claire. I am. You shouldn't have just stumbled upon them like that. I'm surprised this is the first we're hearing about it. Why have you kept it a secret?"

"Why have I kept it a secret?" Claire said. "That's rich. Why have you kept it a secret is the question. Furthermore, I didn't keep it a secret. I was planning to confront you the very next day if you must know."

"Calm down, Claire," her dad said.

"Don't tell me to calm down," Claire raised her voice.

When Boots said, "You have every right to be upset," Claire was confused. Boots never took her side.

"I demand to know what happened. Why would you do this to me? Why did you keep me from her for all these years?" Claire was doing her best to keep from breaking down.

"Okay, Claire. Let me explain. It is not an easy story to tell. When you were three years old, your grandmother became very ill, and Sophie flew home to be with her."

Claire was startled to hear her mother's name spoken. It had been that long since she and her dad had talked about her.

He continued, "When she died, Sophie called to tell me she needed to stay a while longer to help with the funeral and the estate. Not that there was much of an estate to speak about, but that's another story. After a few weeks, I started to worry. I considered flying over, but you were so little, and I was in the middle of residency. It was a very chaotic time. It's when Miss Harriet used to babysit you, remember?"

"I do," Claire said, memories flooding back to her nanny who served her lunches on what she called "party trays," which transformed turkey, cheese, carrots, and apples cut into little pieces into something special Claire could eat while watching *Sesame Street.*

"After a few months, it became apparent that Sophie wasn't going to return. She stopped answering my calls. Remember, this is before the age of social media and cell phones like we know it today. This was back in 2004, 2005. Texting wasn't a thing like it is now. I mean, it existed, but it wasn't the primary means of communication back then, especially not for adults. If someone wanted to disappear, it was much easier to do so then than it would be now," her dad said.

"Why didn't you go over there and just get her?" Claire said. "Maybe she needed help. Maybe she needed you to convince her to come back."

"I was planning to," her dad said. "I was in the process of getting tickets when I got the news. Your mom had made a new friend. Not a good guy. He was a con artist who took advantage of your mother. He was a drug smuggler who got arrested, and when he did, Sophie was with him and detained as well."

World Gone Mad

"A drug smuggler?" Claire asked.

"I know it sounds farfetched. It did to me, too. I mean, what do I know about international drug smuggling? I was just a medical resident from Ohio. I had only been to Europe once, and that was my junior year in high school with the German Club. You know I met Sophie at a coffee house on campus when she was studying at Ohio State for her year abroad, and I was in medical school. What started as a whirlwind romance turned into something far more serious when she got pregnant with you, and we got married."

"You got pregnant before you got married?" Claire asked. "How did I not know this before?"

"Because I never wanted you to feel anything but loved. That's what this whole thing has been about, Claire. Not wanting you to feel abandoned and then ashamed that your mother is in prison for a stupid, careless error in judgment," her dad said.

"She's in prison?" Claire asked. "Like, still? Now?"

"No," her dad said. "When she had served her time, she returned to Paris. She isn't allowed to leave the country. We hid the letters from you to protect you. It was in your best interest. It was so hard for you when she left. And then, I had to separate you from Miss Harriet when I took the job at Maywood Hospital. So many changes at once. Do you remember how difficult it was when I met Boots? How you refused to speak anything but French until Mrs. Thompson took you under her wing? How was I going to tell you your mother was in prison? It was hard enough for you to deal with being abandoned."

"We planned to tell you," Boots interjected. "The plan was to tell you on your eighteenth birthday, but then Drake died, and the pandemic hit, and I don't know. It's not an excuse, I know. I'm just trying to explain why it's taken this long to come out. Of course, we didn't know you had found the letters in January. You should have told us."

"Should? Should?" Claire yelled. "Don't tell me what I should and shouldn't do, Boots. You are such a hypocrite. You act like you've been this fairy godmother when in fact, you've been nothing but a step monster my whole life."

"How is protecting you and not wanting you to feel shame a bad thing?" Boots asked.

"Because it's bullshit. You didn't want me to feel ashamed? It is more like you didn't want to be embarrassed in front of your Junior League and your stupid fucking blog followers. How would it look for the Queen of Gracious Living to have a daughter whose birth mother was in prison for drug smuggling? Don't act like you did this for my benefit."

"That's enough—" her dad interrupted.

"That's not enough," Claire said. "You have no rights either. You have no idea how awful it's been, thinking my mother didn't even think about me all these years. At least, I could have written her back and had a relationship with her in that way, which would have been better than what I've had my whole life, which is nothing."

World Gone Mad

When Chris walked into the dining room, Claire said, "Is there anything else? What about Chris? Did his dad join the circus or fall off a cliff or something, and you don't want to tell us that, either?"

"Chris knows exactly where his father is," Boots said. "He can reach his father anytime he likes, and he knows it. Last I heard, he had left the logging ranch in Oregon and was living in a meditation center in Santa Fe."

"He's in San Diego now," Chris said, keeping his eyes averted from Claire. "He said he had enough of deserts and yogis and missed the ocean. I just spoke with him last week. He called to congratulate me for graduation."

Claire whipped around and snarled, "You didn't tell me that. What is it with everyone in this family and their secrets? You make me sick. All of you."

She didn't turn around, even when her dad called her back. Instead, she closed her bedroom door, pulled out her duffel bag, and started packing.

45
wound

"Claire says we can use all the paints we need," Taylor said.

"Chris will meet us at her studio door."

"She's not home?" Josh asked.

"She's still at Calico House. She and Sam will meet us on campus tomorrow," Taylor said as they walked to the Cutler's house to retrieve the supplies they needed for their Black Lives Matter signs for tomorrow's protest at the Maywood branch of Ohio State campus.

The week after graduation, on May 25, 2020, the news exploded with the report of a forty-six-year-old African American man named George Floyd, who was murdered at the hands of police officers outside a convenience store in Minneapolis. The political movement Black Lives Matter, which had been bubbling for some time, gained momentum. People, not just all over the country but worldwide, were flooding the streets in protests. Fires, looting, and riots had erupted in many cities. The Minneapolis Police Department's Third Precinct was burned down, which prompted the mayor to request the National Guard deployment. Violence escalated when the news broke of Breonna Taylor, a young black woman in Louisville, Kentucky, who was gunned down in her apartment in the middle of the night. An innocent woman was killed practically in her own bed, yet none of the police officers were facing charges. Cities instituted curfews, and the president threatened to deploy the military to stop the protests that were gaining in momentum, not declining.

A list of police brutality victims was too long to print on t-shirts, but they tried. The music industry responded by blacking out on Tuesday, May 26, which included Phish canceling their weekly stream in solidarity. Taylor and Josh would not have watched the stream anyway. Instead, they gathered with about a hundred other protestors on campus, chanting "I can't breathe" and a response that rang, "Hands up" to the cry, "Don't shoot."

A minister spoke through a bullhorn before introducing a hip-hop artist who delivered a passionate speech about the need to respond to police brutality and fight to stop the injustice of racism in the United States. Claire and Sam found Taylor and Josh in the crowd.

"What did we miss?" Claire asked from behind her mask. Everyone was wearing masks, of course. However, nobody was practicing social distancing as they crowded around the front of the main building on campus. "Are we going to march from here?"

"I don't think this protest is as much a march as it is a rally," Taylor explained. "The protest in Dayton on Saturday will be a march."

"And you're still planning to go with Josh's family?" Claire asked.

"No," Taylor said. "My parents want to go. You know my dad grew up in Dayton. We'll be meeting family there, which is not the greatest excuse for a family reunion, but there it is. My Uncle Joe and Aunt Connie will be there with their kids. Josh's family isn't even going to be in Dayton. Mr. Gentry was requested to speak at the rally in Cincinnati, so they'll be there."

Taylor didn't mention that Eric Sutherland, the host of Holler Poets, had reached out to Taylor to read a poem at this rally. Taylor accepted the invitation immediately, of course, but didn't want to exacerbate her anxiety by telling anyone other than her mother what she was planning.

Claire, Chris, and Sam were stunned when Eric introduced Taylor's name, and their friend pushed her way through the crowd to stand on the makeshift stage in front of the microphone. She elbow-shook Eric's elbow, grabbed the microphone, and said, "Hello, My name is Taylor Thompson." The crowd quieted in response, and Taylor launched.

With one fist raised, she cried, "Hands Up!" The call was responded with the crowd replying, "Don't Shoot!" Then, Taylor read:

World Gone Mad

Should not be
the call and response
my baby brothers
learn before they even
learn how to drive
but the rules
they must learn:
not to hold Skittles
not to run
not to move
not to hide
while driving black
while walking black
while living black
while being black

are rules that have
been broken
we are broken
lives are broken
hearts are broken
screams are...

Stop! I can't
breathe, he
cried, we cry,
shout, scream, mourn,
fight, rally, holler
on deaf ears our
government doesn't
want to hear, nor
do they care even
as we chant their names
calling up their spirits
holding them close
to our hearts shattered
in a breath not taken
lives stolen.

B. Elizabeth Beck

In the name of:

Emmitt Till, Trayvon Martin,
Alton Sterling, Bothom Jean,
Atiana Jefferson, Dontre Hamilton,
Eric Garner, John Crawford III,
Michael Brown, Ezell Ford,
Laquan McDonald, Akai Gurley,
Tamir Rice, Antonio Martin,
Jerame Reid, Ahmaud Arbery,
Tony McDade, Dion Johnson,
George Floyd, and Breonna Taylor

We hear you. We shout your names
into the heavens, praying your souls
are lifted as we are grounded
in an unjust world, judged by
the color of our skin and not by
the content of our character

civil rights a broken promise
Dr. King would weep tears
black brothers and sisters
and white brothers and sisters
do not sit together at the table
of justice years after he shared
his dreams deferred into shambles
Maya Angelou flies like a caged
bird freed to the top of Baldwin's
mountain where all the flowers
are the color purple and every
black soul is free.

Of course, the crowd cheered when Taylor listed the victims' names, much like she anticipated. She didn't usually write in slam style, but she knew call-outs were always crowd-pleasers. She smiled behind her mask when she received the response. She bowed her head, raised her fist in the air to the applause at the end before she stepped down from the stage.

"That was unbelievable," Claire said, pulling her into a hug.

"Incredible. Powerful. Right on," Chris said.

Sam and Alex joined in, exclaiming over her poem and her reading, each hugging and patting her. Josh held back. Taylor read his expression behind his mask, and even though he said, "That was awesome," his eyes read, "How could you not have told me?" Taylor knew he felt betrayed, but she knew even telling him would have put so much pressure on her, she might have backed out. Reading a poem at the Holler stage was entirely different from reading a poem at a rally. Even a small one in Maywood was a much larger crowd than Taylor had ever read to.

She tried to explain it to him later that evening when they were alone, but he brushed her off, saying, "It's fine, Taylor. Amazing. Great writing." How could she confess she wanted this moment to be private? That she didn't feel compelled to tell him every little thing that happened to her. Wasn't that how couples should feel? Taylor just didn't know.

Because her family surrounded Taylor, she felt less afraid than she would have without them when they arrived to protest in Dayton. It was unlike the peaceful demonstration in Maywood, which was attended by mostly well-meaning white people with barely any police presence. In Dayton, the police were armed in riot gear, replete with shields, helmets, and pepper spray. Their presence felt menacing as intended. Some of the younger men protestors shook their fists, screamed obscenities, and jumped up and down in the officer's faces before running off.

The ministers who spoke were eloquent and passionate. The crowd surged and fueled the simmering rage everyone felt in the face of injustice. The march was ten blocks from Second Street to the Oregon District, chanting "No Justice. No Peace."

Her dad and Uncle Joe walked arm-in-arm, their fists pumped in the air. By the time they marched the ten city blocks, the crowd had doubled in size. The mayor of Dayton addressed the crowd, thanking them for their peacefulness and calling for a change in the country for black lives who matter. When everyone kneeled, one hand on the back of the stranger in front of them, the crowd hushed to a silence that was more powerful than the chanting. Taylor saw her mom wiping tears with the back of her hand.

Taylor and her family returned to their parked car and drove back to Maywood before the violence erupted. The police were shooting bean bags into the crowd and pepper spray to disperse everyone from the streets. Taylor looked back to TJ and Tristan, their heads bent over a phone, playing a video game, and felt a bolt of fear for them. What if one of her brothers was gunned down for holding a bag of Skittles?

"So, you and Uncle Joe used to protest together, back in the day?" Taylor asked her father as he was driving.

"That's right. Today was close to what we used to do, except for the Million Man March in D.C. Now that was something else altogether. I have never seen so many black people gathered together

World Gone Mad

in one place in my life. Uncle Joe and I drove his old Dodge straight to D.C., without a plan, of course. No hotel reservations. Nothing. Just responding to the call of the Reverend Louis Farrakhan," Dad said. "We heard Rosa Parks speak, Taylor. The actual woman. And Betty Shabazz and Maya Angelou. Now that was a treat. You would have loved it."

"Where did you stay?" Taylor asked.

Her dad laughed and said, "Nowhere. We crashed in the car for a bit and then drove the whole eight hours back to Dayton. We were young then."

"And dumb," her mom added.

"Yes," her dad agreed. "Young and dumb. Those were the days."

Taylor's mom turned around to look at her daughter. She said, "Taylor, I have a favor to ask. Tomorrow, we will sit the boys down to have the talk, and I thought since what you went through with Josh in the fall, it might be a good idea to have you participate. Share your experience. Explain the rules as you know it."

"Of course, Mom," Taylor said. "May I invite Josh? You know they love him and will probably listen to whatever he has to say more than anything we could say."

"That's a good idea," her mom said. "Ask him for Sunday dinner. We can have the talk and then eat."

Much like Taylor predicted, TJ and Tristan hung on every word when Josh spoke, their eyes wide with fear. Josh was very patient and reassuring, but he emphasized the importance of their primary goal: to get home safely, to stay alive, to give the police no reason to shoot.

"But what if they do?" Tristan asked. "What if they shoot anyway?"

The room went silent. Nobody had a response until their father stepped in. He said, "The point is to keep your hands visible at all times and never to talk back. No matter what. Do you understand? Do not talk back."

"I talked back," Taylor said quietly, keeping her head bowed. "I made a mistake by talking back. It almost got Josh and me into a lot of trouble, and it would have been my fault for being mouthy."

"What did you say, Tay?" TJ asked.

"I questioned the officer for calling Josh 'boy'. I had no right to do that, but I did, and it was the wrong thing to do."

"But you didn't get shot, right?" Tristan asked.

"No, I did not get shot, but I was terrified," Taylor said, finally looking at her brothers' sweet faces. "We were lucky. I'm home safe with you, but I know better now. I do. I learned my lesson."

Their mom said, "You need to listen to me closely now. Taylor does not have the privilege to mouth off and say anything that comes to her mind when dealing with police officers, and neither do you. That may sound harsh, but it is the truth."

Their dad closed his eyes, took a deep breath, and said, "Okay, Sons, it's time to tell you about your Aunt Tyfini, my little sister. When she was nine years old--"

"I'm nine!" Tristan said.

World Gone Mad

"I know. That's why I'm telling you this story because you are a big boy now and can understand. My little sister was a dancer. If you ask me, the world's best dancer, but she never had a chance to grow up. She was practicing pirouettes in the front yard, which is not like our front yard. We lived in the city. The houses were close to the street. Anyway, she was dancing in the front yard like she always did, when a car drove up and started shooting. They weren't shooting at her, of course. She got caught in what's known as crossfire. I thought by moving you kids here to Maywood, you would be safe. Safer than the neighborhood I grew up in, for sure. But now I don't know anymore. You may not get shot by a stray bullet in a drive-by as my little sister did, but you are not anymore safe here than anywhere else in the United States because you are black. Public Enemy Number One."

"What does that mean?" TJ asked.

"It means we are perceived as a threat merely because of the color of our skin," Josh said. "You may be the biggest gentleman or the kindest person in the world, but it may not always matter. You won't be judged on the content of your character. We are still judged by the color of our skin."

"I like the color of my skin," Tristan said. "It's darker than Mommy's but lighter than Tay's."

"We like the color of your skin, too," their dad said. "But when white people look at you, they are only going to see a black man. Meaning, they won't know you love spaghetti or got an A on your Math test, or even that you say your prayers at night. The only thing they see is black."

"And you'll notice if you pay attention," Josh said. "A white person will cross the street not to have to pass you, or in a store, they will follow you around so that you won't steal."

"A white woman may pull her purse closer when she gets into an elevator with you for one reason only," Taylor said. "You are black."

Tristan frowned and said, "But Claire is your best friend."

"She is my best friend," Taylor said. "Not all white people are racist."

"But you should always be careful," Josh said. "Never assume any white person has your best interest at heart. Even your own best friend will throw you under the bus if she has to."

"Claire's gonna throw you under a bus, Tay?" Tristan asked.

"No," their mom said. "Claire is not going to hurt Taylor, and I think that's enough for one conversation. Why don't you go outside and play? There's still an hour or so until dinner will be ready."

The boys dragged Josh to play basketball, and because Taylor's dad was home for once, he joined them. Their mom shooed Taylor out of the house as well.

"Go get some fresh air. Have fun," she said, waving Taylor away.

When Tristan saw Taylor, he called, "Join our team, Tay. Join us. Josh is terrible."

Josh laughed and said, "He's not lying. I am terrible at basketball. We didn't have a basketball hoop at our house growing up."

World Gone Mad

"What did you play?" TJ asked.

Taylor's dad chuckled when Josh said, "Tennis. I play tennis. My brother plays golf."

"Regular old Arthur Ashe, are you?" Taylor's dad teased Josh, who laughed in return.

"Judge Gentry is a firm believer that more business gets done on the tennis courts and the golf course than in the boardrooms," Josh explained.

"And then along came Barack Obama, right?" her dad teased. "Your dad could not have expected the first black president of the United States to be an old baller on the courts, right?"

Josh grinned and said, "That's great. I'm gonna use that with Judge. I've gotta."

Taylor watched the four men of her life, cutting up, laughing, modifying the game to accommodate TJ and Tristan's shorter heights and Josh's lack of skills, enjoying the peace that comes with bouncing an orange ball and shooting it into a hoop until their mom emerged from the house and called them all in for dinner. Her dad held back a moment, put his hand on Taylor's arm, and whispered, "I like him."

"I like him, too, Daddy," Taylor said.

46
surrender

Claire looked up from her sketch pad when Sam approached her. She had been perched at the elm tree for most of the afternoon, enjoying the balmy June weather while Sam helped Luke, who was busy converting the old barn into a working studio for his furniture making, and while Aunt Karen disappeared into her studio. Before Sam could speak, Claire pointed to the line of ducks on the pond. A mother duck and her ducklings, Claire presumed. Sam leaned down and kissed her. He asked, "Would you like to collect eggs with me? I'm going to make pasta carbonara. Chris gave me the recipe."

"Of course," Claire said. She abandoned her sketchbook and markers and took Sam's hand. The chickens greeted them as they opened the door to the yard outside the coop. "Hello, Gertrude,

Frieda, and Virginia. Hello, Alice, Georgia, Donna Jean."

They collected the eggs, filled the troughs with feed, and checked the water supply before carrying the filled basket to the kitchen. Sam chose the SPAC Phish show he and Claire loved the most from last year's tour from the LivePhish app to play through the speakers in the house. Claire recognized the first notes of "Fluffhead" and said, "Our show."

Sam busied himself unearthing the big pot to boil pasta, the skillet, and the colander while Claire sliced an onion. "Should I use a bit of the basil?" she asked, indicating the herbs Aunt Karen planted in pots in the kitchen windowsill.

"Oregano only. Never basil. Especially not basil. Something about how eggs and basil do not belong in the same dish. I was told not to question," Sam said.

He laid eight pieces of bacon on a stone pan to bake in the oven so the stovetop would be free to sauté the onions in olive oil with crushed garlic. He opened a jar of roasted red peppers for Claire to dice and poured a small amount of frozen green peas into a bowl to warm to room temperature before tossing it into the pasta and dumping grated parmesan on top to serve.

"It says to crack two egg yolks with one complete egg," Sam said, frowning. "That seems weird. Two yolks and not whites? Okay."

Claire yelled over the food processor, grating the parmesan because Chris insisted they could not grate the cheese ahead of time. "It's like a hollandaise. Yolks, not whites."

Sam whisked the eggs in a large bowl. He poured more salt than he thought was necessary for the water, but Chris was very specific with his instructions again.

"It should taste like the ocean. Saltwater, because you'll use a half cup of it to thicken the eggs. It's what cooks the eggs."

Before the last song of the first set, the bacon was crisp and laid on a paper towel to drain. The water was simmering, ready to be brought to a full boil. The cheese was grated, and the onions were soft and translucent.

"Whatever translucent onions are supposed to look like," Claire joked.

She and Sam poured glasses of iced tea to take to the patio. They settled on the porch swing to listen to the last song of the set, "Drift While You're Sleeping," as the sun descended over the pond.

Although Sam and Claire would begin their life together in New York in August, Sam would forever consider Calico House his home and felt grateful to have stolen these extra months here, something he had yet to admit aloud. The global pandemic had devasted too many lives to pretend these past three months weren't tragic times. Sam considered himself very fortunate his father hadn't gotten ill, that he had Aunt Karen and Luke as extended family, and the love of his life snuggled next to him as dinner was ready to be served. Fortunate life.

"I don't think there is anything wrong with finding the silver lining in a time of grief," Aunt Karen said when Sam expressed his thoughts at the dinner table after he and Claire loaded everyone's

World Gone Mad

bowls with the pasta. "That's called humility and humanity. Humility because you feel guilty for finding joy in darkness and because you feel guilty at finding any peace in the face of others' suffering. Humanity because you care so much. There aren't many people who give a damn today. What's happened last month is evidence of how awful society has become in the past four years. We have to vote that man out in November. It's the only way."

"I'm waiting to apply for my absentee ballot," Claire said. "They haven't opened the on-line application yet. Have you applied for yours yet, Sam?"

"Yes," Sam said. "It will be our first presidential election. Of course, we'll vote."

"It's a shame it will be mostly mail-in voting this year. Luke, remember the first year Obama ran? It was like a party at the polls. Lines for days, people so excited to participate in making history happen in our lifetime. And the celebrations when he won. The moment he and Michelle walked out to accept his presidency? Incredible," Aunt Karen said.

"Those were magical days, for sure," Luke agreed. "We haven't seen that kind of dignity in the White House since."

Aunt Karen changed the topic of conversation by asking Claire about her dad and Boots. "Have you spoken to them yet? It's been a week."

"I haven't. I'm not ready to talk, but if you need me to leave, I can always go to Taylor's house," Claire said.

"You are welcome here as long as you like, Claire. That wasn't what I was trying to imply. I'm just checking in to see how you are feeling and to ask what you are thinking because I know you've been thinking down there at the elm tree every day."

"I have been thinking, but I haven't made any decisions yet. I don't think there is a decision to be made. I feel betrayed by their decision to lie to me. I feel shaky what I thought I understood about my mother wasn't the truth, and in fact, the truth is even worse. I have a mother who was in prison. Prison. It's beyond comprehensible, and I'm having a hard time wrapping my brain around it all. I feel hurt and betrayed and duped to an extent. Like I was an idiot or like the proverbial ostrich with her head in the sand or whatever."

"Time," Luke said. When they looked up at him, he continued. "Things like this take time. At least, in my experience. I mean, I never went through what you're going through, but I do know what it feels like to be betrayed."

"I just don't want you to leave for college without making some kind of peace," Aunt Karen said. "Trust me. I watched my sister leave when things weren't good between her and our mother, and I think it helped destroy her. Sam, your mom carried such unresolved pain from the grudge she carried. Claire, I'm not saying you have to forgive them or that everything will be magically okay again. It won't, perhaps not for a long time, and you have every right to feel the way you do. But do stop and consider your dad. It couldn't have been easy for him as a young doctor with a small child, abandoned and alone. He did the best he knew how, and he always has your best interests at heart."

World Gone Mad

Claire didn't say anything. She sat quietly, absorbing Karen's words. As mad as Claire was, she knew her dad loved her. It hurt that he lied, but that was also mixed up with her deep love and affection that she'd always had for him. As for Boots, she expected nothing but what she got. Although she had to admit, Boots insisted she was in support of telling Claire the truth earlier, and she did good, picking out the charm bracelet Claire had not taken off since she received it.

"I'm confused, but you're right," Claire said. "Not tonight. Maybe not even tomorrow, but I promise I will make peace with my dad before I leave for school."

Aunt Karen stood, gathered the empty bowls, and said, "We'll take care of the dishes tonight, kids. Thank you for cooking."

Claire followed Sam to the porch to settle on the swing.

He said, "You know what tonight is, right?" When she looked confused, he reached into his pocket, handed her a little box, and said, "Open it."

Nestled on a bit of cotton was a small brass skeleton key charm on a black cord. Claire lifted it to inspect it. "Thank you," she said.

"You're welcome," Sam said. "It's not the actual key to Gramercy Park. It's not the literal key to my heart. It's not the keys to the city. It's not the key to anything. Instead, it's the key to everything. Meeting you a year ago was the key to my life, in a way. I wanted to give you something to symbolize that."

"A year ago today? It's been a year?" Claire said as she pulled the cord around her neck on top of the Love necklace she never removed and kissed Sam.

He reached for her hand and said, "You know where we're going next."

Sam texted Chris and Taylor to be ready, so they were both masked up and waiting at the end of their driveways when Sam and Claire pulled up. Nobody was at the trestle because of quarantine. The mayor had even had all the basketball nets removed from the public parks to deter groups of kids from gathering to play, so the trestle's recreation area was deserted as well. Prepared this time, Sam opened the trunk to unearth towels and blankets he and Chris carried to the log where they smoked their first joint together. The four of them walked to the center of the train tracks that ran over Lake Juniper. They held hands, yelled, "in omnia paratus," and then jumped together off the bridge into the water below, swam to the surface, and laughed in the summer air.

World Gone Mad

ACKNOWLEDGEMENTS

Creating a story is a solitary endeavor. Making a book requires collaboration. I am grateful for my tribe, who support my writing life. Tomica Chitterson and Tyfini McGowan, mentoring you inspired me to become a teacher. Imagine my delight, all these years later, when you became my teachers. I could not have written this book without your careful eyes, sharp insights, and generous hearts. Thank you to my writing partner, Jay McCoy. Hope we'll continue slinging words together for years to come. I treasure my friendship with Jessica Topper, who guides me with wisdom and humor. Good looking out, Marc Silverman. You are a pal for talking me through all things dental school in the 80s. Carrie, our connection carries me through. Forever grateful. Thank you, Cassidy Senefelder, for your thoughtful edits. Elisa Allechant, keep rocking the radio, sister. You are a good friend. I appreciate Matthew Zapruder for permission to include "Prelude." You wished for a Flying Pizza poem, and Taylor responded. Chris Davis, if you ever get tired of my poems and my stories, I will be lost, my gentle reader. As for my men, Kevin and Carter, you are my everything.

ABOUT THE AUTHOR

B. Elizabeth Beck is a writer, artist, and teacher who lives with her family in a home on a pond in Kentucky. Her dogs love to chase the geese and ducks who visit, and the highlight of any day is spotting the blue herons that grace her dock.

She taught English and Art History in public schools for over twenty years. Devoted to community service, she founded The Teen Howl Poetry Series in 2011 and the award-winning Leestown OUTLOUD Poets in 2014. She also volunteers her time teaching writing workshops.

Elizabeth has published three books of poetry, *Interiors* (Finishing Line Press 2011*), insignificant white girl* (Evening Street Press 2011), *Painted Daydreams: Collection of Ekphrastic Poems* (Accents Publishing 2018). Her poems and essays can also be found in various anthologies and journals. In 2020, she launched her debut novel, SUMMER TOUR. She continues the adventures with the same characters in WORLD GONE MAD.

Visit her online at elizbeck.com

- facebook.com/B Elizabeth Beck Author
- instagram.com/Elizabeth__Beck
- goodreads.com/B Elizabeth Beck

Made in the USA
Middletown, DE
30 March 2021